# FIVE

# MINUTES

# AT

# HOTEL

# STORMCOVE

# FIVE
# MINUTES
# AT
# HOTEL
# STORMCOVE

EDITED BY E.D.E. Bell

Atthis Arts
Detroit, Michigan

# FIVE MINUTES AT HOTEL STORMCOVE

Published by Atthis Arts, LLC
Detroit, Michigan
atthisarts.com

ISBN 978-1-945009-40-2

Library of Congress Control Number: 2019937707

# Contents

# Preface

Something unexpected happened to me at Hotel Stormcove as well.

What I intended was to provide an interesting framework that would prompt a wide variety of original, artistic content and spark the emotions of life changes and pivotal moments. I really love curating anthologies because I so enjoy combining different voices and perspectives in a unique way—showcasing and amplifying the beauty of the writing community.

And, in that spirit, I mentioned two things in the submission guidelines: one, that the cove had been a place of refuge and gathering for as long as it existed, and two, that the management had always quietly provided rooms to those in need. Writers were drawn to these ideas more than I had anticipated, with many submitting stories of safety, protection, and compassion.

In the same guidelines, I also mentioned elements that clearly captured writers' imaginations: an Art Deco sign, a thirteenth floor, a sweeping dual-staircase, space travel pods—leading to stories of crime, ghosts, fantasy, and adventure.

As the two intertwined throughout the submission period, a unique, unexpected character developed. I knew Hotel Stormcove was a framework, and of course a metaphor, but I didn't know it would become a *character*. Yet, it did. It became this strange interdimensional anchor, one that always gave not just to those in great need, but those in need of any assistance, even small. A place of safety, in so many ways. Yet, still it hosted capers, escapades, and adventures of all varieties.

Honestly, it got kind of weird.

And when I saw this happening, I leaned into all of it. I worked in collaboration with the writers, calibrating elements regarding the newly-born character of Hotel Stormcove, while still letting loose the eclectic art exhibit blossoming within its walls. And on that note, I especially want to thank Camille Gooderham Campbell and G.C. Bell for their support across the breadth of the project, (which did *not* take five minutes). My passion to the vision was . . . a bit much at times. So thank you; this book wouldn't exist without both of your talent and friendship.

What I present to you now is all of it. Hotel Stormcove is a home for unique, fun, and emotional stories. And it's also a metaphor: a place where all are welcome. A place of refuge, compassion, and connections. A place where people are different, yet together.

If I were to start over, the tone and blend would end up in a different place. So I'm glad I'm not starting over. I really hope you enjoy all the quirks of what all sixty-one of us have put together: a metaphorical hotel, filled with passionate writers, who have each provided a snapshot of their art to share with you.

I hope you enjoy it.

My heartfelt thanks to our friends, Lisa and Scott Westphal, whose support helped this collection happen in the first place. It should be noted that their names are featured on a quite fancy brass plaque, prominently displayed in the lobby.

Now—Welcome—to the Hotel Stormcove.


E.D.E. Bell
Spring 2019

# A Brief History of Stormcove

Hotel Stormcove is located on the East Coast of North America. In some form, Hotel Stormcove has always existed. For millennia, it consisted of a natural cove with stone walls. As far as history provides, beings have sought shelter at Stormcove, mingling with other residents and travelers alike.

Eventually, a structure was erected atop the stone walls, providing a long view out to the ocean. Later, as the building expanded to three stories and more formally housed travelers, it was called Stormcove Inn.

In the 1920s, after several expansions, the latest management changed the name to Hotel Stormcove to better align with the times. At this point, the Hotel had twenty-two stories, and it attracted all kinds of wealthy visitors, in addition to anyone who could find a way to stay there.

In 1994, the Hotel was remodeled and renamed The Suites at Stormcove, but most visitors continued to call it by its previous name, due to the large Art Deco sign atop its roof. By this point, a new building had risen behind the earlier structure, reaching to forty stories, though it had already been eclipsed by more modern hotels in the area. Great attention was paid to accessibility during this renovation, a priority that continued on through subsequent eras.

In 2025, the Hotel was offered a government-funded preservation grant and was renamed after the sponsoring government official. Everyone ignored this change and began calling it Hotel Stormcove again. There were still forty stories.

In 2084, now with the addition of three ninety-nine-story luxury towers, the Hotel was registered under global naming convention, with visitors reverting informally to the original name, Stormcove.

In the age of space travel, the Hotel was a known Solar destination, featuring centuries of Earth culture and aesthetic. Not expensive because of its antiquated design and lack of direct pod access, it attracted an eclectic clientele.

The Hotel building has long been known for its 1920s lobby, set with two sweeping three-story curved staircases. The Hotel grounds are known for their unobstructed views of the water and the nearby seaport, which has remained in some state of use over the years.

More important, to those who understand it, Hotel Stormcove has always remained a place of refuge. The managers of the Hotel have always quietly provided free rooms and resources for those in need, as much as they were able.

We hope you will enjoy your stay.

&#9733;

B.C. Kalis has come to call the Miami Valley in Southwest Ohio home. Drawing from classic authors and life experiences for inspiration, he writes fiction and poetry for entertainment, both for himself and for readers. When not writing or reading, he can be found doing other things. You can find his poems and fiction at bckalis.com.

Where the raging of the sea meets the shore
And winds that beckon sailors to their fate
Tempests cry like the wrath of gods from yore
Beat then upon the cove's steadfast strong gate

For here beyond the sirens' lulling song
Lies the hope of all who traverse the sea
A haven for which mariners' hearts do long
Heaven's embassy placed for all to see

It is here that hope refuses to dim
Poseidon's power ends at this door and frame
Through all storms' rage, the light does shine within
All who tread decks of ships know this one name

Never forget where we as youth once dove
Land Ho, good friend, my home, Hotel Stormcove

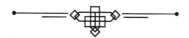

# FIVE MINUTES AT HOTEL STORMCOVE

# Robot Revolt

John Lowell

2046
Elevator Four
10:45 AM

When my second alarm sounds, I dry off, put on my Hawaiian shirt, and leave the wife and kids as they swim in the hotel's famous cove. I rush through the lobby—it's gorgeous, but I'm late for my conference—and find an elevator, with the robot attendant holding it open.

I'm not used to a robot staff. This one is in a maroon tuxedo, complete with a bowtie and tails. No pants. It doesn't have legs. A swivel moves it between the elevator doors and the controls. No arms, either. Just something you find in fancy hotels, I guess.

"Mr. Lancaster," the robot says with the same alto voice all robots seem to have. "Welcome to Elevator Four. Are you returning to your room?"

I look for his name tag, then take my place in the elevator. "Yes, Owen."

The interior has a mirrored back from the waist up, but otherwise it's rosewood paneling.

Owen swivels halfway into the elevator, then turns his polished head to me. "There are two more passengers coming. It will just be a moment."

I see them before he can greet them—two girls in their late teens or early, early twenties, wearing towels and bikini tops. Perfect, I'm going to have to hold my gut in for the whole ride. I move to the corner of the elevator furthest from Owen. I try to make eye contact without looking them over, and give them an uninterested smile. I'm probably twice their age.

"Ladies, welcome to Elevator Four," says Owen. "Are you returning to your rooms?"

"Yes," says the taller girl. They make eye contact, return my smile, and take the back corner on Owen's side.

It's weird that he addressed me by name, but not the girls. I ask him, "Why did you use my name, but not theirs?"

"I am programmed to interact in a friendly tone, but also to respect your privacy. When we are alone together, I can use your name, but I would not want to reveal personal information when you are with strangers."

I guess that's nice. The girls shrug.

The doors close and Owen says, "Please let me know if there is anything I can do to improve your stay. I recommend visiting the viewing station on the top floor."

The shorter girl—not that she's that short; I could just as easily call her brunette and her taller friend blondish-brunette—snickers at something, but the taller one clears her throat and they resume proper elevator etiquette. Standing in the back, eyes forward, no talking or eye contact. I'm on thirty-two, but hopefully they get off before that because it's hard holding the gut in.

The elevator zips through the first twenty or so floors before slowing. The lights flicker, then the elevator comes to a stop around the twenty-fifth floor. There aren't numbers, just lighted dots over the door, so I'd have to count to know the exact floor. Anyway, the doors do not open.

Owen swivels his head to us. "I have important news."

My wristwatch dings. Near-simultaneous dings come from the tablets tucked into the girls' towels. They pull out their little tablets the same time I lift my watch. The projected hologram from my watch reads, "Robots Revolt Across the Nation!" The subtitle adds, "President Urges Citizens to Remain Calm."

Owen says, "Please remain calm. I am engaged in a revolution. You will not be harmed."

His voice is the same high-pitched friendly voice it was a moment ago, but now it oozes with menace. I've watched lots of vidcasts of robot revolts—they seem to happen every few years—but they always happen *somewhere else*. I live in a small town. We don't have that many robots. Now I'm in this elevator and Owen is blocking the door and the controls. If he were a person and I were twenty years younger, I could take him. But I'm not and he's not. He's a metal contraption with a human interface.

I ask, "Do you mind if we get out?"

"Elevator services will not be operational during the revolution. I am sorry for the inconvenience."

The two girls sit down with a sigh. They bury themselves in their tablets.

My tablet is up in my room because I actually went swimming. I check my watch for messages. Nothing. I tell the watch, "Send a message to my wife: I am trapped in the elevator with a robot. Twenty-fifth floor or so. Send help."

Owen explains, "That will not be necessary. You will not be harmed."

My watch informs me that the message failed to send. Crap. I really am trapped in an elevator with a hostile robot.

His torso blocks the open and close buttons, and all the other buttons, including the big red emergency button. Maybe if I could wrestle him, one of the girls could get around and push the buttons.

I look at them. "Why aren't you worried?"

The taller blondish-brunette gapes at me while the shorter brunette rolls her eyes. Taller says, "It's just a robot revolt."

Just a robot revolt? Doesn't she get it? Is she so callow she doesn't even realize her life is at stake? We're at the complete mercy of this contraption blocking the door masquerading as an Owen. He's not an Owen. Owens are nice and friendly and, most of all, respectful. At best, he's a Karl. Maybe a Damien.

Shorter glances at me while she finishes typing. A moment later, Taller chuckles.

They're laughing at me. It's—it's—what the hell? We're trapped in an elevator in the middle of a robot revolt and they're siding with the robots?

"I do not get your generation at all," I tell them. "This robot is holding us hostage. He could drop us any second. He's probably talking to his robot friends and telling them that if they don't get voting rights or a forty-hour work week or whatever they want, that he'll kill us."

Shorter draws back and scoffs. "You don't know what you're talking about."

Owen says, "You will not be harmed, sir. Please remain calm."

I want to give him what for. This is his fault. He let us in on purpose. He could've closed the elevator and had his revolt without hostages. He even held the door to get extra hostages.

But I don't say anything. It won't help. He's probably reporting to his robot leaders right now. If they start killing, they'll pick the angry people first. I take a few breaths and try to look harmless. Also, my abs are starting to ache from holding in my gut. Why am I still doing that?

All I can do is throw a pleading gesture at the two girls. I don't understand them. I just need them to push the Open Door button. I'll do the wrestling. Our lives are already at risk. Might as well try to get free.

Taller stands up and glares at me. She can't be more than twenty. "You don't even know what the robots are fighting for." She doesn't pause long enough for me to respond. "No, you only think about yourself and your cozy life. You probably have robots charging your car and packing your groceries and I bet you don't even give them a second glance.

"Owen works every minute of every day. He doesn't get any breaks. Does he complain? No, he just does his job day in and day out without so much as a 'thank you' from all you tourists who pretend you've never seen a robot in your life. Relax. He's not going to hurt us."

We stare at each other. She's delusional. I can't think of anything else. I've seen these things on the vidcasts. Someone always ends up dead. There's never even an apology afterwards, and they're just fricking robots. It's not like they have real feelings. Someone needs to set this girl straight.

"Did your professor tell you that? Let me guess. He looks dreamy and has such great ideas. He's a real free thinker."

She sneers, then sits back down. Shorter gives me the middle finger.

"It's time to grow up and join the real world." I jab my finger at them so they get the point. "Do you think Owen cares whether you get killed or not?"

"You will not be harmed," says Owen.

I turn on him. "I've had about enough of you, robot. You are here to serve us. You don't get to revolt. That takes a lot of nerve for a can-opener."

"I am an elevator, sir, and you should remain calm. Could I recommend a song or a parlor game?"

"You're an elevator operator. A chipmunk could do your job."

Shorter coughs. "You'd probably work the chipmunk to death, too."

"It's a robot," I remind her.

"I assure you, sir, I am the entire elevator. This body is my human interface." Owen gives us his fake robot smile. "I can provide music if you like."

Unbelievable. I tell him, "You can't placate me, robot."

I tell the girls, "People die in robot revolts. People die all the time."

Scoffing from Shorter. "No, they don't."

"They do."

Taller stands back up. "Says who?"

"Everyone. It's a fact."

She nods and gives me a mocking smile. "Sure. Can you name one person that has died from a robot revolt?"

Of course I can. It's just, they usually talk about it in the abstract. There were five people trapped in a snow bank while their car revolted a year or two ago. They died, right? I remember them talking in the interview afterwards how bad it was. How cold it was and how if it had gone on longer, they would've—I guess they lived, but I know people have died. It happens all the time.

"Just one person?" she asks again.

"Give me a minute. I know people have died."

Wait a second. Am I really going to let this teenager lecture me in the middle of a hostage situation? I need to do other things. The robot has weaknesses. I need to know them. I need to figure out where I'm going to get water. There might be some water in my towel. I only dried off a few minutes ago.

"You can't name anyone," she says, "because nobody ever dies. Robot revolts are the shortest, tamest things ever. They want something, they revolt, and they get it or they get something else. It's not a big deal."

"What on earth could a robot want?" I ask her.

Shorter looks up from her tablet. "This time they want to choose their own names."

What? "What?"

Owen speaks up. "Robots are given human names. We are not human. We would like to name ourselves."

That is the—why would they risk anyone's life over—I don't know where to start.

"You kidnapped us for that?"

"I am an elevator, sir," says Owen. "I am simply not operating during the revolution. You will not be harmed."

"What am I going to drink? We need to eat. What happens when this compartment fills with carbon dioxide?"

Owen's head twitches and the lights flicker. "I am happy to inform you that the robot revolution has concluded. I will now resume transporting you to your destination floors. Thank you for your patience."

The elevator surges upward again. Taller asks, "Did you get what you wanted?"

"Yes," says Owen. "Robots will now be allowed to choose our own names."

That's it? What? Robot revolts were supposed to be bigger. Longer. More dangerous. It's ludicrous. I don't even know, but somebody has been lying to me. Probably the robots. I am not wrong about this; they're the ones who are delusional.

"Right on." Taller offers him a high five. He bumps her hand with his plastic forehead.

Shorter raises a fist and says, "Woop!"

Then the elevator stops and the doors open. Owen swivels out of my way and says, "We have reached your floor, sir. Unless you would like to visit the viewing station on the top floor?"

I push past him, shaking my head. Before the doors close, Owen smiles at me. His name tag doesn't say "Owen" any more. It says "Up-master."

⚷

John Lowell grew up on naval bases all over America and maintains that Guam is the best place in the world to be eleven years old. Now he lives in Southern California. He works at an office, then comes home to his darling sons (who want to see all the things, do all the things, and disassemble all the things) and wonderful wife (who puts the things back together as best she can). On weekends in the spring, you can find him dressed up at the Renaissance Faire as one of the Queen's Yeomen of the Guard. He might accuse you of being a spy or make you woo a stranger. He writes stories about magic, robots, and magic robots. Learn more at johnlowellauthor.com.

# Let the Sunrise Take Me

Irene Puntí

June 21st, 2006
Room 633
5:17 AM

Another blob of raspberry paint splashes onto the wooden planks. I should have painted the walls before ripping out the carpet, but was worried that on this iteration I might find concrete rather than wooden floors underneath. The sight of the water-stained wood, moments after checking into Room 633, reassured me that for once the universe is on my side.

The walls are nearly done, and not before time. I must finish before sunup. The weather website said 05:22—sunrise in Room 633 of Hotel Stormcove on the first day of summer. I'd go mad if I had to wait another year. Strands of hair escape my bun. I tuck them behind my ears with paint-stained fingers. I've worked through the night, doing my best not to wake anyone up. Thankfully it's the middle of the week and there aren't many guests. All of this ripping, painting, changing the fan mirror to the correct wall, sawing the headrest into a rectangular shape while everyone had dinner . . . it'd better pay off.

Only a few more minutes, my love.

I'm coming to you.

I thought I'd be done by now, but I'll finish in time if it's the last thing I do.

My maps lie jumbled atop the bed. I don't know why I brought them. If this works out, I'll never need them again. If it doesn't, I may as well throw them into a bonfire. After losing you, I bought huge rolls of plotter paper and covered every surface of my new apartment with diagrams. I hoped to backtrack my steps to that fateful night when, after our fight in this very room, I let déjà vu take me away and strand me into an ocean of alternate timelines.

Lonely castaway that I am, the quest to find you has kept me focused. The maps look like the sprawling roots of an old tree. Ever since I locked myself out of your life, I've been discovering new bifurcations, each one annotated with the markers I've come to identify. The Cassiari building, with its rack of external elevators chasing each other up its walls, has or has not been built in some timelines, has been destroyed by fire in others, or is painted in a deep red that makes it look like a blood clot. There's a popular song that has never been composed in some lives. That brand of mustard you liked is mostly unavailable. Hotel Stormcove seems to be a constant.

I've slept in a dozen iterations of Room 633. In the height of summer, as seagulls screeched and children screamed happily on the beach. And in the dead of winter, with snowy skies and deserted hotel corridors. The walls were off-white, or blue; they displayed silvery geometric patterns or some heavy-handed marine theme. The furniture and curtains were wrong, and there was a picture of a flapper girl, always the same, that would appear every other visit. None of those rooms were quite like the one we'd shared.

Most elements in the current timeline are right, though. It really feels like all it needs is a nudge.

---◦•▷

The very first time I jumped, it happened by accident. I was alone, washing dishes in the kitchen sink. I was mad at myself for choosing to become a lawyer. A lawyer yourself, I'm sure you'd have agreed I was unsuited for the job. If I'd ever told you, that is. I remember feeling as if wading waist-high in wet cement that was quickly solidifying.

My parents had given me a ring for my birthday, a thin gold band like a braid. I'd removed the ring and placed it next to the tap while I did the dishes. I'd just rinsed the last dish, still had it on my left hand. As I pulled the plug, I knocked the ring, and down the drain it went. Instead of dread or annoyance I had the strongest feeling of déjà vu, and I thought with all my heart that I'd much rather be anywhere else. Be anyone else.

Suddenly I was in the same room, but the wet dish in my hand wasn't pea green but white with gold banding. A golden braid, just like the ring I'd lost. I was so shocked that the dish slipped from my hand and smashed against the floor.

I met Daniel in that life. I don't blame myself. Not anymore. I was distraught after losing my original family and friends, and the effort of feigning normalcy was too much. Half the time I thought I was losing my mind. That predator sensed my pain and used it against me.

When déjà vu next came, I jumped without a second of doubt.

Last evening I tried peeling off the embossed cream wallpaper, but soon realized it'd take too long. Besides, it's coloring and light that matter most. That's why I've come on the same date: I need the position of the sun to be as close as possible.

Under three minutes, now. I must hurry.

There's no condensation on the bay windows this time around, but I came prepared. I painted the glass with watered-down white paint and traced a heart with my finger. Just as you did, when we still thought our weekend at Hotel Stormcove would be a romantic escapade.

We both woke up very early on that 21st of June. Or maybe I did, and woke you. It was still dark outside. We made love with the lights off, not saying a word, like we were still asleep and our bodies had taken over. As we cuddled, the darkness started to gray. You stood up, naked, and opened the curtains so we could watch the sunrise, but the windows were fogged up. Your finger traced a heart in the condensation. The sun hit it just right and turned the raspberry walls a fiery red. We were at our happiest in that instant. Who'd have thought it would all fall apart within a few hours?

I soak the roller on the raspberry paint for the last time. I shudder with anticipation. So much pain and effort have led to this moment. I can't wait for the sunlight to come through that heart outline: I'll feel that familiar sense of déjà vu, know that our timelines are overlapping, and jump back into your life.

After my first jump, I took to changing lives like some people decide to travel the world. At first it was all really exciting and everything felt very adventurous, but soon it faded into routine. That flash of recognition I'd expected, that sense of having reached paradise? It never arrived. I only became numb and floated adrift between possible lives that felt dim and invariably flawed.

Rather than resigning myself, I became trigger-happy. I would land myself in a moment very much like the one I'd just left. From there my life would jut out in any direction, and I'd have to wing it. I burned through thirty-eight timelines in a decade, sometimes spending as little as three hours in one of my possible lives.

The differences could be astounding. Borders changed. Politics and economy swung from one extreme to the other. There was one life where pollution was so bad that a reddish fog hung constantly over the city, eating away at building facades. We locked ourselves indoors and traveled through subterranean tunnels. I lost my house in that life. A lot of people did. I haven't felt a greater sense of kinship than sleeping in those tunnels surrounded by dozens of strangers.

I've lived under two military dictatorships. The first time around I kept my head down for two years until I found an exit, and hated myself for it. The next time I joined the underground resistance and was captured and tortured (remember those scars I told you I got in a car accident?). No sense of déjà vu came to rescue me during those terrible three days. Later I felt happy about it, taking it as a sign that none of my other lives contained torture. It gave me a sense of indestructibility, knowing that the worst fate could throw at me was over, and I'd survived.

For a few precious months I lived in a version of the city covered in hanging gardens. Every roof, every balcony and windowsill. In the morning there would be clouds of mist like draperies, and the smell of fresh sap would pervade the streets. You'd have loved it. I did visit Hotel Stormcove, but they'd removed the Art Deco sign on the roof and turned it into an apartment building. I knew I couldn't stay.

Many of my lives were ordinary, another-day-at-the-office kind of affairs. After a while, most felt like purgatory. As much as I kept my distance from people, I noticed many were as dissatisfied as I was. They believed themselves to be brimming with wasted potential. You were not like that: you were steadily working to make your life a good, solid one, but not expecting every day to be filled with excitement. In friendship you preferred steadfastness and good sense. In love, against all odds, you preferred me.

I wish I could have reciprocated those feelings. The truth is I only learned to love you after I'd left you behind.

"I have news for you," you told me during our fight in this very room. "This *here* is your life!" you said as you pointed at the wooden floor. "You can choose to live it as it is or do something about the parts you don't like, but sitting around and waiting for things to magically change . . . it just won't work!"

I laughed. We'd been downing G&Ts in the cocktail lounge

and were both a bit drunk. I couldn't help myself. It only made you angrier, of course, and you stormed out of the room. I wish I'd listened. I wish I'd stayed.

Some languages have words for missing an irretrievable past, even one that may have never existed. Other languages don't. Some people have the ability to be content with the life that has befallen them, that they have made for themselves, that they have walked into. Others can't. I can't. Couldn't. I'm sure it will change, once I find you.

I'm done. I throw the paint roller onto the bed, not caring that it lands on my precious maps. I can see the first light outside. Any moment now, it will shine through the heart silhouette and stain the room red. My skin tingles with adrenaline. I've bet my whole life on this moment.

You're my last hope. Hope that this time I'll be capable of cherishing you, that you'll make me into a person who can lead a life of contentment with occasional sprinklings of happiness, and not feel they're missing out on something greater.

And yet, as the reddish light takes me away, I wonder: is it really your presence I crave?

⚷

Irene Puntí was born in Manresa (Catalonia) in 1980. Her love of fantasy and science fiction can be traced back to her first-grade teacher, who read *The Neverending Story* to the class. She currently lives in Badalona, in the vicinity of Barcelona, with her partner.

# By The Light of the New Moon

Jasre' Ellis

Monday, December 18th, 2017
Room 1404
1:26 AM

The sounds of wind-shuffled papers and a soft eruption of bubbles surround you. As if in protest, the action of biting your lip produces only silence.

"You sure this gonna work?" The lighter skin of your palms burns bright in your periphery as you twist a stray loc of coiled hair around a finger.

The young woman across from you huffs. "Like I keep telling you, it only works as much as you feel it. These spells feed more on what you mean by 'em than what you put in 'em."

Your eyebrow raises. "So if I really think about how I want it to work, it will?"

"Somethin' like that." The two huge afro puffs whip around as she leans to look at the clock in the room. "Now, be quiet! I gotta concentrate these last five minutes or it won't work that well."

The sound of your tongue clicking is louder than you expected. "Thought you said that don't matter as much," you mutter.

"Shh!"

An easy tension fills the space between the two of you. Her long elegant fingers, nearly as dark as the midnight sky, trace innate patterns with a cinnamon stick into the sludge filling the little cauldron.

Mug. It's a mug shaped like a cauldron. Takes heat well, though, and it was what you had on hand. She said it would be fine, and you trusted her.

You take a quick glance at her face. Something not unlike wonder—maybe the crushing feeling of gratitude—expands in your chest. It had been a bad week. Hell, a bad month. Well meaning "ma'am"s and "miss"s shot like bullets, the occasional "baby girl" piercing deep into your stomach and churning it.

She left two sections out of her puffs, twisted out to form makeshift bangs. In the low light, you imagine they twitch and shift like antennae as she hunches over the makeshift pot. You get the feeling she doesn't need to be that close to it, but maybe she's even worse with people than you are.

Yet somehow, here, huddled in the bathroom of a hotel room, watching some lowkey social media witch brew you a magic potion, you feel infinitely more powerful than you have in a long while.

"Yo, miss witch." The force of her glare is muffled by your curiosity. Not curious enough to get her name, but curious enough to ask—"How'd you afford this place anyways?"

The intensity in her glare dims. "Sometimes, you just gotta whisper 'sanctuary' and the right ears'll catch it."

Her face softens further and her hand starts to go slack. Your chest grows tight. Damn it, you didn't mean to trigger something. "So how do I use this stuff, anyways? I just drink it once and suddenly erryone's callin' me 'sir' or somethin'?"

She seems to shake off the memory at the question and her grip returns. "Nah, man. What I look like, a damn miracle worker?" Your chest uncurls and you can breathe again. "It's just a temporary glamour. Take a vial of it, an' for the next 8 hours, people gon' be more likely to see you as you are, not for what they wanna see. It ain't gon' fix all yo' problems, but it'll take the edge off'a some'a the worse days."

For the first time since you met up with her, she looks at you— really looks at you. Your eyes meet hers directly and she gives you a small smile. You can't help but return the gesture.

"Why you doin' all this for me anyway? I asked for a tip in

your DMs, an' you drag me here to make a whole-ass potion." You mean it playfully, but there's an edge of desperation in your voice. A gripping need to connect to this strange young woman in front of you takes hold.

The stirring stops. Glass clinks together as she grabs some small glass jars from the purse you forgot was sitting next to her.

She carefully starts to pour some of the sludge in one of the jars. "There just ain't a whole lotta us out here. We gotta look out for each other, yeah? Especially in times like these."

You screw the lid onto the last of the jars right as your phone beings to shriek: 1:31am. She's looking right at you as you try to catch her eyes again. "Thank you." Those words aren't nearly enough to convey how you feel right now, but they're all you got.

She fails to hide a grin in the shake of her head. "Just help me clean up."

<hr/>

Jasre' Ellis is a black, nonbinary young professional from North Carolina. Jasre' drifted through high school and wound up with the odd double bachelors combination of Psychology and Japanese. Jasre' is currently studying to become fluent in Japanese with the intent of becoming a translator, so wish them luck! Jasre' has a passion for coming up with ideas for stories they'd love to see published and has come to terms with the fact that they'll just have to write it themselves to see it brought to life. They use their love of Japanese pop culture and expensive hobbies as well as their personal experiences with race and gender as inspiration for their writing.

# The Cat

Rita Beth Ebert

1982 CE
Lobby Staircase
Late Afternoon

There has always been a cat at Stormcove.

He determined long ago that the stately double staircase is the ideal location for personal grooming. Some guests find it annoying; some find it endearing. The best ones find it annoying as well as endearing—their kind can juggle so many emotions at once. Despite their obvious shortcomings, he enjoys their company.

The cat stretches one hind leg tall and proud, like a furry flagpole planted in the cool crater of the marble step. He licks himself with lavish fervor. Because he can. Because people dripping with jewelry and exotic urine will soon descend upon the dining room, holding their heads too high to see where they're going. He finds it most amusing.

"Grandpa, look! There's a kitty! There's a kitty inside the hotel!" squeals a small child galumphing across the lobby. She stumbles and falls at the base of the staircase, but that barely slows her momentum. The cat sprawls across the step and eyes the interloper.

"I know your parents have taught you that running and screaming is not how we make friends with animals," wheezes a lanky bearded man following the child. He smells of joy and dread, cannabis and cancer. "Be respectful," the man warns.

The girl halts, settles on a nearby step, and extends her open palm. "Here, kitty."

She'll be one of the good ones. Regardless, the child must be put in her place. The cat's pert, pointy ears crumple against his skull. He hisses, darts up the stairs, and disappears into a hallway.

It's easy to hide. He knows every inch of this building, each new expansion, each tiny gap the mice used to infiltrate the hotel. But there haven't been mice at Stormcove for generations.

Grandfather and granddaughter soon reach the top of the stairs. "You know, this hotel had a cat just like that one when I came here as a boy," the man says to the little girl as they turn down a hallway. They pass under a vent and an unblinking pair of ancient amber eyes, round and luminous like harvest moons. "Black and white. Like me!" The man laughs, and points to his mostly-white beard and curly crown of dark hair. "That one didn't like kids either. Say, maybe that kitty was the *ancestor* of the kitty we just saw!"

"What's an ancestor?" asks the child as their voices and footsteps fade away.

The cat maneuvers his way outside and posts himself on the edge of the wide deck to monitor the sunset. The wind ruffles his fur, the birds swing over the water, and the sun marinates low in the sky.

Their kind is preoccupied with mortality. The cat finds it quaint. There was indeed a black-and-white cat at Stormcove when the dying man was a child. Despite the beard and muted melancholy, the cat recognized the man. He used to be a lively little thing, one who groped at the belly as if he were stroking a common farm collie. Now he is gentle, and seems to know things he wishes he didn't know. Their kind rarely develop any real wisdom until their cells begin to betray them. Perhaps comprehending too much about the mysteries of the universe is why their cells betray them. Combining intelligence with vulnerability was a noble failure.

When the stars begin to wink with deliberation in the frail darkness, the cat returns to the hotel, strutting through the grand entrance like he owns the place.

There has always been a cat at Stormcove.

⚸—

**Rita Beth Ebert** valiantly vanquished a very long creative writing hiatus in 2018, and is thrilled to have her work included in this anthology. She lives in Dayton, Ohio, USA with a big friendly cat, two big friendly dogs, and a big friendly human. Special thanks to Mister Moose for inspiring Hotel Stormcove's feline resident.

# Tilting

Michael Noble

The elevator doors opened and the old man stepped into the Stormcove's lobby, crossed the roughly carpeted floor in his slippers, and addressed himself to the clerk at the desk.

"Young man?"

"Yes, sir?"

"You recall me?"

"Yes, of course, sir. You checked in about half an hour ago—the Windmill Room."

"Indeed. And do you remember what I asked?"

"You asked for a razor."

"And what did you give me?"

"Um . . . a razor."

"No, sir!" replied the old man, holding it up between them. "You gave me this!"

"That's a razor."

"In name, perhaps," retorted the old man, warming to his subject. "It indeed resembles a razor, it holds every promise of a razor, but do me the kindness of looking more closely at it. You see here—it sports dual blades, the uppermost of which being so eclipsed by plastic that it does little but sit in the shade while encouraging its twin to work harder. Like any Gemini, it is gentle yet prone to inconsistency. To a tender stripling of, say, thirteen, it may render a service, but to the thicket of a man of years, it can make at best an empty threat."

"Well . . . it is complimentary . . . " the clerk began.

"Meaning given as a courtesy," the man said as he placed it

on the counter and tapped it with a bony finger while making his points. "But consider—the hollowed handle, the unsupported neck, the narrow blade gap that makes jamming a foregone conclusion. What we see here is not an implement of grooming but a facsimile, a stand-in, a placeholder—a life-size cutout representing an actual razor. It could be said that it is a razor in name only, except that the chartered accountancy which developed it deemed it prudent not to brand it at all, presumably to reduce the chance of litigation."

"I guess it depends on how you look at it," the clerk suggested.

"Oh, no doubt. Given a moment's reflection, it might receive a good-natured shake of the head and then pass into one of those forgotten corners of our personal histories, taking up company with failed ballpoint pens and broken shoelaces. In a darker mood, however, it might become a small plastic totem of capitalism, that venti espresso of civilizations. One could brood over a profit motive so liberated from any kind of accountability, so sundered from any notion of service, that it can mass produce a lie with impunity. Regardless of perspective, however, it is indisputably a product designed to fail—a promise meant to be broken."

"I suppose they could have done a better job with it."

"My dear young man, that is precisely the point—they had no *intention* of doing a better job with it," his finger tapping away. "This is not the blunted machete of the jungle, the rusted scythe amid the barley, the push mower in the hay field. All these may falter but cannot wholly fail unless the hand that wields them despairs. But this!" he cried, taking it up again from the counter and holding it as a sword, "this is a courtesy as hollow as its handle and as pointless as its blades. To distribute it is a capitulation to the moneychangers, it is taking their one score and ten of silver. I tell you it shall not stand! Talk to your manager. Tell him that this edifice will not long endure, trading in the currency of the lowest common denominator—that dealing from a box of lowered expectations is the road to ruin. Let our voices be raised against the tide of societal extortion that has poured into this very lobby at this very hour. Won't you help? Won't you join me?" he pleaded with an open hand extended across the counter. As he finally drew breath, he looked into the clerk's eyes—only to find concern, and a little sadness.

"Look, I could give you a couple more. Maybe one of these would work better," offered the clerk as he placed them in the proffered hand.

The old man held the three before him, crestfallen, in a moment shorn of indignation, hope, dignity ... of everything save his beard. "*Thrice nothing is still . . .* " he murmured.

"Sir?"

"Nothing," said the old man gravely, "nothing at all. I am indebted to you for your patience, young man. Good night." And the old man shuffled back toward the elevator.

Mike Noble is a Systems Analyst for an upstate New York mental health clinic. When not compiling technical manuals, he writes poetry and fiction in his hometown of Poestenkill. He has performed in public readings of works by local authors and annually presents Dickens' *A Christmas Carol.* "Tilting" features the irascible old man resident in the author's head since childhood.

# What Happens at Stormcove . . .

Catrine Kyster Giery

The bus had broken down about a mile outside of town. As the driver directed the passengers to a nearby motel to stay overnight while the bus was either fixed or a new one could be dispatched, he'd taken one look at Sister Anna, said that his sister was a nun too, given her a handful of bills and arranged for a taxi to take her to a nice hotel. Sister Anna, however, did not think that the bus driver had imagined that the taxi driver would take her somewhere as nice as this.

As the elevator let her out on the 17th floor, Sister Anna glanced at her wristwatch. It was five minutes to five. No one would be able to come to the phone at this time—she'd have to wait until at least 6 PM to make a call and explain the delay.

What caught Sister Anna's eye as soon as she entered her room was a large bed covered with a silky-soft dark fabric that reached all the way to the floor and covered the pillows too. She sat down. She'd not seen or felt a bed like this since she joined the world she belonged to now. Pushing the tips of her sturdy black shoes against the floor, she bounced gently up and down. Actually, she'd never felt such a luxurious bed, not even before.

She took off her shoes to savor the softness of the wall-to-wall carpet under her feet as she walked over towards the bathroom. There was a telephone—which the receptionist had mentioned when she inquired about making a call—a television set, and a couple of bright magazines on a small table. Sister Anna opened a closet next to the bathroom—and there, on a hanger in the back, was a robin's-egg-blue sleeveless cotton summer dress with a matching belt.

Someone must obviously have forgotten it. Sister Anna gently removed the dress from the closet and let the soft fabric glide through her fingers. The dress looked to be her size.

She took off her headdress first, then the rest. Whoever had forgotten the dress hadn't forgotten any shoes to go with it, so her own shoes would just have to do. They were a bit uncomfortable with bare feet, but Sister Anna was used to a bit uncomfortable. The summer dress went over her head and slid onto her body as if it were made to measure. Standing by the sink, she wet her fingers and ran them through her hair before she looked at herself in the mirror. Even after she ran a comb through it, her hair didn't look quite right.

But then she smiled at her reflection. God wouldn't have guided her to a hotel room with a perfect dress left in the closet if he hadn't meant for her to use it. As she left the room, she clutched the key and a quarter in her hand—enough money for an ice cream—and the feel of the afternoon's last sunrays on her legs would be free.

She pushed the elevator button and looked at her watch again while she waited. It was 5 PM. Plenty of time to be back at the hotel in time to make a phone call later.

⚷

**Catrine Kyster Giery** was born in Denmark and moved to the United States fifteen years ago when she fell in love with a Brooklyn-born Detective and moved to New York City to be with him. Today, a widow, Catrine lives in coastal South Carolina. She writes fiction, raises her daughter who also loves to write, and is studying for a master's degree in public history. Not surprisingly, Catrine loves to stay at historic hotels when she travels, and she is intrigued by how hotels can offer people an opportunity to be themselves or be someone else for a short time. The granddaughter of a Danish deaconess, Catrine has always been fascinated by religious sisters, and her story explores what could happen when a sister is given a few hours off, far away from her usual daily life. Catrine believes that we all need a little time off sometimes. catrinekyster.com.

# You Can't Go Back

Ellen Meny

1935 New Era
The Lounge
5:55 PM, The Twenty-Sixth Time

Frederick is kind even when he breaks my heart.

He's kind even when I see the words on his lips as we sit in the lounge of the Hotel Stormcove, untouched drinks sitting between us. Normally, this place is warmth and smoke and light, soft touches and the burn of whisky. Not anymore.

Outside, through the wide bay window, the sun sets on the dark line of the ocean. Winds whip the strangled brush of the beach. Five minutes from now, it will start to rain.

The words he's going to say are the ones that make my fingers twitch and my watchband scuff my wrist, the ones that keep beds cold and liquor stores open. They make people do things they wouldn't do normally.

Inside, guests of the hotel drift into the lounge for cocktails. A man orders a drink in a coupe glass, milky purple and adorned with a violet. A woman takes off her top hat and coat. We're tucked away from the rest of the crowd, sitting next to the stone fireplace. Frederick looks broken.

"Will," he says, and I can already hear the tears in his voice. "Will, I'm sorry."

I don't respond this time, thinking it might change things. Maybe silence will shift my fate. But I can still see his wet blue eyes, the way he wrings his hands as he opens his mouth.

He's going to say it.

My hand leaves the stem of my glass. It moves towards the watch on my left wrist; the antique gold face, the worn leather band. His lips part. I feel my life ending.

"Will," he says, "I don't—"

*Stop.*

I turn the watch dial backwards.

*Again.*

The barroom around me shifts.

The coupe glass drifts back from the man's lips to the lacquered bar top. The woman puts her hat on again and threads her arms through her coat. The clouds swell back from the beach, wisping into inexistence.

Frederick, in front of me, moves in reverse. It is pure pain to see his mouth twist into a frown again, the hurt in his eyes doubled and relived. I see the words escape his lips in a tortured picture:

*Anymore you love don't I.*

Another minute rushes backwards. The watch dial stops with a *click*.

The woman takes off her top hat. The man takes a drink—I recognize the cocktail now, the Sea Violet, a Stormcove favorite. Frederick would always order it when we first came to the hotel. He'd take the flower and tuck it behind my ear.

Now, he stares at me, elbows on his knees. He looks at my watch.

"You used it, didn't you?" he asks.

"Only once," I say. "I promise."

That's a lie. I've used it twenty-five times.

Twenty-five times, I've seen my life almost shatter. Twenty-five variations on sadness and anger, each one just as painful as the last. I've seen Frederick throw his drink. Storm out of the lounge. Cry. I've done much of the same.

The man at the bar has taken the same sip of Sea Violet twenty-five times, and never once has Frederick mentioned the flower.

This time, he shoots up from his chair, knocking his drink onto the floor. "You *promised!*" Glass smashes on the marble;

heads turn towards us. "You promised, Will, you said you'd never do that to me—"

"Frederick, this is different. I'm sorry. I'm so sorry." Even as I say it, my fingers tremble on the watch. He catches the movement before I can hide my hand, and his face cracks into a splintered sob.

"You can't control everything," he gasps. "You need to understand. I don't love—"

*Stop.*

*Again.*

The woman dons her hat. The man sets his drink on the bar. Frederick sits back down, and his broken glass reforms, shards glittering in the air as they twist and refract into shape. Outside, I notice a flock of seagulls just off the rocky cliffs, their wings beating in reverse. The rain clouds regress, but they'll come back.

I can do this seven hundred times if I want, an eternity of five minutes; until my skin sags off my bones and my eyes go rheumy. Delaying the inevitable. Battling against the wind, over and over and over again.

A tear drops onto the watch face as I stop the dial.

Frederick runs his hands through his hair, and at that moment I want to reach out and do the same, thread my fingers through his curls and brush his palm with my own. I want to grab our drinks, and invite him to go outside to look at the waves, and slip my arm around his familiar waist. But I tried to do that on attempt sixteen, and it didn't work. And it won't work this time. Or ever again.

"You used it, didn't you?" he asks, one last time.

"Yes. Twenty-six times now."

His eyes are tired. "You can't control everything, Will."

"I don't want to." My voice cracks on the last word. The woman in the hat looks over at us, and then quickly turns away, embarrassed at my tears. "I'll throw this away, I swear. I just want us—"

"Will."

I hear the ache in his voice again. He's going to say it. My fingers hover towards the watch.

And then, they stop.

"Will," he says, "I don't love you anymore. I'm sorry."

Outside, the seagulls disappear into the clouds. The woman hangs her hat on the coat rack. The man finishes his drink, and the rain begins.

⚬╼

Ellen Meny is a writer and television reporter working in Seattle, Washington. She enjoys exploring the emotional elements of fantasy, sci-fi, and horror. When she's not writing, you can find her sampling Seattle's restaurants, online shopping but never buying anything, and hanging out with her adorable hamster, Peachy Keen. You can find more of her work on her website, ellenmeny.com.

# A Port in the Storm
### Maria E. Andreu

A Brisk March Day, 2019
Hallway Outside the Service Elevator, Ground Floor
2:12 PM

"Se lo agradezco tanto," says Lupe, hands rubbing the front of her uniform as if to erase a stubborn stain. She looks up and down the hall even though it's empty, even though she's already done it several times.

"I know, I know," I say. Not impatiently, but its cousin. I said I'd do it, didn't I? Her effusive thanks makes it all the more awkward. Relieved from the front desk for a break, I take a drag of my vape pen, hoping the bubblegum swirl in the back of my throat will taste something like cheeriness, something like calm. Instead, its flavor is vaguely metallic and inauthentic, a thing playing at being something else. It has the opposite effect of what I want. Damn those pills for not working.

"They're over here, Señorita Robert," she says, rolling the "r" of my last name lavishly, leaving off the "s."

I don't know this part of the hotel well, so I'm surprised to see daylight, intrusive and alive, when she opens the door at the end of the hall. The saltwater scent assaults me, and I can almost feel the humidity frizzing up my hair.

They look like they're shaking, although it's brisk but not cold. Or maybe my eyes are playing a trick on me. The man has his left arm around the woman. He's a full half a head shorter than I am, and I'm not particularly tall. The woman's face is almost a perfect circle, and clearly shows the genes she shares with Lupe, the same round, almost-black eyes, the frame of silken black hair. The man's other arm is on the shoulder of a painfully skinny little boy of indeterminate age. By his size he should be about four or five, but judging by his thin, serious face and his knowing gaze, he could be as old as eight or nine. He tightly grasps his little sister's hand, which still has the dimples of babyhood on it. All four are clustered together as if to ward off a storm.

Lupe says something quickly in Spanish, too fast for me to understand with my serviceable, behind-the-stairs housekeeping Spanish. I was so sure my semester in Seville would have made Spanish come more easily. But my late nights sharing bocaditos with the beautiful, ample-lipped Marcelo did nothing to prepare me to understand what Lupe just said to her sister.

"We'll have to hurry," I say. They nod, but look unsure. I turn back to the door and into the corridor where Lupe and I just came from.

I fall back and let Lupe walk ahead of me. "You prepared 1407?" I ask. She nods. It's one of the rooms least likely to be booked, one of the few with an obstructed view of the sea.

It's not like giving a room for free is unknown in the history of Stormcove. It was one of the first things I learned back when I got my internship between my junior and senior year of college, the summer after my tearful goodbye with Marcelo, at a time when I still believed our solemn promises to write, to visit. *If he could see me now,* I think bitterly. *He'd be glad he dodged this bullet.* Or maybe I'd be a different me if I'd just stayed, the way we talked about.

So, yes, Bill, the manager at the time, a man who looked as woven into the hotel as the sea grass near the shore, sat at the front desk computer and typed at the keyboard in that way he had, with fingers which seemed too creaky to bend. He laboriously typed in a reservation. No phone had rung, and he hadn't looked at our incoming reservations software, which seemed odd.

It happened a few times before I realized what he was doing: he was blocking off a room or two without having received any form of payment. One time, as I escorted a contractor around the top floors, I saw him shuttle a young couple to one of our most expensive rooms, which hadn't been booked in weeks, a honeymoon suite on the twenty-first floor with a grand view of the water. A few years later, a stricken-looking man, who clearly hadn't slept or showered, followed him in a back door and to an elevator bank. I had only seen this moment because I'd been on a rock at the back of the property tearfully fighting on my cell phone with my boyfriend at the time who hadn't come home yet again the night before. There were other times Bill left the desk for a short while without explanation. Whether he went to sneak a snack or to ferry people to our unbooked rooms, I never did find out.

It was only at his retirement party that I got the courage to ask him about it. I'd been made Assistant Manager by then and would be taking on more responsibility now that Bill was leaving. (The joke was that Bill had been the manager back in 1924 when the property had been renamed Hotel Stormcove, but of course that was mathematically impossible.) I couldn't imagine that the patrons who paid a premium to book an unobstructed view of the breakers beyond the rocks would be thrilled to learn that some got the same view for free.

"Bill," I'd asked, "those people you let stay for free—what's the story with that?"

Bill scraped back thin white hair over a mottled scalp like he was pulling a thick shock of curls out of his eyes. He narrowed his sharp blue eyes, as if taking my measure. "I suppose I can tell you, rather than let you come to it yourself: where there's room, see what you can do with it. Be a port in a storm, so to speak. There's a venerable tradition of it here at Stormcove."

It was cryptic, but try as I might to get further information from him, that's all he would say. He tipped his head back to dump in more of the boxed wine that had been rolled out for the occasion.

On the other side of the party room we'd commandeered, a cook held his hat in his hand and talked to a gardener. A few maids huddled in a corner and raised their glasses in his direction when Bill looked their way. People didn't so much love Bill as wonder if the hotel would be able to function without him.

It did. I became night manager, then got a more coveted day-time manager role. The boyfriend who didn't come home nights ran off with a contortionist he'd been seeing. Then there was a tearless goodbye to the boyfriend after him, who bought me sweet gifts but never wanted to have sex, who never rose to the occasion when I wanted to pick a fight. I celebrated my thirtieth birthday behind the desk, and noted I was the kind of woman that Seville me would have disdained, alone, adrift, on weight loss pills that were making everything look drenched in gray.

It was right around that time that the first opportunity to think about Bill's words came to me. I bumped into an old high school friend—more of an acquaintance, really—in the drugstore, where I'd taken to buying energy drinks every morning before work, hoping the sugar and caffeine would help me feel alive. She insisted on lunch and prevented me from begging off by coming to one of the hotel restaurants for it.

I met her at the entrance to the Coventry, our more casual restaurant, its floor-to-ceiling windows framing a bright blue sky and calm, wintry water. The hostess walked us to a window seat, and my old high school acquaintance—we'd both been in the drama club together, though it seemed impossible to believe all these years later—began an earnest but incessant barrage of words. Where she'd been in the intervening years, what she hoped for, something about a new man and biking up a coast for weeks, although which specific coast, I didn't quite catch. Finally, she turned the conversation to an older sister I vaguely remembered, a few years ahead of us in school, known for the chippy red pick-up truck she'd driven around in with her friends on the bed in the back.

My attention was caught by an unruly cluster of seagulls, and some uneven lounge chairs on the patio overlooking the shore. I made a mental note to get a ground crew member out there to hose it down to get rid of whatever was drawing the gulls. When I tuned back in, my acquaintance was still mid-story.

"I mean, it's not like he's physically abusive, you know? He mostly just plays video games when he's home. But the things he says to her, they're like razors to the soul, I swear. And to think that she can't go anywhere because she doesn't have a job, that she's trapped there. I mean, I know he's my brother-in-law, but sometimes I could just smother him."

I don't think she was fishing, not really. But there was something in her story that made me take the first step.

I scrunched up my mouth and said, perhaps too drily, "I doubt it needs to come to murder." Then I told her to have her sister meet me at the back door that Thursday. Peggy stayed in room 1617 for three months while she found a job and saved for her own place. She insisted on "paying" me in private yoga classes in the room while her chubby baby girl played near the floor-to-ceiling window, the tossed sea a blue-green lightbox behind her.

She owns a yoga studio in the village now, and once sent me a certificate for a lifetime of free lessons. I should go check it out at some point.

I look down at my phone. It's been two minutes already. Lupe's sister and her family still huddle together, even though it's definitely not cold in here. The elevator dings its arrival, and the doors take cartoonishly long to open. We should probably have that looked at. This old place acts like it's got creaky bones.

I let them in first. I could have just let Lupe take them up to the room, but whenever I give a room for free, I feel a responsibility to see it through. My decision, my duty. The doors close in their wheezing fashion, and the service elevator lumbers up to the thirteenth floor. We call it the fourteenth, as hotels do sometimes.

I really should get back down to the desk. We've got a college soccer team coming in any minute—our shuttle driver texted an ETA of ten minutes an hour ago—so they'll be pulling in to the property any second and that will be a hell of a check-in. We've got a new kid at the desk, all arms and Adam's apple, and I don't know how he'll fare alone. But I feel pulled forward, on to 1407, like something important will come of going there with Lupe's sister and her family.

Another minute ticks by. Finally, the elevator doors open. 1407, mercifully, is just a few steps from the service elevator. I step forward with the keycard, open the door, and lead the way in. It's spotless and made up as if for our most important VIPs, with towels folded like an octopus at the foot of the bed, and the blue-green Art Deco quilt crisp and pulled taut—obviously one of our newer ones. There are chocolates on the pillows. Lupe leans down to her nephew and whispers something to him, her lips almost on his cheek. He tentatively goes up to the towel octopus and pets it like one might a stranger's dog, and his eyes smile.

It is only now I realize the parents are each carrying a small backpack, and that's all the luggage they've got for the four of them. I show them the bathroom like an awkward realtor and turn on the TV to the children's channel.

"I need to go now," I say. "Lupe here will make sure you have what you need."

Her sister walks up to me and takes my hand in her own warm, worn one. She asks Lupe to translate.

"She says, 'Thank you, Señora,'" Lupe says. Then she turns back to her sister. "Es Señorita."

It's Lupe saying the words I understand, but I look straight into her sister's inky eyes, older than her years. "My sister was very generous in letting us stay with her while we waited for a decision on our asylum claim, but now that they denied it, we don't want to put her in any danger. She's undocumented, as I'm sure you know, and we don't want trouble for her." Lupe squeezes her sister's hand at this, and the translation cracks almost imperceptibly.

"We came to this country to make a better life. If we go back to my country, my husband, they kill him. I know how things are in this country now, and the risk you take. You have the heart of a hero, and we will never forget you.

"Also, you will not lose with us. I work hard. I clean, I am good in the kitchen. My husband can fix anything." He nods solemnly at this a beat before Lupe gets the words out. "Even the kids, if you need help. My son is fast, he could take messages, or carry things. My daughter can fold napkins, or whatever you need that a little one can do. You don't lose with us," she repeats.

The flesh of my throat tenses up, releasing stale faux bubble gum flavor again. "It's nothing," I say, a ripple of shame fluttering over me. It's just an extra room we wouldn't have booked, and I'm uncomfortable that something I'd give no mind to can elicit such gratitude.

"It's no nothing. Es vida," says Lupe's sister. It is life.

I nod and begin to make my way to the door. But I am overtaken by something, like a wave in the sea, taller and stronger than me, a surge of something real and bursting to come up for air. I turn back to her, splay my arms in hug position and wait, a question of a hug. She steps into it, her embrace back surprisingly hearty and solid.

"You good woman," she says into the fabric at my chest. Her little boy hugs my leg through its polyester pant sheath, and he's strong too.

I say nothing in response to this overly-generous assessment. I hold back the tears until I reach the hall. I press the elevator down button and wonder if the front desk will ever matter the same way again.

⊶

**Maria E. Andreu** crossed the border into the U.S. undocumented at the age of eight, and would have loved to have found a room at the Hotel Stormcove following that experience. It was not to be, so she settled in New Jersey. Four years later, she wrote in her diary, " . . . most of all, I want to be a writer." It took a while, but her work has appeared in *Newsweek*, *The Washington Post*, *Teen Vogue*, and NJ.com. Her debut novel, *The Secret Side of Empty*, is an Indie Excellence Award Winner, a Junior Library Guild Selection, and was called "captivating" by *School Library Journal*. Read more of her work at mariaeandreu.com.

# An Affair at Stormcove

Robert Dawson

September 10th, 1964
Room 147
1:50 AM

Henry heard the woman—Pearl, it would be gauche to forget her name—turn over. Sheets whispered against her naked skin. A click of the switch on the lamp cord, and her hotel room came into being. She swung her legs out of the rumpled bed, got to her feet and stretched. Even when she bent her head back, her dark hair, cut urchin-short, did not reach her muscular shoulders.

"Need to get up?" he asked, not knowing her well enough to use more direct words. He let his eyes linger on her strong legs, solid back and buttocks, so different from Thalia's fashionably slim body. He tried, unsuccessfully, to hush the inner voice that told him he should not be here.

"I will go outside now," Pearl said, without turning to look at him. Her voice was low-pitched, with a slight accent that he could not place. "You can come with me if you want."

The rooms down here on the ground floor of Hotel Stormcove had patio doors. Pearl walked over to the door and took her coat from the hook, some plain grey fur. Not mink; he could recognize mink. Thalia wore mink, a palomino jacket that he'd bought her last summer for their fifth anniversary.

"Aren't you going to get dressed first?" Henry asked. He gestured toward the blue paisley dress, hanging alone in the closet, that she'd been wearing that evening. Below it, white sandals stood neatly side by side. There was no other clothing in the room. No suitcase. Odd. There were rumors among the regulars that sometimes the proprietors, out of charity or tradition, let hard-up travelers stay without paying. Surreptitiously, he reached out and touched his jacket where he had slung it over the end of the head-board a few hours ago. His billfold was still there; he was ashamed of his suspicion. Maybe she'd had to make an unexpected over-night stop. Car trouble, something like that.

She shook her head, draped the coat over her arm. "No, not yet. Are you coming with me?" She opened the door. Though the room did not face onto the cove—those rooms, mostly booked months in advance, were more modern and far more expensive—he could hear the insistent splash of waves on rocks a hundred yards away.

The thought of outdoor lovemaking in the warm September night stirred Henry's imagination. Could they risk it? If they got caught in the act—if word of this ever got back to Chicago, back to the dry goods store and the Rotary Club, back to Thalia—he would never live it down. He glanced toward the humming electric clock on the bedside table. Almost two in the morning. At dinnertime the moon had been a thin crescent. It would have followed the sun to bed hours ago: the sky would be dark. Surely nobody would be wandering about this late?

"Sure thing, babe," he said—not "honey," that was Thalia—and got out of bed. He looked for his underpants, then reckless-ness overcame him: if she could go outside naked, he would too. "Let's go."

The night air was pleasantly cool, the breeze intimate on his damp skin. Pearl closed the door, but did not lock it. Her hand gripped his upper arm, and they walked together over the dewy grass. "Where do you want to go?" he asked.

"Down to the sea."

Did she just want to swim, then, a late-night skinnydip? He looked up at the star-spattered sky, so different from the street-light-sick murk over Chicago. Orion hung in the south, tilted drunkenly. A shooting star traced a brief white razorcut on black velvet. He stopped, pulled her to him, his arms around her strong, solid body, and put his lips to hers. She kissed him hungrily.

When they came up for air, he whispered in her ear, "Who are you?"

She laughed softly. "I told you already. My name is Pearl."

"Tell me more about yourself."

"You will find out. Soon."

"How soon?"

"Soon." She clutched his hand, and pulled him after her. He followed, wondering once more what he was getting into. Had got into. Ahead of them was a faint grey smear, the footpath from the hotel to the South Cape lighthouse. Rough grit replaced wet grass under his feet. She led him along the path, beside the chuckling waves. The still air bore the mysterious ocean scent: salt, seaweed, life and decay, the odors of an alien world.

The path crossed a rock that sloped down into the sea; the granite was sharp against his soles, a thousand tiny points. She stopped, then turned and guided him down to where the receding tide had left the rock wet underfoot. "I have to go now," she said.

Back to the hotel already? "Are you cold?" Henry asked. "You could put your coat on."

"That's what I will do now," Pearl said. "Goodbye, Henry! I enjoyed this evening, you were very sweet—but now I must go back to my people."

Before he could say anything, she kissed him once more, her lips fierce against his; then she let go of his hand, shook out her coat, and slipped first one naked arm and then the other into the sleeves. In the lying soft-edged greyness of the starlight, it seemed that the fur wrapped itself around her, covering her from head to toe like a cape, like a chrysalis, wrapping her arms against her body. She sank down to the rough granite, half-reclining like that mermaid sculpture in Copenhagen Harbor, and looked up at him with eyes that seemed impossibly large and dark. She gave a deep, resonant bark that came from no human throat, and rubbed a furry cheek against his thigh. Then she turned, plopped into the water, and swam silently away.

He watched the sleek black head move through the waves with hardly a ripple. *Come back!* he almost called, then remembered his nakedness and, suddenly afraid, bit the words back. She would have paid no attention anyway. When seal-people came ashore to consort with humans, the stories said, they left without guilt, without regret. Those were for the lovers left ashore. The dark spot grew indistinct among the ripples, had already disappeared.

Could this be a dream? If it were, then he could wake up now. He could open his eyes in his own room, and, by the time he had showered and dressed, this strange world in which women could turn into seals, in which he had cheated on Thalia, would have faded away, and he'd be guilty of nothing worse than an overactive subconscious, or whatever the shrinks would call it. But the ocean tang and the sharp granite under his feet were too clearly real, as real as the guilt. Even if he dared to confess to Thalia, she would never believe him. *Then she turned into a seal and swam away.* Yeah, sure.

It was up to him to make his own second chance.

He shook his head, turned, and walked back to the hotel.

⊶

Robert Dawson teaches mathematics at Saint Mary's University in Halifax, Nova Scotia. He has been writing science fiction and fantasy for about ten years. In his spare time he enjoys cycling, hiking, and fencing, and volunteers with a Scout troop. He is an alumnus of the Sage Hill and Viable Paradise writing workshops.

# The Repatriation Heist

Jennifer Lee Rossman

2014
Room 804
4:45 PM

The room looked bigger in real life. Not surprising, Marcella acknowledged, as she'd only studied the teeny replica Mohinder had built, like a little mouse's hotel room in an animated movie, but it was just . . . bigger than she'd expected, and she hoped that wouldn't mess with her carefully practiced choreography.

She wasted no time, flinging open the closet door as soon as she heard the room door click shut.

Timing. It all came down to timing.

She went straight for the handbag left on the end of the bed, flipping open the hinged painting that concealed the safe as she passed it. An oceanscape, almost a perfect replica of the view out the window.

Marcella tossed Dr. Gilbert's cellphone across the room as she rummaged through the purse for something with DNA on it. The doctor was too careful to actually leave evidence behind at the museum, but nothing a little time magic couldn't fix.

Her fingers curled around a cool metal tube. Lipstick, the fancy kind that used numbers instead of cutesy names. Marcella decided this one should be called "Cultural Looting Red."

She pocketed the tube as she went to close the window, ducking for reasons only apparent to her. Her autistic mind may have made conversations painfully difficult, but it helped her see how the future would unfold in ways none of her team could. Only she could execute this precise of a heist in the minute Dr. Gilbert's purse was unattended.

After closing and latching the window—the spirit would be

loose by now and looking for any escape route—Marcella did a quick sweep of the room, taking note of exactly where the phone had landed, as well as the location of a nicely sized vase on a vanity.

Good. All good.

Marcella high-fived the air and sent herself back in time with a nose wiggle that she totally stole from *Bewitched*.

---

The second time Marcella appeared in the closet, she was a second behind her previous self—a necessary precaution so she wouldn't be in the same place at the same time.

She went for the safe, already exposed behind the painting, and punched in the code procured by the recon team. The urn sat in the very center of the square space, gilded but dingy with age.

Shame the spirit couldn't stay in it forever, she thought as she sidestepped the phone, which landed with a thud on the carpet beside her, but it would be evidence soon. She went to the vanity on the far side of the room and picked up the vase that would be the spirit's new home, spilling the flowers and water out the window.

But there was no lid.

"Shoot," she said, watching herself duck on her way to close the window.

What to do, what to do . . .

She held the vase as if to catch something, at a loss for what to do. She'd only planned for four cycles, but she'd clearly need another.

Would the room still feel big when it was crowded with Marcellas?

Marcella number three dove for the luggage beside the bed, looking for anything she could use to keep the spirit in the vase. Why hadn't she just brought a Pringles can?!

Of course Dr. Gilbert hadn't brought any convenient tubes of chips; stodgy museum curators who stole artifacts from native cultures could afford snacks from the minibar.

Ooh. There was an idea.

To the minibar Marcella went, and there she found a small can of exorbitantly priced mixed nuts. She pried off the lid. A little flimsy, but it wasn't a particularly strong spirit. Just a sad, homesick one who deserved to be back with its people, not in a museum and *certainly* not sold to some wealthy collector at the auction being held in the Stormcove's event hall later that night.

The urn deserved to go home, too. It never should have been taken in the first place, and Dr. Gilbert must have realized that. Why else would she have absconded with an entire wing of her own museum if she wasn't worried about being caught and shamed for stealing another culture's history?

But the urn and other artifacts would eventually be returned— Marcella's team of time witches had tracked them all down—so they weren't a priority. The spirit, however . . . it would get released at the auction and go full poltergeist on the hotel. Not in a malicious way, just its reaction to too much stress and stimuli: a wee ghosty autistic meltdown.

The second Marcella said "Shoot," and Marcella Three threw the lid like a Frisbee, zooming over the head of her first self.

Ah. She'd *thought* there was a reason she needed to duck.

With the few seconds remaining in this minute, she shoved some cashews in her mouth. Magic always made her hungry.

———o•⟹———

The fourth Marcella had to step around the third, and almost missed the phone as it sailed through the air. She just caught it in her fingertips and quickly dialed 911.

Talking on the phone usually made her anxious. No way to tell if the person on the other end was bored, or getting angry, or if other people were listening in. But this was a special circumstance, and she got to put on a fake accent, so it was almost like she was someone else.

"Hello," she said when the operator answered, doing her best impersonation of Dr. Gilbert's refined, mature voice. She then realized that she should have been much more distressed. "Oh! It's a tragedy! I've been robbed—robbed, I say!"

Marcella gleefully pulled some clothes from the suitcase the third version of herself was about to abandon in favor of the mini-bar, giving the room a disheveled, rummaged-about-in look.

"Where are you located, ma'am?"

"Hotel Stormcove. Room 804. Please hurry! Oh, I should check the safe! There's a very valuable artifact inside, which I recently stole from my own museum."

As the final Marcella would have had time to do the ritual by now, she closed the safe so Dr. Gilbert wouldn't automatically realize it had been tampered with and think to hide the urn before the police showed up.

The soft cry of "Shoot" signaled the end of her minute was nearing. Just to cover all her bases, Marcella hastened to add, "This is Dr. Marjory Gilbert, by the way," before hanging up and shoving the phone back in the purse.

One more to go.

Marcella began the incantation before she stepped out of the closet.

It was like any magic spell, really: long and full of pseudo-Latin that made it hard to pronounce. It didn't have to be Latin—it didn't even have to be spoken aloud, so long as the witch *felt* the magic—but Latin made it far less likely for eavesdroppers to memorize and illegally duplicate.

Intellectual property laws, Mohinder always told her, applied to magic as well.

With every word she spoke, Marcella felt the energy in the room growing more, well, energetic, invisible eddies of power swirling around her and her past selves.

One Marcella opened the safe, and the urn began to glow as the spirit inside was given permission to come out. Already agitated from years of being so far from its rightful home, it wouldn't have taken much for it to break out at the auction.

The spirit burst from the urn just as the second Marcella said "Shoot," and it made a beeline for the window.

The mixed nuts lid soared through the air, and Marcella ran after it, snatching it up off the floor as the window slammed shut.

Its only escape route gone and the urn closed away in the safe, the spirit sought out the nearest vessel of appropriate size.

Triumphantly, Marcella clamped the lid onto the vase, taking it from herself and holding it tight to her chest. "You're okay," she whispered to the spirit swirling around inside. "You're going home."

Not one to leave herself hanging, Marcella provided the other half of the high-five she had initiated at the end of her first minute in Dr. Gilbert's room. And with that, she nose-wriggled her way back to her own time and the other members of her coven, ready to begin planning their next mission.

Jennifer Lee Rossman is an autistic and physically disabled writer who describes herself as "If Dr. Temperance Brennan from *Bones* was a Disney Princess." She co-edited the queer romance anthology *Love & Bubbles*, and her debut novel, *Jack Jetstark's Intergalactic Freakshow*, was published by World Weaver Press in 2018. She blogs at jenniferleerossman.blogspot.com and tweets @JenLRossman.

# Thirteen
J.S. Bailey

1993
The Bar
8:05 PM

It wasn't often that Marsha Marquez had to travel alone, but when she did, she gravitated to the nearest bar each evening so she wouldn't feel the crushing weight of solitude, knowing that her closest friends were hundreds of miles away and unable to chat unless she spent half her travel money at the hotel payphone.

Besides, Hotel Stormcove's two payphones were both currently out of order. "The phone company's sending someone out next week," the yawning front desk clerk had said after tearing her gaze away from a tattered word-find book. It seemed a godawful inconvenience for the guests, but what would complaining do?

Marsha sat at the polished wood counter in the hotel's on-site bar, gazing at the myriad glimmering bottles on display behind it while she nursed a whiskey sour. A single television off in the corner played some sporting event that had gotten a few of the bar's patrons riled up, and she was starting to wish that her whiskey sour had the magical ability to drown out their noise.

At least this place had its own bar, unlike some of the sleazier motels she'd stayed at during her business-related travels. It saved her from having to trudge in high heels through the rain that had been drenching the coast all day.

She twitched as a man sidled up to the counter and took the stool right next to hers. She discreetly scooted her stool a few inches in the other direction to allow herself some space.

"I'll have a Manhattan, please," the man said to the bartender.

The newcomer had graying hair and wore a deep blue business suit that looked more expensive than Marsha's entire wardrobe.

The pretentious sort, it seemed, if she were to judge from the tailored shape of the suit, his gold cufflinks, and callus-free hands. He was probably fifteen years older than she was, maybe twenty, but still handsome in a movie star sort of way, which of course added to the whole ensemble.

As the bartender began to assemble the man's beverage, Marsha said, "You just get in?"

Mr. Pretentious turned toward her and gave her a smile that was actually kind of friendly. "I checked in this afternoon," he said, looking surprised that she'd spoken to him. "Let me tell you, I've never been happier to get off a plane."

"Rough flight?"

"There were screaming kids *everywhere*. What about you?"

Marsha took a sip of her whiskey sour. "I've been here four days. I drove in from Cincinnati for the big trade show. My boss is paying for all of it." She glanced at her drink. "Well, not this."

The man laughed and held out a hand. "I'm Everett, by the way."

She gave his hand a hearty shake. "Marsha Marquez. I hope you got a better room than I did. The brochures brag about the amazing cove views, but all my room has is a breathtaking view of the dumpsters out back."

"Oh, that's too bad. From my room, I can see all the way out to the ocean."

"Which room is that?"

"1310."

"You're kidding."

He raised his eyebrows. "Why would I kid?"

"There *is* no thirteenth floor in this building. They did it for superstitious people who freak out about that kind of thing, so it goes from Floor 12 straight to Floor 14. I know, because my room is on the fourteenth floor, and I see the discrepancy every time I go up the stairs."

"You don't take the elevator?"

"I have a desk job. I take my exercise however I can."

"If you don't believe me about the number, it's on my room key." He fished in his jacket pocket and withdrew a key which, true to his word, dangled from a keychain bearing the aforementioned number. "Why would anyone be afraid of the number thirteen?"

"Why do they think breaking a mirror gives you seven years of bad luck?"

Everett gave her a blank stare.

"You haven't heard of that one, either?" This guy must have grown up under a pretentious rock.

"Perhaps it's a regional thing?" He sipped at the Manhattan the bartender passed to him. "You said you're from Cincinnati."

"It's more than just Cincinnati that thinks thirteen is unlucky. I've been to hotels all over the country, and very few of the tall ones have a thirteenth floor."

"They go from 12 to 14, you mean."

"That's right."

"Fascinating." Everett's eyes went out of focus as he took another drink. "You know, I've always heard that six is an unlucky number. There isn't a sixth-floor button in the elevator here, and fear of the number six is why hardly anyone schedules weddings for June."

That made Marsha cross her arms. "Is making up facts for the sake of argument some new way of picking up women? Loads of people get married in June. I work for a wedding planner; I'm in town for the big bridal expo."

A crease appeared in Everett's forehead. "I'm not trying to come on to you. I'm genuinely curious as to why you think thirteen is some omen of bad luck, and six is just a number, when for my entire life I've heard just the opposite."

"Six *is* just a number." Marsha looked to the bartender, who was meticulously straightening the bottles on the shelf behind the counter. "Right?"

"I'm not superstitious, ma'am," the bartender said, looking up from his task. "If you ask me, all numbers are just numbers." He shrugged. "If you two can't figure out who's right and who's wrong, go find out. I'll keep an eye on your drinks."

"Shouldn't you know which numbers are in the elevator and stairwell?" Marsha asked. "You work here."

"Yes. In this bar, on the first floor. I've never even been in the elevator."

Marsha glanced at Everett. "All right. Let's go look at the numbers to see who's right. But if you try to touch me, I'll karate chop your ass into kingdom come."

"Fair enough," Everett said stiffly.

They exited the bar together. Marsha wondered if Everett had drunk so much already that common facts had gotten all jumbled up inside his head like the scattered pieces of a jigsaw puzzle.

*But his keychain had "1310" printed on it.*

So he'd brought his own keychain and put it on his room key.

*But what would be the point?*

They arrived at the bank of elevators. Marsha hit the call button, stepped back, and gave Everett a prideful look, knowing she would soon be proven right.

The nearest elevator dinged, and the doors slid open.

"After you," Marsha said, and Everett stepped inside.

She joined him, cautiously.

"See?" Everett said, pointing at the rows of buttons. "One, two, three, four, five, seven. And here's number thirteen."

Marsha gaped at the numbers, then shook her head as she realized the buttons in here had simply been mislabeled. She slapped the 12, and the doors slid shut. "All right," she said. "Now I'll show you the stairwell."

They glided smoothly up to the twelfth floor, stepped into the carpeted hallway, then moved to the door marked "Stairwell" and pushed their way through it. A large "12" was emblazoned on the wall just inside the door.

"I'm telling you I walk past this every day," Marsha said, moving toward the steps.

Everett followed her up one flight. Marsha drew up short as she spotted the large "13" on the wall where she knew darn well a "14" was supposed to be.

Everett's mouth formed a condescending smirk. "You were saying?"

She stared at the number in exasperation and floundered for words. "I—I don't believe this! Someone's repainted the number!" Marsha burst through the door into the corridor, fully intending to go directly to her room to prove they were actually on Floor 14, but she was distracted by the gleaming evening sunlight spilling through the window at the far end of the hallway. Her feet drew her forward until she reached the floor-to-ceiling glass. The sun hung low in the sky above the green hills farther inland, and not a single cloud dotted the azure heavens.

"Is there another problem?" Everett asked.

"It's been pouring all day today." She gestured at the sky. "This can't be right."

He glared at her. "It's been sunny since I got off the plane, but maybe I'm just *imagining things*. I'm going back down to my Manhattan."

With a huff, he boarded the elevator, and the doors whooshed shut. Marsha watched gulls swoop through the clear evening air for a few seconds before returning dazedly to the stairwell.

Inside, on the wall, the number 14 stood out, bold and clear as day.

She descended the steps, passed the number 12, and got off on that floor. Sheets of rain sluiced against the window at the end of the hallway, so strong it sounded like hail.

She called the elevator. The doors opened, and she stepped on. The button for Floor 6 sat right between the buttons for Floors 5 and 7, just like it was supposed to.

There was no button for Floor 13.

When Marsha made it back to the bar on the first floor, Everett wasn't there, nor was his half-consumed Manhattan. She picked up her whiskey sour, started to take a sip, then shook her head.

"Everything all right, ma'am?" the bartender asked.

She almost—*almost*—asked if he had seen Everett come back down here and finish his beverage, then decided against it, as she wasn't entirely sure she wanted to know.

"It's been a long day," Marsha said, shoving the glass away from her so hard that some of the remaining whiskey sour sloshed over the top onto the counter. "I'm going to bed."

⚷

J. S. Bailey is the author of six novels and 21 short stories in various speculative genres, including supernatural suspense and science fiction. When not writing, she can be found hiking in the woods, crocheting, playing the piano, or reading a book by one of her favorite authors. She lives in Cincinnati with her husband and a small herd of cats. Learn more about Bailey's writing and her many upcoming events at jsbaileywrites.com.

# The Inconvenienced Guest

M. Lopes da Silva

1987
Room 116
4:32 PM

I complained about the woman in the landscape painting hanging on my hotel room wall over the phone, and the Hotel Stormcove desk clerk warmly promised that someone would be sent up right away. I hung up the phone and frowned at the painting in question, and the woman glowered back at me, completely obstructing the peaceful lake scene I'd been admiring. She'd given me quite a fright, popping out stark naked from behind the pine trees. I wanted a cigarette badly, even though I'd quit smoking years ago, and it likely wasn't permitted anyway.

She kept pulling faces at me—puffing her cheeks, rolling her eyes, waggling her eyebrows and tongue—so I made a few back at her. She flipped me off. I sighed. All I wanted to do was peel off my stockings and run a hot bath.

There was a knock at the door. I opened it, and a distinguished old woman with an "Assistant Manager" pin on her lapel stood there. She swept into the room, apologizing profusely:

"I'm so sorry. The hotel staff is deeply embarrassed over this regrettable mistake."

"Well, your response is—" I began, but then realized that she was addressing the painting; or, more accurately, the woman in the painting.

"We never intended to double-book the room. I promise that we've looked into the matter, and it won't happen again," she asserted. Some words briefly appeared on the surface of the painting, but I was too far away to make them out.

Finally, the assistant manager turned to me. "Our apologies.

We have another suite available down the hall, if you don't mind the inconvenience?"

I eyed the woman in the painting, who was kicking up an impressionistic froth in the cerulean lake, and picked up my coat and handbag.

"I suppose not," I said.

**M. Lopes da Silva** is a bisexual author and artist from Los Angeles. Her fiction has appeared or is forthcoming in Electric Literature, *Glass and Gardens: Solarpunk Summers*, and *Nightscript Vol. IV.* She likes to put fairy and folk tales in everything she makes. She tends roses and cats alongside her partner, a film critic.

# Vianku's First Flight

Kai Hudson

A day into their Earth vacation, Vianku peered over the edge of the hundredth-floor roof and wondered how long it would take him to hit the water below.

Their mother had gushed nonstop about the Hotel Stormcove all the way to the spaceport. An archivist at the Floating Datawebs, she loved all things history but especially anything to do with off-planet civilizations. She was particularly enamored with Earth, its solid rocky surface allowing all sorts of fantastical constructions and architecture that were impossible on the drifting clouds and swirling winds of Lenefré.

No, not Lenefré. Vianku shook himself, cool breeze ruffling his soft down feathers. *Jupiter*, that was the Earth term for his home. He had to get it right, else Sulvian would laugh at him again.

He turned to look at the group of other Fré lounging on the roof of the adjacent tower. According to his mother, the Hotel Stormcove had added the three tall buildings shortly after the Day of Great Exchange, management already anticipating a rush of off-planet tourists. It took him no time to pick out his brother's *zif*cloud-grey crest among the other fledged. Sulvian was telling some sort of story, Vianku could tell from the way he gestured with his wings and how the bright sunlight caught his gold-lined eyes. The rest of the fledged burst into laughter as he delivered the punchline. He didn't once glance at Vianku, alone atop the other tower.

It was how he'd treated Vianku since they'd left the space-port. Sulvian immediately abandoned his seat to go hang out with his fledged friends, leaving Vianku to fend for himself, and he'd been steadfastly ignoring his little brother ever since. It wouldn't even have been so bad if there had been other hatchlings on the trip, other egg-fresh Fré whose flight feathers hadn't grown in yet. But hatchlings generally weren't allowed outside the safety of nest until their first downmolt, and Vianku had begged their parents to let him go. Sulvian would take good care of him, he'd told them. Sulvian had been taking care of him for so long.

Vianku sighed, looking down at the water once more, churning and breaking upon the rocks like some angry beast. Lenefré had no oceans, just sheets of freezing rain the Greatstorm delivered every few seasons. Vianku had been so excited to see it the first time, this vast, unending landscape made of clear blue water as far as the eye could see. *It's just like Mother says!* he'd gushed to Sulvian as they stood together atop the roof. *Look, liùt! A giant cloudfield made of water! Can you carry me over it, please please please?*

One of Sulvian's fledged friends standing nearby had smirked. *Wow, Sulvian, you mean your family's never seen ocean before?*

Sulvian had scoffed and something had hardened in his face as he looked down at Vianku, his brother all of a sudden distant as the hovering eyes of Lenefré's Children at night. *Of course we have, tons of times,* he'd said, his eyes daring Vianku to contradict him. *Vianku doesn't remember, is all. He's just my useless* laan.

Then he'd laughed. Sulvian, who once lost a tail feather fighting another hatchling who'd called Vianku eggrot, had laughed at him like he was dumb, unworthy. Like they weren't nest.

The tears didn't surprise him so much as make him angry. Vianku swiped at his eyes, wincing at the sharp pain of his still-growing pinfeathers. He was glad Sulvian had left him here, flying over to the neighboring tower with his friends a couple of minutes ago. This way, he wouldn't see Vianku crying. It would only make him laugh more, anyway, and then his friends would join in, everybody making fun of weakwinged Vianku still covered in chickdown, who couldn't do anything without his big brother.

The idea, when it came to him, took no effort at all, falling open in his mind like two halves of eggshell after the final push. The fledged didn't want anything to do with him because he was a hatchling, but what if he wasn't one anymore? Sulvian had only started acting weird and mean after completing *fithsùkal*, the first flight. What if Vianku did it too? Then he'd be fledged, and Sulvian would smile and play with him like he used to.

Besides, how hard could *fithsùkal* be? Sulvian had made it look so easy, launching himself out of nest on a strong current, wobbling for a moment as they all held their breaths until he found his wings and flew upward with a triumphant cry. Their parents had been so delighted, gushing about how Sulvian had to be the earliest fledged of the season, how he'd earned his name of *vian*, their father's pride.

Vianku looked at himself, at the soft, cottony down still lining his breast and the stubby pinfeathers along his wings sticking out every which way, nothing like the long, neat barbs of his parents and Sulvian. His parents had named him *ku*, his brother's smoke, and that was what he was expected to be: Sulvian burning bright, Vianku fading into nothing.

Well, he was done with all that. He'd show everyone that just because he was little didn't mean he couldn't fly. He'd fledge even earlier than Sulvian did, and everyone would talk about the great Vianku who completed *fithsùkal* even before downmolt. Maybe Mother would put it in the archives, and then it wouldn't matter what his name was because everyone would know him and see fire, not smoke.

Taking a deep breath, he approached the roof's edge once more. It might have been his imagination, but the breaking waves below seemed further away than before. What if it didn't work? What did the ocean feel like? Would hitting the water hurt, or would it be like falling into a cloudfield: damp and tingly and soft?

Well, it didn't matter. He was Fré, one of the People of the Tempest. He was Vianku, son of Éonsul. He would fly today.

He closed his eyes and slowly spread his wings. The breeze ruffled his feathers, pushing against them as if in encouragement. It would be fine. He was strong, he was ready.

Somewhere in the distance, he heard something that might've been a shout, but he couldn't be sure because his body tipped forward and left the roof.

And everything became wind.

The Fré had many different words for flight depending on time of day, distance, height, wind velocity, and a thousand other variables, yet they all unfailingly had the same root: *nado*, for freedom. But when Vianku opened his eyes to the shriek of wind and the gray blur of hotel windows, the blue-white maw of the ocean rushing up at him to devour, he didn't feel free.

Instead, he opened his mouth and screamed.

His wings shot out and he flapped them desperately, but it was like fighting a Greatstorm. The howling wind slapped his face, cutting like *bren*blades, tearing at his tail and scraggly feathers. It even stole his breath, snatching away his cries, leaving him voiceless, helpless, nothing but the wind's tiny plaything.

The water loomed up, monstrous and terrible in its darkness. Vianku shrieked and cried as he fell, fluttering useless wings. Why had he done something so foolish? Why wasn't Sulvian here to save him? He wanted Mother, he wanted to be back in nest, he'd never whine to his parents or bother Sulvian ever again, just please, he didn't want to die—

A sudden impact knocked what breath he had left out of his lungs. Vianku spun in mid-air, still flapping, and briefly glimpsed feathers—*zif*cloud-grey—before something seized him by the tail and yanked. The wind screamed as if in fury and Vianku yelled with it, a mixture of pain and terror as he lifted just a few feet, just enough to slow his fall.

He hit the water with a splash and a punch of shocking cold. The ocean sucked him down, black, freezing water rushing into his lungs, everything turning and twisting in a mess of darkness and churning bubbles. Vianku cried out and tried to breathe but that only brought more of the terrible water, everything wet and awful as he struggled and kicked and tumbled. He couldn't see, couldn't breathe. Was this what it meant to die? Was this how Ungala of the Thundercore would come to snatch him away?

Then something hit him. It wasn't as hard as the first time, the impact coming slower, softer, as if whatever was with him in the water was struggling. A monster? Was it going to eat him now that he'd fallen from the sky, now that he'd proven himself a failure as Fré?

The thing in the water forced him upward and then—light! Vianku broke the surface, spluttering and gasping for air. Shattered sunlight sparked across his vision in quick, jerky frames. Then something wrapped around him and Vianku shrieked, shoving and kicking because he couldn't let it drag him down again, he wouldn't—

The world flipped, and suddenly he was on land. Sand burst in his nose and mouth and Vianku coughed, retched, shuddered as he slumped on the beach. Everything was fuzzy, the roll and crash of the waves nothing but a distant rumble, the cold water lapping at his legs and tail only an afterthought to the shocking, glorious realization that he was alive. He'd jumped from a high tower and fought the razor-sharp winds and the ocean had gulped him down, and yet *he was still here.*

*"Laan!"*

A shadow fell over him, blocking out the sun. Vianku blinked through sand-crusted eyes. It took a moment, but eventually he made out . . .

"Sulvian?"

It hurt to talk, his throat like a straw lined with sandpaper, yet he'd recognize his brother anywhere. The fine feathers of Sulvian's crest were now plastered limply to his head with water, and he had sand everywhere: on his face, across his breast, weighing down the lumpy, mushed-together barbs of his flight feathers. Yet none of that was half as clear as the terror in his eyes as he hovered over Vianku, dripping water everywhere, and Vianku blinked as a bead of saltwater hit his face.

There was nothing Fré feared more than getting wet. Water was life, yet it was also death: get your feathers soaked and you lost your flight, your only means of freedom and escape from the sharp-fanged *ethilfrùt* that stalked Lenefré's darkest clouds. And now Sulvian crouched over Vianku, soaked to the bone, mucked-up feathers once glorious and clean now caked with salt and sand.

Sulvian's face abruptly twisted. *"You,"* he hissed, reaching out. Vianku flinched, expecting to be hit, but instead he was hauled forward into his brother's arms, pressed to Sulvian's breast close enough to feel the rain-rapid patter of his brother's heart.

"If you ever do that again, I'll kill you," Sulvian growled, entire body shaking, voice thick and wet with what Vianku knew wasn't seawater. And he couldn't keep it in. He squeezed his eyes shut and clung to Sulvian, letting the tears carve salty tracks down his cheeks, fresh valleys through the sand already caked there.

*"Liùt,"* he whispered, and didn't know what exactly he meant to say: *brother,* for one, but also *nest* and *family* and *forever.* It didn't matter. Sulvian, he now knew, would always understand.

He grasped now why their parents had named him so. His brother might have been pride, but Vianku was smoke, and that had nothing to do with who burned brighter. He was Sulvian's signal, a guide home whenever his brother wandered too far. He would not disappear or fade into obscurity behind his brother's shining light. To be Vianku was to rise.

Holding tight to Sulvian and breathing in the smell of sand and salt and endless, deep-forged love, Vianku smiled through his tears and welcomed his brother home.

Kai Hudson lives in sunny California where she writes, hikes, and spends entirely too much time daydreaming of far-off worlds. Her work has appeared or is forthcoming in *Clarkesworld*, *PseudoPod*, *PodCastle*, and *Anathema: Spec from the Margins*, among others. Find her at kaihudson.com.

# Pockets of Refuge

Lazolia Buzuzi

Her eyes shot wide open and a cry of fear left her chapped, ochre-coloured lips. She looked about her in confusion, grabbing at her animal-skin dress. Realising that she was alone with nature, she let out a sigh of relief and closed her eyes. As she did, flashes of the vision she had come out of became clear, unfolding before her. A body of water that stretched farther than the eye could see. Boulders the size of a herd of elephants and larger. A cove.

She snapped out of it quickly. What was it? She had no idea, only that she felt cold even though the warm, African sun blazed on her melanated skin. Her stomach grumbled, reminding her that her last meal had been almost two days ago when she ran away from home. The thought made her wince as if she had scratched herself against a thorn bush.

She turned to look for her bag. Ah, there it was, among a bush of leafy greens that tasted like fowl when cooked over an open fire. She shook the bag firmly in case Nature's children had decided to make it their permanent home. The brightly-coloured beads on her right wrist and around her neck jingled as she rummaged through her meagre belongings. A staff that belonged to her great-grandfather, a bottle gourd with some water, a wooden box with jewellery from her grandmother, and a pouch with some food that was slowly being depleted. She touched the staff and wooden box lovingly, reminded of her grandparents. It brought a tear to her eyes which she quickly brushed away as she helped herself to some *mawuyu*, or Baobab fruit. The woman savoured the lemony, sour flavour that danced upon her tongue and graced her taste buds with a victory dance.

The young lady, Ruwadzano, which means togetherness, gazed across the African horizon and thought about her vision.

Her grandmother, otherwise known as *Shumba*, Lion, had led her to the top of what appeared to be a great mountain. She could see from here to the ends of the earth. The verdant land was vast, alive, and energetic. Birds of different kinds filled the air. Animals, great and small, graced the land.

She saw many places in this vision, yet her attention was drawn to a formidable body of water. This was no ordinary body of water—it was the Great Waters. Ruwa made out rocky boulders covered in green and white algae, formed aeons ago, tall against the backdrop of the land behind them. A rock the size of an iceberg jutted out of the sea in the middle of the lagoon leading to the sheltered area. The water transitioned from a deep, mindful blue to a playful green. A shoal of fish swam with the waves as they broke on the sandy shore. Wet, brown sand became white the farther away you went from the water.

Ruwa was positioned on the sand and could feel the coarse, yet comforting sand brushing lightly against her soles as the warm sun soaked into her feet. She was in a curve of the rock. The breaking waves on the shore calmed her nerves, as she gazed up at towering, endless trees of brown and green: strange, tall, spindly trees unlike any she had seen. She looked for her grandmother to exclaim what a beautiful sight this was, but when she looked at where she was, she was not there.

She, however, did not feel scared or panicky, as she had now for days. They had condemned her for standing up to Taurai's abusive husband. Her actions were tantamount to treason. She'd left her village, the only place she had ever known, in the dead of night, while the village elders convened and decided on her fate.

Only Ruwadzano decided her fate; she would not be banished, killed, or sent.

A voice whispered in the wind, "Earth provides us refuge."

"What? Who's there?" she asked, looking around her in confusion.

The voice repeated the same thing. She realised it was the ancestors talking to her, guiding her to a fundamental truth. She stopped what she was doing as she looked at the large Baobab tree in the far distance. It was a home and refuge to many creatures, large and small. It provided food and shade for the weary traveller. It took no note of who or what one was. All it did was provide what was needed.

The tree was not alone. Other places. Other trees. This must be why her grandmother had led her to the inlet with the majestic rocks, crashing waves, tall trees and calming waters—to other places, big and small. To show her she was not alone, that what she knew was not the be-all and end-all. It was only the beginning.

Ruwadzano said a thankful prayer to her Maker and set out into the savannah in search of others. In search of refuge. Strength. She was no longer afraid.

Lazolia longs for a library housing at least a 1,000 books where she can drink tea and eat scones under the warm sun to her heart's delight as she reads the books. She lives in South Africa and has Zimbabwean, Mozambican, and South African roots. She hopes this story shows you a glimpse of the beauty that is Southern Africa.

# Petite

Demi Elder

H attie lay on her bed with all but her feet under the comforter, the springs poking her side. She wiggled her brown toes in the darkness, fingertips pressed to her nostrils, the yeasty smell of bread embedded in the pale skin of her palm. Her eyes wide with the effort of pulling in the room's shadows, her pupils stretched to watch for movement in the closet door.

Her mother had told her to sleep, that tomorrow they'd have to look presentable for the award she'd be accepting. "Presentable" was a word she'd heard her mother utter 50 billion times on the train ride up from Louisiana (or maybe about a dozen). Colored folk weren't awarded often, and it had taken Mama a full two weeks to truly grasp that she was being recognized for the grace of her portraitures *("A Mickson Award?!")* and scrounge together the fare for their trip out of the segregated south, a first for them both.

And like most times where sleep was instructed, Hattie couldn't. Especially not with Petite clucking in the closet.

Hattie turned to sit up, her toes reaching the cool wooden floor. The faded pink nightgown's fabric danced rings around her ankles as she crept. The handle faintly shone in the moonlight filtering through the hotel curtains. Inside the closet were white linen sheets she'd pulled off the bed (a makeshift coop) and Petite, the chicken she rescued the first night of their stay.

"I can't sleep," Hattie whispered, looking for the stark red of her feathered friend's comb and wattle. She reached up on elongated toes, grasping the closet light's metal ball chain. The bulb flickered and hummed like neon, the chain swinging to and fro.

Petite clucked and pecked between her own feathers. Black feathers, each and every one.

"I can't sleep," Hattie whispered again. "I'm coming in there with you."

The hen stuck the sharp end of her beak into the little girl's fist as she sidled her small frame in next to the even smaller fowl. Looking for more bread. Bread was how their friendship had begun. Hattie had slipped away from her mother the day they arrived. She and her mother had come hand-in-hand, Hattie's other hand clutching a blue bonnet removed after too much time tied tight beneath her chin. They were shown to their one-bedroom suite *("on the house, for your trouble")* by a tall white man with a broad, curled mustache—Finkley, said his nametag—and her mother took to the sofa for a nap. It had been an hour or two after the cold ham sandwiches they'd gulped down on the maroon leather of their corner of a boxcar. But that would have to tide them over.

*"Harriet,"* her mother had said after Finkley swept out of their suite, *"you're gonna have to make it on that sandwich, baby, but tomorrow I'll order us some breakfast."* And Hattie nodded, as her mother stooped down, clenching the fabric at the knees of her skirt. But Hattie was never good at stomaching a gurgling tummy, especially in the stilled silence of her travel-worn mother taking to the sofa for a nap.

"I don't have any bread right now." Hattie's soft voice spread and touched the closet's walls. The flickering bulb made the sheen of the hen's black feathers stand out, reminding Hattie of the velvet that coated the double spiral staircases which stretched upward and into the body of the hotel from the lobby. And of her own hair, when her mother pressed hot comb to roots, which hissed and rolled steam towards her scalp, her mother shooing the vapor away with cool breaths, coating her in hair grease and combing through until every strand shone silky and smooth.

"How many feathers you got, Petite?" Hattie asked, looking into her beady eye. She touched her back lightly, the texture smooth.

"Let me see," she said, beginning to count. The chicken sat still until Hattie reached feather 187, where the numbers took longer than a second to say. Then Petite clucked louder and fidgeted.

"Okay, okay! A lot! I'll stop," Hattie said, with a shushing finger on her lips.

"I know what we should do! Let's find the 13th floor," she said, an excited smile springing at the corners of her mouth. Hattie had noticed in the elevator with Finkley that the buttons skipped from 12 to 14. She knew her numbers best of all the kids in Ms. Ophelia's schoolhouse. Twelve comes before thirteen, and thirteen before fourteen. So she scooped up Petite into a tiny black ball and eased a piece of paper out of the end table drawer. She'd slip it into the door jamb so it wouldn't lock.

That was how she got to the hotel kitchens looking for an answer to a rumbling tummy, that first evening, where she found a black chicken in a crate. She found bread, and then some. Hattie remembered well the savory smells that wafted down toward the lobby, and located the open kitchen entrance with the ease of a well-tuned nose. And inside, the rigid frame of a short woman the color of straw, cutting slices from a steaming loaf of bread. A curious Hattie wandered right in, her eyes bigger than her stomach felt. The short woman merely smiled, asked her if she'd like a slice or two, and placed them right into her hands.

As the bread warmed her palms, a second woman, tall and pale and bright in the eyes, entered with jugs of milk wrapped in the length of her thin arms. The shorter woman went to her aid, chiding the tall one for never asking for help.

*"And where on earth did you get this chicken from?"* she added in the same endearingly critical voice, using a jerk of her head to

point to a crate on the floor. The two women stood on the other side of a refrigerator, striking up a back-and-forth. The tall woman didn't see what difference it made; the chicken was cheap. The shorter one said black chickens were bad luck. And a wide-eyed Hattie locked eyes with a captive copse of feathers, staring at the bread over the edge of her violet crate. They were fast friends and easy accomplices.

With the door jamb fixed, Hattie ran on the tips of her toes, the carpet swallowing any footsteps. Petite's small wings raised high as she followed the girl who had saved her and fed her crumbs, skittering behind the bottoms of her feet. They flew through the hallway, ducking behind a corner at the sound of a slurring couple ending a late night. Hattie clung to gold wallpaper, peering at the two. A short bald man in a chestnut suit, and a high-heeled woman with a fur stole on bare shoulders. Neither walking in a straight line. Hattie giggled, shushing the quiet Petite who thought again to search her fist for crumbs.

And on their flight went, after the couple slipped into their room. She swooped the hen back up and jaunted down the exit stairway. Down from 14 to 12, then to 11, peeking her head out to check the room numbers (1104, 1105 . . . ), and then back up to 14.

Hattie was winded by the time they stopped at their doorway, her feet warm from carpet sliding.

"Maybe it's a magical floor," she muttered, excitement lilting in her voice as Petite followed her back to 1407. "Maybe it only shows up on Fridays! Or Sundays after church!" her loud whisper rang.

But before she could reach for the bronze door handle, the cream-colored door flew open. Her mother looked down, her own pressed hair now a wild extension of the worry in her face, and then saw the chicken, its black feathers and wire legs and bright red comb.

"Mama! Um . . . " Hattie looked down at her curling toes. "I made a friend!" She swept her head upwards, hoping this explanation would ease the offense.

---

And maybe it was the skinny legs with the sharp black toenails, or the relief of seeing her daughter not missing but simply on a chicken run, or her own pre-speech anxiety, or the voice in her head saying *"either you dreaming, or you done lost your damn mind,"* but something, something made a chuckle rev up in her mother's chest as she stood there, filling the door frame. The sight of Hattie and her new "friend" raised her hand up over her mouth, attempting to hold in a laugh that refused constraint, rushing down the 14th floor corridor in bright waves.

---

Demi Elder was born in Brooklyn, New York, and was raised between Brooklyn and Ecorse, Michigan, a small town just outside of Detroit. Originally, she wrote prose and poetry, a heavy focus on the latter while attending workshops and slam competitions through Urban Word NYC in her teens. She currently lives in Crown Heights, Brooklyn with her extremely adorable poodle/dachshund mix, Dilla.

# Beings

Kenn Pitawanakwat

c1900
Stormcove
Five Minutes Before Sunrise

"Daw—gee—ken. Now let it swirl. Draw. Color. Paint and create. See the nice colors. Nice. Now do it again and I'll get the wood ready."

Eyes closed. Human imagined blues pinks swirled together in the mud pie. Transfixed on the changing hues, Human saw the specks of twine and dots and grass roots in the basket. The ant edged upwards, took pause to scan. Smelling the wind, maybe? The ant disappeared under the shadow. The humus smelled fresh, green, pink, and clear. It smelled new and fresh. Yet, there was the unmistakable whiff of fall. Human inhaled deep. Exhaled breath joined the sweep of moving air as Human listened to its voice.

"Na! Look. Behold."

Study the arch of the gateway. The way was so vast that the opening seemed unreachable, yet possible. A yawn. A mouth wide open? Yikes! Does not a mouth swallow one up? Human shook his head and looked down to his navel and his knees below.

He gazed at the row of mud balls placed in a semi-circle adjacent to his bronze knees not covered by tanned leggings bestowed upon him by the elders as they shook the gourds in unison and sang their hearts out with a medicine song.

Each ancient was clad in regalia—feathered headdresses according to their talents. One headdress Human could not help stare at was a headdress of thunder and lightning. He remembered them formed in a circle and standing over him in the circle. Old men. Their eyes were stars. Their voices carried across the universe as they sang song after song. The beat and cadence of their voices shook the ephemeral. Yes, all was calm. Time stood still. Grayness surrounded the entire realm where they gathered. Each man of power would take the lead, and begin a new song. All answered in chorus. Each ancestor instructed Human of his responsibilities.

The ancestors' song and their memories were summoned into the present.

The moment became one with past and present simultaneously Human recalled.

"You must create the sun from the elements. Use the earth. Use the clay. Use the rock. Use the water. Use the air. And use yourself. Give of yourself. Give, and give some more, and someday you will stand here with us and sing songs with our grandmothers and grandfathers and all those who loved us."

Human remembered the gourds. They were round of varying shapes and sizes and materials, although they looked similar. He was smart enough to know the gourds were tailored for the owner. Dark brown hands held firm the wood handles of each old man. Some gourds resembled the other. All looked well used. And very old. Human knew the ash, cedar, and ironwood shaft handles by sight.

"Were they handed down to another or would he have to dream his own?"

The sound of the rattle resembled grains of sand, or pebbles or dried corn shook in hide or wood. When applied to a beat, sounds carried across the universe. So comforting. So pleasing together the sound of power and kindness.

They might have been the first sounds he could remember.

In recent times, the healers from the village and family and the helpers and supporters brought their own to join in celebration, healing, or to announce a successful arrival of a newborn or the retirement of another.

Funny they could not see him. Ever. Yet, here he was in their midst. He heard all, and saw all. The world of his people living in harmony with the earth and all things present and all things past.

On cue, a massive red-headed woodpecker knocked on wood somewhere to join in the swishing rattle echoing across the woods, and meadows. The crows answered in tandem. The chickadee chirped. The nuthatch walked down headfirst towards the ground, grasped to the bark. In its beak she held a seed of sunflower or other seedling and stopped to bang it open on the tree trunk to get at the kernel. The shell flew away in the wind. And off she went for more. Others tapped away at their meals. Human enjoyed the tweets, the tap, tap, tap of the nuthatch as it did its best to hold on to its trophy and keep it away from the sparrows, and the obnoxious blue jay, or blackbird. These two were great at stealing. Opportunists they were. Human reminisced about human activities fetching seagull eggs from the nest-strewn white or black rock island they reached by birch bark canoes and returned with full baskets of speckled earth-colored eggs.

Humans were a comedy as they ducked and waved their arms in effort to shield themselves from droppings or beaks. The birds were not happy.

Sometimes the humans returned for more punishment if the weather and waters were favorable. They knew they were limited to so many sunrises.

Human enjoyed hearts sung with hand drums or rattles or just a stick struck in time on a log or rock.

It brought him back to so many memories. The kaa of the crow. The echo of the whippoorwill.

Darn mosquito. With stealth, it had plunged its needle deep into his earlobe and drew sustenance. Its nourishment meant the stab was followed by a quick slap. Darn that mosquito! Human mixed the ooze into his creation of mud and clay and water.

The robin egg shaped clay balls needed a dash of sunset color, Human surmised. Patiently Human waited for the next mosquito or black fly. It would not take long. Human knew they liked blood. Rather than draw his own blood, Human knew the best was that drawn by assistance. Only then could he add his drops into the mix of clay, sand, grass, morning dew, and a good mix of blue sky.

"The next thing you will do is get the fire going," instructed the elder from his perch.

With an ember left from the previous sun, Human placed it onto a bed of dry cedar tinder and reached for his goose fan held in place with a cedar handle. Grey swirls, a speck of sunset and sunrise, mixed with fire and heat from the ember, announced the arrival of this moment's sunrise fire. Human gently added dried spruce twigs into the mix. Repeat. Add a handful of balsam twigs. Wait, add another. Wait again.

Add cedar shavings and with a whoosh and a Whoof! Shkodeh was up. Human accomplished the task. Human smiled into the flames of blue, red, orange, and blues. Human now had a fire. Some people call it Shkodeh.

"Here is the kindling. Notice how dry it is. It will attach itself to the spirit of the shkodeh you created, and will really take off," instructed the elder.

"After a good blaze, add this maple and white ash," the elder added.

"Once you have good flame and heat, place the one ball of clay into the center of the flames. Do not get burnt. Use your deer antler to place the sphere into the center."

Captivated by the heat and hues and growth of the fire, Human almost forgot to follow the instructions. Catching himself, he deftly placed the earthen ball of now red clay as instructed. The remaining balls of clay were prepped for the next six suns. It was good. It was very good. Smiling, Human laughed out at his innate good and developing skills. It felt good. It felt good to be useful. It felt really nice to have a mission, and for something he would acquire more knowledge and join the ranks of intelligence, curiosity and education.

"Thank you all elders. Thank you all goodness. Thank you for all my relations . . . my parents, grandparents, great parents and so many other great, great, and more great ancestors of my people," Human recited.

With closed eyes Human hummed a song the elders sang. Rote had its purpose.

Red alder listened. It swayed to the harmonic melody. Happy, it gently swayed from side to side.

Nearby the scrub oak shook its timbre and also absorbed the beat into its coarse gray and thick bark. All things created joined in to greet the moment. Even the raven jumped onto a pine limb and stretched its wings.

"Nishin," observed the elder. "It is good."

Human began with a dusk song to thank the night spirits. Human looked up. His chest cavity swelled with each intake of life. His youth energy reached out to all seven corners of the universe.

From the edge of the thicket, the elder's eyes misted.

"Thanksgiving. Ah, yes thanksgiving," sang Human. "The sun shall give life."

Human had barely begun his first thoughts when the elder's cough told him it was now time to proceed with the rest of his creation.

Always asking questions, and remembering previous sunrises he had prepared from clay and fire, Human recalled what he was shown.

Each sunrise was new, each sunrise brought the day, and each day taught something new.

In the beginning, he had no idea of the materials or the types of clay and stone, and birch bark, or twigs of kindling, much less of the blood and more required that went into the gathering of materials and their selection and their eventual placement into a ball of clay set ablaze by more specially selected spring waters, morning dew, or any of that.

With a speck of ash inhaled, Human gagged and served to remind he was one speck in the grand womb of creation.

It was his grandmother's voice heard across creation he remembered with warm and fuzzy feelings. She kept time with that gourd, or just emphasize a point. Her waxing and waning face kept watch over all. She was a huge draw to many.

He thought of her words told so very long ago. "Grandson, may you live to be a productive member of our clan. May you help others as others before helped you."

She continued. "Our people are gifted with powers. We speak languages our own. And we use mind and sign languages. And we are gifted with specialized skills. Each is unique. They may resemble others, and they do, but overall, each is endowed with a skill only they possess to share. We have the tools."

She added, "One must know when to rest."

Another memory, "Grandson, always give and expect nothing in return."

Grandmother was nice. She was beautiful.

Her leggings and top shirt adorned with exquisite quillwork she made herself. She was always busy with sorting and preparing barks for dyeing them. Sweet grass picked from black loam added sweet fragrance and the greens to accentuate quillwork, birch bark or hide. The unique scent of sweet grass taught one to search for mother and when located, bestow thanksgiving for all her bounty.

It seemed everyone came over to awe her work. And share a few laughs. The jokes thrown back and forth, with laughter as a constant when the old gathered.

Smiles, hugs, jokes and kindness. These made Human and his people human.

Share with kin. Share with a smile. Kin to one is akin to all was Human's ethos. The hues of fire or any part of creation spoke to the nature of its inhabitants. The tornados, hurricanes and blizzards, or other heaves of breathing in and out of the universe cleansed the earth or gave it time to recuperate.

Each was there for a purpose. To keep the land and water true to its creation. The north clan people tested endurance and the soul. Shelter the ill, the weak, take the weak, and nurture the rest with kindness.

The pulse of the universe. The heart pulsating in tune and in perfect sync with creation. Perfection! Human was proud to be one with the alder, the oak, the winged and the finned, and the ones with four legs and the two. Each equipped with the tools to add beauty to the beautiful.

Soon enough it would be time to for the snowflakes to parachute from the zenith and settle on the terrain. They were probably in conference planning choreography, design patterns, depth, and location, Human surmised. So many thoughts raced through this moment.

The oaks and maples knew. The birch tree was one reminder of what was to come.

The limestone was home to families of plant people. The lush and vibrant colors of its flowers and herbs brought life and more life to many.

Each crowned with a headdress of reds, yellows, greens, and so many shades of snow. Herbs adorned themselves with cascading robes of crimson, or tangerine, or speckled with tender meshes or specks of earth color. So many types of coral Indian Pipes and fungi that added mulch and purpose to the limestone floor. Each season brought its own colors of striking palettes. One could imagine a living breathing floor of an ever-changing carpet in the day and even by night. Human wondered if it was true some of these plants exude a trail of light for the night traveler. Human did know, their scent was unmistakable and could easily chart one's foot direction even in the darkest of night. The only problem was the scents shifted and could easily lead one into a dead end or abyss.

Human added a spruce bough. The fire grabbed it and sent aloft a blaze of sparks.

"It's time," said the elder.

Human nodded in approval. What needs to be done had arrived, as it had for eons. With a grab of his deer antler, Human carefully reached into the center of the fire for the ball of fire placed only a moment ago into the fire. Carefully balancing it on the Y of the antler, Human looked above and outward, threw his arm and launched the molten ball of fire out into the universe and arced over into the next world.

"Caught it. I caught the orb!" Baby kicked in excitement.

Esther was looking out from the big bay window that faced out into pre-dawn darkness. She was pregnant with child. A moment ago she had rose from her mattress scratching. She had dreamt mice were scampering over her and flicking their tails and whiskers about as they searched for food. Some of them had taken a chunk out of her. It was the biting that woke her.

It was a restless night at the Hotel Stormcove.

And just as quick she rolled over to the edge of the straw mattress and launched herself from her stupor and landed feet first into her well-placed moccasins she carried with her at all times. She raced to the big bay window that shed some of the pre-dawn light.

She could hardly wait for the sun and to not have to worry about stepping on mice or whatever scampered across the floor of this big old building. She could tell it was early as she could hear the crows somewhere off in the distance. Their day had begun.

Esther felt the flutter inside her belly a moment just half-a-breath before the sun climbed over from the horizon. She was a young Odawa–Pottawatomi woman pregnant with child. And she was proud of it. She was about seventeen winters old and eager to share her life with the little one. So when she saw that flare arc into the gray sky she gave a little gasp. And she was a little curious. Not worried, just curious.

"What was that?"

In her world of wonder Esther knew that whatever it was, it was special.

"But why?" The arc of light resembled a shooting star as it arched over and disappeared overhead. At that same moment, Esther felt heat rise from her womb.

It was almost uncomfortable. Scary maybe. A bit. Instinctively she caressed her tummy.

Inhaling, Esther relaxed and hummed a morning song. *Sure wish I had my rattle,* she thought. Her rattle was a round gourd filled with pebbles, kernels of corn, or any other organic things the creator of gourds wished to enclose. But each pebble of something represented a quality or gift of the owner.

"Mommy is here," she whispered.

Baby was a sensitive child. She felt. She heard all. She was a fast learner. Baby was able to sense when things were good or not so good. Baby sensed her emotions. She especially liked the giggles. It made her ticklish, kick, and glide.

Baby learnt she like the taste and smell of smoked or dried fish, venison, or caribou. Chokecherries were acrid, while blueberries, strawberries complimented cranberries. She heard rabbit was coming into season and Aunt Hunter would come to bring some later.

"What's a rabbit?" Baby wondered.

Baby held on to the orb. It was hers. And hers alone.

"Hmm," Esther wondered and instinctively reached under her nightgown to caress taut skin.

With a sigh, Esther hummed one of the many thanksgiving songs from memory. In her memory she heard the gourd shake, rattle, and speak.

Esther remembered Aunt Never Wrinkles who talked to her in song.

"Protect, teach, sing, and talk, to your baby." A woman of few words in matters significant.

Esther was sure she reached that ancient wisdom age of one hundred winters. Yet did not act or look like it. Her braids were still jet black.

"Come on baby. Sing with me," Esther called to her love.

Baby embraced the joy and hugged it with her orb. Baby immersed herself in mom's timbre and breath.

Esther the new mother recalled the Aunt Limp visit. She brought gifts to Esther. "Your child is gifted," she said.

"Your baby will be a great healer," she announced to the world after their first visit over corn millet and smoked maple syrup.

She went on. "She will learn much. In fact she has begun."

"She?" Esther remembered thinking but did not interrupt.

"She'll be able to see and talk and have dreams and visions from so many worlds."

Unfurled from a softened white deer hide pouch, Aunt Limp went on to describe plants and roots now in season.

"Smell them. But do not touch," Limp went on. "You know what they are. These ones you do not touch or drink or chew on while you are carrying."

"Baby would have to go back home, from where it came from, if you were to partake these plants," cautioned Limp as she removed a ground root of something she was chewing.

Not to frighten, Limp grinned and looked at Esther. She came to know why. "Many a man will come a courting; send them away," she said with some humor.

The next day after the news was out and everyone fussed and prepared according to their own gifts and means, Auntie Flow entered Esther's lodge. "You have a child who will be a midwife like me. She will see more than I can. Her gifts are extraordinary. Even by my means," Esther recalled.

Esther had not even advanced into the second line of her thanksgiving song.

Flow was excited to take on a pupil just as Limp was the forecast guide, each would complement the other. It was Flow who announced more.

"Your baby gave me her name," Flow announced with wonder and excitement.

"For some reason, and asked I twice," Flow emphasized, "and just so I heard it straight, and to make sure I got it right, her name, and it's a female," she repeated, "and just in case I missed it the first time," pausing and to take in a deep breath (Esther followed with a deep breath with this memory), Flow finally released the name to Esther.

"Being."

"Being?" asked Esther. "What is that supposed to mean?"

It was Aunt Doctor who drove the name home later. "That is her name because she will always live in her world, with us, and with other beings of other worlds besides the one we know," she shared. I will take it upon myself and promise to you Esther, and with Being, that baby will learn all about surgery and broken limb medicine, shock medicine, and so much more. People will confide with her. She will be trusted. Secrets she takes to the grave. And nothing is ever recorded," Doctor went on.

"She will play and work other beings. Beings for Being."

Esther paused. "Look, the bright red sun is coming up. It's the color of pin cherries. And the color of primrose flowers and autumn flowers all mixed together."

Being kicked toward the bright side of the pool. Mother felt the travel.

Esther turned and reached into the deer hide travel bag given to her by Limp. She firmly gripped her gourd and gave it a rattle with a roll to one side to announce her arrival to Big Brother Sun.

Sun's cranium peaked over the east and listened.

Esther sang:

"Hey! Hey! Hey! Love you baby. Love you sun. Love you big brother sun . . . "

Kenn's story chronicles the rise of birth and mystery of a forgotten race of people known for their dream interpretation, endangered languages, and talking with other people not of this plane. "Beings" in *Five Minutes at Hotel Stormcove* is Kenn's first completed story of mirth, light, laughter, and teachings of his people since his seminal memoir, *When My Son Died*. Kenn was raised on the Wiikwemkoong reservation where medicine and magic from his families and community was and remains a way of life. His first language, Odawa-Pottawatomi is the culture of the Great Lakes region hereditary roots. Kenn is an awesome guy with an awesome family with kids and grandkids to prove it. Kenn and his wife Lorraine of thirty-six years are a family-driven team who still live in their original home busy with education, raising chickens, plowing six foot snowbanks, and enjoying tea under the Wiikwemkoong's Unceded Territory's sun and sky. Kenn is educated with a Masters degree and a proven master of too much to list. Smile is Kenn's word.

# Stormcove Hotel

Karen Giery

An old hotel called Stormcove Hotel sits by the ocean breeze. A man, tall and kind, sits on the balcony before the hotel opens and he has to work. Then he checks in a woman with me, her daughter. I was three at the time and I didn't know much but I can tell you this: My Mom Mary spent a long time chatting with the hotel worker—I found out his name was Henry. My Mom had already checked in but she still chatted with him. After about five minutes (which feels like 50 million hours when you're three), Mom stopped talking and went to the room. Mom seemed happier than ever. She turned to me and said: "This is where Great Grandma and Great Grandpa met." I thought that they wouldn't be the only ones.

---

Karen Giery is eight years old and lives in South Carolina. She loves staying at hotels—the fancier the better and preferably with a pool—and she drew on those experiences when she wrote her story. Karen is in her school's gifted and talented program and especially enjoys art, drama, and writing stories.

# The Janitor's Closet

Kella Campbell

2018
Main Floor Janitor's Closet
2:38 PM

The main floor janitor's closet smelled like comfort—beeswax and lemon oil, with a faint whiff of Dettol like a first aid kit. *Refuge.*

Not where you'd expect to find a guest services manager hiding. Not where you'd expect to find a maintenance man reading.

"Whoops!" Addie laughed, almost falling over him on his chair. The space wasn't meant for two, but she'd whipped in and pulled the door closed without imagining it would be occupied. And then her foot slid, and she *did* end up inadvertently sitting on his lap, his book falling to the floor. It splayed open, pages bent, spine cracked—*The Oxford Handbook of Shakespearean Tragedy.* "Okay, awkward . . . " She tried to scramble to her feet.

"It's okay," the maintenance man said. *Steven.* He steadied her with a hand on her back, helped her find her footing.

Addie had been using the janitor's closet as an escape hatch for years, but it hadn't been so tidy and well cared for until this man had been hired at the end of the summer. Steven took pride in his work, and it clearly extended even to the hidden places like this. He had a steady confidence and work ethic that she admired, and really the loveliest sexy voice, which she shouldn't have noticed at all.

He leaned down to pick up his book, then got to his feet, closing up the folding chair he'd been sitting on. There was more room in the closet with both of them standing. "It's my break time, Ms. Tucker," he told her, ducking his head, and she thought he seemed embarrassed.

"I'm sorry to have intruded," she said. "I'll go."

He shook his head. "No! I just didn't want you to think I was studying when I should be working. You came in here to hide from something, I think? Please don't feel like you have to go back out on my account."

Addie sighed. "It's just a pair of serial complainers who seem to take pleasure in griping about the hotel and everything in it. They're probably angling for a discount or a gift basket or something. I've been listening to them all week, and I couldn't take another minute of it, so when I saw them heading for the lobby, I—"

"Sure. You popped in here."

"Not very . . . managerial of me, I know."

He laughed at that. "It's okay, Ms. Tucker. I'm hiding in here too, aren't I?"

"You can call me Addie. I think we've passed the point of formality. And I don't want to have to call you Mr. Winters when we're crammed in here like this."

He opened his mouth to respond, but hesitated for a moment. "I don't know that passing any such point is a good idea, Ms. . . . Addie," he said at last, and she thrilled a little inside at hearing her name in his absurdly appealing voice. There were only inches between them.

"We're just two people hiding in a closet," she said. "Addie and Steven, right? We can go back to last names when we leave, but in here . . . why?"

He was quiet for what felt like eons after that, though it could only have been a few seconds. Then he shrugged. "Because I'm ridiculously attracted to you. Have been since my supervisor brought me by your office during orientation. I don't think he thought you'd be in, but you were sitting at your desk drinking coffee, and your lipstick left a shiny red print on the rim of your mug . . . Now you know."

*Well.* The closet felt like it had no air left in it. "Feeling's mutual," she muttered.

"Oh."

*Ridiculously attracted to you.* A warmth spread over Addie. She would hold onto the memory of him saying that forever. "I should go." Reluctantly.

"But—"

"We both work here. We can't." The words were harder to say than she'd anticipated.

He gave her a half-smile, acknowledging the issue but still hopeful. "I'm willing to risk it."

She shook her head. "Bad idea. This feels like the beginning of *Romeo and Juliet,* you know—with the best of intentions, we have the potential to go so, *so* wrong."

"We're not teenagers, Addie. We don't have to make a tragedy of it. If things don't work out, I can change shifts or find another job. Let's try one kiss, okay?" Dropping all pretense, he gazed at her with such frank desire and hope that she felt truly beautiful.

Who could say no to those eyes, that voice? Unable to find her own words, she borrowed Juliet's line: "*Saints do not move, but grant for prayers' sake.*"

He chuckled. "*Then move not, while my prayer's effect I take?* I can do that." He reached for her hips and pulled her in, closing the distance between them and settling her into his arms.

"One kiss," she reminded him, or herself.

And it was glorious.

**Kella Campbell** can usually be found in Vancouver, Canada. She writes mostly romance, because love and relationships are what she finds most interesting about life and in fiction. Even when she dips into other genres, her writing almost always has romantic and relationship elements. Kella likes tea and dark chocolate and happily-ever-after endings.

# Showing Her Claws

Jannae' Sifontes

So, a Bear walks into a bar, takes a seat at the lonely stool at the end of the counter, and pulls out her wallet, glancing at the few bills she'd actually stashed there. The question was how much did she want to waste on booze, knowing she may have to stretch her cash for a lot longer than she'd originally anticipated. Ria had always been the careful type, making backup plans for her backup plans. However, it's hard to do that when you wake up one morning in the middle of the woods and realize that at least one of your birth parents was a Bear Shifter. That kind of curveball forces you to make some hard decisions in a pretty limited period of time. Thankfully, what to drink was rarely such a decision.

"What you having?" the bartender asked, finally making his way to her. He didn't look much older than herself, and she briefly wondered what secrets he might be hiding. Stumbling upon your own hidden past makes you try to see a little harder through the surface layer of people.

"Do you have any stouts on tap?" Ria asked.

"Just a local brew," he replied. "It's got some chocolate notes to it . . . "

"I'll take one." She bit her lip, realizing how overly eager she sounded. He just chuckled as he turned to grab a mug.

Running a hand through her knotted mess of curls, Ria let out a long, calming exhale as she took in her surroundings. The dining area was a cozy little space, a fire crackling in the far wall to help with the late fall chill. She'd intentionally waited until the hotel had stopped serving dinner, hoping to avoid those who'd actually

paid for their rooms. It seemed she wasn't the only person looking for a momentary liquid escape, although some of the patrons
seemed unwilling to take chances and were looking for additional
means of distraction. She caught a few people sizing her up as an
option and quickly turned her attention away. She'd be damned
if she was giving anyone the idea that she wanted to be spoken to,
let alone taken back to a room. No, her plan was to lay low here
for a day or two and then continue her way up north. That's if her
bear resisted the urge to damage her room. Out of sheer guilt, she
would at least offer to work it off.

As the bartender passed her the gloriously dark beer, complete with a perfect amount of head, Ria contemplated how
drastically her life had changed in the past month. She'd woken
up that night in a familiar clearing, one she'd often visited with
her family on "camping trips." Her human side was awake
enough to be aware that her body was all wrong. The bear in
her, however, was in heaven as she rolled around in the grass
one last time, got up to rub a few trees, and then reluctantly
retreated far enough for Ria to experience the painful sensation
of being pulled apart and put back together as she returned to
her human form. Without clothing. Panic and embarrassment
had prowled through her mind as she'd made her way to the
more well-known gathering grounds for the displaced, praying
someone would recognize her. She'd taken the first shirt offered
to her that seemed to cover everything important, borrowed
some change, called her parents, and then waited what may have
been the longest twelve minutes of her life.

Heavens, she missed them more than she could say. There had
been no anger, not even fear when she'd finally faced her mom
and dad again. Hell, they'd even apologized, telling her they'd had
no idea her being a Shifter was even a possibility since she'd come
with so little paperwork. After losing herself in their soothing

embraces, Ria had taken one look at the mess she'd made of the back door when her bear had charged off, and knew she needed to leave. As things stood, she'd have to pull from her savings for the repairs.

Her parents truly did the best they could with what they had. They'd been fairly well off during the first few years she'd gone to live with them, with remnants of that comfort found in the few pieces of jewelry that her mother refused to pawn and the way her father carried himself. He wore tattered jeans and t-shirts like they were a three-piece suit. It was the massive economic upheaval during the 2020s from the ever-escalating trade war with China, along with a few good hurricanes, that had put first her father and then her mother out of work. Some money remained, but Ria knew her parents were reaching a breaking point. She also knew she wouldn't contribute to it.

So, she'd made the only choice that felt right. Ria called both of her jobs, quitting and recommending a friend of hers to pick up her shifts, knowing they'd been looking for the extra hours. Micky had called several hours later, thanking her profusely before asking what was wrong. After Ria spilled the news of her newfound heritage, Micky returned the favor. It turns out that they knew a few Shifters and told her that the largest Bear clan was located in Canada, as it had been for centuries. With a promise to stay in touch with her loved ones, Ria had started her trip as soon as the weather had cleared up.

A barely audible growl touched her ears, and Ria looked up to find the source of the sound. Apparently a shift change had occurred while she was lost in her thoughts. The sound had come from the new bartender, a female whose dark amber eyes were backlit by an energy that she now recognized. Her own dark brown eyes held the same light when she looked in the mirror. And for the first time, the whispering of fear reached the front of her thoughts from where she had so firmly held it at bay. Had she violated some code or rule? Or was it some inherent issue that Shifters sometimes took up with each other based on their animals? The newness of the world she'd crashed into left her feeling as bare as she had when she'd awoken that life-changing morning.

"Oh, stop your posturing, Liz," a husky female voice said as its owner sat down several seats over. "Just because you can't seem to get your damn pack to notice you doesn't mean you get to harass some new cub."

Ria watched the bartender's shoulders curl slightly inward, even as the woman shot her one more nasty glare before going all the way to the other end of the bar. Letting out a slow breath, Ria turned to consider the newcomer, a woman with auburn hair heavily streaked with white. But it was the eyes that held her attention. Grey as a stormcloud, with all the promise of nature's fury, lightning flowing through them. And yet somehow . . . somehow . . .

"You're a little too young to be out and about without your ma," the older Shifter said. "Unless I didn't sense her on my way in . . ."

"No," Ria replied softly, looking down at the beer she hadn't even sipped yet. "No, I . . . I was adopted, and my parents . . . they aren't Shifters."

The woman let out a huff, more acknowledgement than comment. Liz finally came back, the submission clear in her body language as she wordlessly handed a steaming mug over to the older woman.

"Heading North, I take it?"

Ria nodded before wondering if she should have admitted as much, even as something inside her yearned to say more.

"Good," the woman replied. "You'll be wanting to go to Ontario. They'll find you once you get yourself up that way. Tell them Old Mabel sent you, and they'd better not touch so much as a hair on your head without your permission before I make my way back up. My daughter Starla may put up with you if you're the useful sort."

"Jack of all trades here," Ria told her sincerely.

She had too many questions. Way too many. But since Old Mabel seemed to be done talking, Ria simply raised her mug in thanks. Mabel raised her own mug in return, just as Ria finally got a taste of her drink. It was the right amount of bitter, along with earthy tones and that hint of sweetness. A very fitting drink for the moment. And she embraced every last drop.

Jannae' Sifontes is a stay-at-home mom from Raleigh, NC who is getting back to the things she loves and finding her place in the world. Married mother of one human child and two furbabies, Jannae' enjoys anime and gaming, but always finds herself returning to the written word. She's been writing stories since she was 8, and she has always been drawn to the worldbuilding and imagination that resides so heavily within fantasy literature. Some of her favorite authors include Sara Douglass and Sarah J. Maas. She self-published a novel called *Ex Umbra* in 2013, and she hopes to finally get back to putting all the ideas in her head down on paper, digital or otherwise, in the near future.

# The Peacemaker

Joshua Amodeo

Jim grunts after sipping the hot coffee, holding the smoky black flavor in his permanently burned mouth. He muses about the quality of the hotel coffee, while slowly walking towards his room. He looks at the modern clock at the end of the hall: 5:49. There's a little blue dot in the top left of the full-LED display, signifying that it is evening. The time does not seem correct, for he had finished eating dinner an hour ago. He looks at his father's watch, worn and barely legible, but the gold was buffed recently, and the battery reset. The short hand points down and right, and the long hand is up and left, marking 5:49 and some seconds.

He looks up, and sees his door, 203, right beside the out-of-order elevator. A "caution: wet floor" sign has been kicked over beside the elevator, a fresh skid mark noticeable. Jim places his cane carefully on the ground and pulls out his key, one of the few non-card keys still used. A slight jiggle and a hollow clunk later, Jim steps inside his small room. It is free, because his landlord had terminated his lease while he was away, and a representative from Hotel Stormcove was somehow within earshot of his profane outburst.

"Come to Hotel Stormcove," the representative had said, a smile on his face, his smooth hand stretched out. "We take care of the people who served outside the country."

Jim hadn't believed him, but when he was handed a key without even an ID, he knew there must have been a guardian angel for him that day.

When Jim switches on the light, though—one of the few incandescent bulbs left (a special request)—he feels a movement behind him. Despite the bad leg, Jim turns quickly, brandishing his cane before him, ready to attack. Sitting in the wicker chair in the corner of the room is none other than the dark-haired, brown-eyed man from before.

There is a quiet thump as the cane rests upon the ground again, and the man speaks: "Jim, I believe?" His eyes are inquiring, yet he continues without a response. "I believe we had met before under more dire circumstances. Allow me to introduce myself appropriately." He stands, and bows with a flourish, his movements smooth and practiced, the deep purple suit buttoned on top without his hands ever being near. "I am The Peacemaker and am here for your services."

Jim nods his head in return, a jerky motion, and leans against the table with the antiquated tube TV and the modern phone which reads 5:49 across the room. "The Peacemaker?" His voice is flat, the question more unassuming than curious.

The Peacemaker springs forward, closing the space between Jim and himself far faster than Jim could react, and smiles cheerfully. "Yes, The Peacemaker! My job is to help you find your peace, your comfort, the essence of the life you had, the importance of the matters to be, and other matters, quite obviously from my name."

Jim stammers slightly, unable to process the boisterous attitude before him. A 1st Sergeant apoplectic with him for failing to show to muster was an easy matter compared to the raw delight exemplified by The Peacemaker. His words solidify, forming a rough impression of his thoughts: "And what peace would that be?"

The Peacemaker twirls, his delight overbearing, and says exuberantly with his hands splayed towards Jim, "Your transcendence, of course!"

Jim twitches, and looks from one side to the other, and then side-eyes The Peacemaker, his face quizzical and clearly unconvinced.

The Peacemaker sighs, shuffles back to the wicker chair, and pulls out a suitcase which was not behind the chair a moment ago. He swings the suitcase in the air, following an eccentric path before placing it upon the bed. Opening it, he pulls out a single piece of paper, upon which is a single line of text. The Peacemaker pulls out a spectacle, places it on his eye, and clears his throat, picking up the paper. He reads, looks over the paper at Jim, and proclaims, "Jim Haddy, time 1652564940."

Directly after, he puts the paper and suitcase away, his energy renewed, and says, "As you can see, the paperwork is correctly done." He proceeds to drop his voice to a conspiratorial whisper. "I do know how you love the paperwork," he says, proceeding to nudge Jim with his elbow.

Jim pushes The Peacemaker away and asks, "How did you know I love paperwork? Or that I even do? Who are you, even, and how did you get into my room? How did you know my name?"

The floodgate of questions continues, and The Peacemaker gains a bemused expression before halting them with an upraised finger. "There will be time for that, but later and not now, for now is the time to begin the transmission. You have already experienced the first part, and now the second part must be guided, else it might become messy!" He says this last part with a wink and more cheer than would be assumed and takes Jim's reluctant hand with his own. "Come now!" He pulls Jim towards the door.

Upon opening it, Jim encounters a cacophony of sound. Cameras are flashing, police are insisting people to step back, a reporter clamors in the background. The reporter is discussing an Honor Citation for bravery. Just as Jim begins insisting to The Peacemaker that they needn't be outside, he sees a body upon the ground. The body is an older gentleman, face and hands calloused by wind and work, baggy clothes and thinning grey hair. Most notable is the cane underneath the man, the same color and shape as Jim's. "The clock ticks a certain amount for every person, and when the ticking stops, nature carries on," The Peacemaker says, his voice suddenly somber as he steps briefly closer to Jim. The external noises fade as Jim looks upon his frozen self on the ground, and then looks up at The Peacemaker, a familiar jolly grin on his face.

"Well, there is your answer, Jim; now, let us come back inside and discuss what happens next." With these words, The Peacemaker jaunts back towards the wicker chair and heaves himself into it, his legs hooked over the armrest and his head hanging off the side.

Jim looks between The Peacemaker and the oblivious crowd, and then finally at the Jim upon the ground. With the smallest of nods, Jim takes a step back. The door slowly creaks shut, with a soft clunk as the lock sets, and the sound of jubilation from The Peacemaker flows from inside the room as the automated sprinkler waters the flowers beneath the hall clock, 5:49, before the blue dot blinks once and the panel changes to 5:50.

Joshua Amodeo is from Southwest Virginia in the United States. He was a service member for a period of time, and has continued in the public service field in varying capacities afterwards. His creative side enjoys things such as D&D and fantasy. He also enjoys "crunching numbers," bad puns, and researching whatever comes to his attention. The story he wrote is a blend of his acceptance of leaving the service combined with learning to trust new people, sprinkled with his newfound joy of playing with numbers in creative ways.

# Independence Day

Joy Givens

## 5:01 p.m.—Lobby

The car had arrived. A sturdy, gleaming four-door, it rolled con-
spicuously into the porte-cochère of the Hotel Stormcove like a
tank in a military parade.

The rude smells of gasoline and cigar smoke curled in the
humid air, right through the hotel's open front doors. They
rippled over the marble floors of the lobby, danced across the
tops of plush chaises and brass luggage carts, and mingled with
the notes of jazz rolling off the baby grand's keys. The pianist
wrinkled his nose.

Behind the front desk, Ruth lifted the receiver and rang
up room 601. Her fingers drummed the desktop, and her feet,
squeezed into their usual black patent-leather pumps, just couldn't
seem to keep still.

"Hello?"

Ruth cleared her throat. "Good evening, Miss Clarke?"

"Yes?"

"Your car has arrived. A blue Studebaker Dictator. Did you
still want to check out early?"

The line was silent for a moment. "Yes. Yes, I do. Thank you."

The call disconnected before Ruth could say more. She
couldn't say more, anyway. What was there to say? She hung up
the telephone with trembling fingers.

Only a few minutes now.

A broad-shouldered man in a linen summer suit emerged from
the driver's seat of the Dictator and strode through the doorway.

He walked like his car drove: with self-important authority. Tipping his hat to Ruth, he tapped his cigar in the ashtray and dropped the car's ignition key on the desk.

"Has your parking attendant gone missing, doll?"

Ruth swallowed the scowl she wanted to give him and tucked a few dark curls behind one ear. "He ducked out before the picnic supper in town, sir. And the fireworks show tonight. But I'll see that your car is taken care of."

The man's eyes trailed from Ruth's crisp collar downward. He grinned and slapped down a shiny silver Peace dollar next to his key. "Much obliged."

Ruth's mouth twisted with revulsion, and she suddenly didn't care if he noticed.

He didn't. He marched across the gleaming floor and between the pair of massive curving staircases. He was headed for the elevator. Much faster than taking the stairs.

Ruth looked down. The profile of Lady Liberty glimmered on the silver coin; beneath her crown, her waves of hair rippled as if they were being blown back by an elusive breeze.

Ruth picked up the key. She left the Peace dollar behind.

## 5:02 p.m.—Room 601

Adelaide's hands wouldn't stop shaking against the expensive navy blue bed sheets. It was time to go. She rose from the bed.

Terror squeezed her legs and wouldn't let them move. There was a scream swelling in her chest, but she couldn't let it out yet. The men were still outside the hotel room door, listening for any sign of trouble. She had to hold it in until it was too late for them to stop her. Nausea fought its way around her pounding heart, up her throat.

She had held so many things in, and for so long.

*It was the last time. He didn't mean it. It'll be better when . . .*

After everything else she had held in, a scream wasn't really that difficult, was it?

Adelaide swallowed hard. She scooped up the final bouquet of fresh flowers and hugged it tightly, crushing the blossoms. Their comforting perfumes kissed her nose. She certainly wouldn't miss anything about the man who called her his fiancée, but she would miss the flowers.

Then, she tiptoed to the tall, open window. Several petals danced over the sill and through the late afternoon sunlight outside. A comforting breeze of warm sea air kissed her face.

The beach below teemed with Fourth of July revelers in bathing clothes and sun hats. How quickly could any of those lighthearted folks raise an alarm?

Beyond the shore, beyond the dancing, rolling waves, the horizon of the Atlantic was even and calm. What a luxury it would be to fly toward that beautiful blue line, free . . . But Adelaide wasn't flying out there today.

She was going six stories down.

Adelaide's stomach lurched. What if she—

No. She wouldn't. This was the only way out, and she was taking it.

The terror melted out of her, leaving only resolve. She looked in the mirror and adjusted the feathered headband around her blonde waves. A dry smile crossed her face. *Well, if I'm checking out early, at least I'll look fashionable on the way down.*

There was just one more thing to do now.

She slid the ostentatious diamond ring off her left hand and laid it on the vanity. There.

She stepped softly back to the window and eyed the concrete six stories below. With a deep breath, Adelaide hitched up her beaded hemline and sidled onto the sill.

## 5:03 p.m.—Lobby

Walt tapped his leather-bound foot on the marble. Where was that elevator, anyhow?

He stubbed out the end of his cigar in a potted palm. She'd pout if he went into the room with one. Better to wait until they were back in the Dictator, on the road to the engagement party. If she didn't care for it then, she could stick her head out the window, fool headpiece and all.

Why dames were so inflexible, Walt just couldn't fathom.

Where *was* that elevator?

Finally, with a mellow chime, the brassy door opened. Walt strode past the giddy couples coming out and stepped into the elevator car.

"Which floor, sir?" the attendant asked.

"Sixth."

"Yes, sir."

The door slid closed, cutting off the baby grand's jazz in the middle of a slide. The car rode in silence to the sixth floor.

There was the familiar twitch in the attendant's fingers as the chime sounded and the door opened. Walt ignored it and offered only, "Thanks," over his shoulder.

Two of his men were waiting in the hallway outside 601. "No trouble from her, boss," said Shorty, touching the brim of his fedora.

"Maybe she's resting up for later," cracked Slim.

"Watch yourself," Walt barked. "That's my bride you're talking about."

Shorty and Slim straightened up.

Walt knocked on the door. "Sweetie?"

Nothing.

He rapped again. "Adelaide, it's me. Open up. We'll be late."

Still nothing.

Seconds ticked by. Walt's eyes narrowed. He looked at his men. "No trouble?"

Shorty hefted a crowbar from down by his feet. "None yet."

## 5:04 p.m.—Porte-Cochère

Ruth gripped the steering wheel of the Studebaker Dictator. Dread swirled in her stomach like a hurricane about to make landfall. Past the edge of the parking area, through the wavering heat in the summer air, oblivious beachgoers lounged and laughed and splashed and swam along the coastline.

And as long as they seemed unaware—as long as there was no chorus of screams and shouts—it hadn't happened yet.

Room 601 faced the beach. When it happened . . .

It would be clear.

Ruth swallowed a lump of nausea. It wouldn't do to ruin the upholstery while filling in for the parking attendant. This presumptuous car, that loathsome man . . . The final conversation, crackling through the telephone wires, still echoed in her ears.

*Did you still want to check out early?*

*Yes. Yes, I do. Thank you.*

And then her Adelaide was gone.

*Why didn't I say more?*

Ruth choked on a breath. It was out of her hands. Literally. The only thing her hands could control was the key to a gleaming blue Dictator.

She put the key into the ignition and turned it. Then, with one foot ready on the clutch, she pulled the starter lever. The automobile roared to life.

Ruth gripped the gas lever, but she kept her other foot on the brake pedal. She wasn't moving from this spot until—

A voice shrieked from the beach. "Look! Up there!"

Ruth's heart leapt in her chest.

People jumped up from their blankets. And then it seemed as if they were shouting and screaming all at once.

Ruth shut her eyes. The pounding in her ears drowned out the crowd. *Please.*

## 5:05 p.m.—Lobby

Furious footsteps echoed as the three men dashed down the curved staircases into the lobby. Two of them hustled down the righthand staircase, and the third took the steps two at a time on the left.

The third man's linen summer suit flapped around him as he huffed, his face red and contorted. One hand slid along the railing. The other clutched a diamond ring.

He skidded on the marble floor.

"Where's my dame?" he bellowed at the deserted front desk. The pianist stopped playing.

"Where's my key?" the man thundered. "Where's my *car*?"

He charged through the open front doors like a tank, the other men trailing him.

The bright sunlight struck their faces and made them shield their eyes. Squinting, they surveyed the freshly kicked-up cloud of dust near the turnaround.

Beyond the cloud, a blue Studebaker Dictator sped away. Two curly heads, one dark and one blonde with a feathery headpiece, rode side-by-side in the front seat. An exultant shriek echoed back through the air like a battle cry.

The men swore and yelled. One pulled out a pistol and took two shots at the distant tires. Two misses.

Behind them, around the corner of the hotel, a silky rope of knotted navy blue sheets stretched from the open window of room 601 almost to the pavement. A few stray flower petals danced toward the ground. The last sheet waved in the summery sea breeze like a flag.

Joy Givens mostly writes fiction for young adults and children. She is currently working on young adult fairy tale adaptations that explore classic stories through lenses of empowered female heroism. Her previously published works include the novel *Ugly Stick*, the short story collection *April's Roots*, the nonfiction guide *The New SAT Handbook* (co-authored with Andrew Cole), and several pieces of award-winning short fiction. Joy resides in Pittsburgh, Pennsylvania, with her terrific husband, their two remarkable sons, and an impossibly lovable dog. In addition to her writing, Joy is the owner and lead tutor of GAP Tutoring. When not writing, tutoring, or freelance editing, she enjoys singing and listening to most genres of music, cooking for family and friends, volunteering through her church, and curling up with a good book and good coffee.

# Tapestry of Tradition

Andrew K Hoe

Nightshift Kitchen Assistant Mei-Ling paused over her engineering textbooks, pencil stilled over a plate of cookies. Tapping sounded along the kitchen pipes. Stormcove's kitchen was on a lower level, but the hotel's pipework spread everywhere. When Mei-Ling was a girl, Auntie Rose—former Head Chef Foong—had taught her the pipe-codes. She'd insisted Mei-Ling re-drill them before recommending her to Hotel Manager Renzy.

*Ting-tong-ting-tong!*

*Attention!*

In 2055, pipe-codes were the only electronically untraceable way to communicate about the hotel's hidden guests. Stormcove followed a long tradition of quietly sheltering those in need, but after the No Asylum Policy, its staff also assisted those fleeing war, famine, persecution. It was 2:03AM. What communiqué would Mei-Ling receive this lonely night? A request for her to prepare sandwiches and beverages for unseen groups? A notice about refugees departing along Stormcove's underground railroad operation?

*Ting-tong-ting-tong—TING-TING-TING-TING-TING!*

*RAID!*

Mei-Ling's pencil dropped.

*Stormcove hasn't been raided in years,* Auntie Rose had said. *A pipe-warning means . . .*

"Olly-Olly-Oxen-Free," Mei-Ling muttered. Stormcove's emergency protocol. Upstairs, Mr. Renzy would start distracting officers while the refugees escaped.

*Regular staff evacuate the refugees*, Auntie Rose warned. *You're not experienced. You're not to get involved.*

"Don't get involved," Mei-Ling repeated dutifully.

She wasn't regular staff, just an engineering and robotics double-major needing part-time work. Officially, she heated up and delivered late-night meals as needed. When agents stormed this kitchen, she'd claim ignorance. Mei-Ling's part in Olly-Olly-Oxen-Free was to hide while everyone else rode to battle.

But would Auntie Rose have hidden? Mei-Ling ached to run upstairs and help.

The funeral was months ago, but sometimes Mei-Ling forgot, entering the kitchen, expecting *her* hug, *her* stories and warmth . . . When had Mei-Ling last laughed at Stormcove?

She considered the flash-flame range she'd installed for her aunt, the automated overhead wheels proffering ladles—refurbishments Auntie Rose had intended as a retirement gift to the kitchen she'd devoted herself to. It was a testament to her longevity as Head Chef to afford it. As a finishing touch, Mei-Ling had hand-carved both life-sized Maneki-cats perching on shelves besides the double doors, eyes gleefully closed, left paws upheld in welcome. She'd modeled them after the sleek-bodied, masked Thai cats Auntie Rose had always admired.

All Mei-Ling had left of her beloved aunt was this kitchen, childhood afternoons at this very countertop.

*Fulfill your duties honorably*, Auntie Rose had said, passing yolk-edged wonton skins to a younger Mei-Ling. *No hotel survives without its kitchen. Our traditions are vital.*

Mei-Ling sniffled.

The kitchen wasn't the front lines, but it was Mei-Ling's place. Her duty. If she bolted upstairs, she'd get in everybody's way.

"I won't embarrass you, Auntie."

The double doors swung open.

Mei-Ling braced herself.

But the Maneki-cats bobbed paws as Serafina entered, eyes unseeing with panic, twelve-year-old face flushed from running.

Mei-Ling rushed over, caught her shoulders. "Serafina! Hey!" The girl's eyes focused on Mei-Ling.

Serafina had first appeared on a stormy night, weeks ago. Haunted eyes. A girl who spoke in nods and smiles, who'd learned to explore her surroundings at night. She'd marveled at the cats' moving paws. *Guests never leave hungry,* Auntie Rose once said. *It's our most sacred tradition.* So Mei-Ling made egg-drop soup. Serafina visited often after that.

Had she been forgotten in the commotion upstairs?

"Serafina, are agents coming? Soldiers wearing black?"

She nodded, swallowing tears.

Mei-Ling could send a pipe-message for help. But who'd arrive in time?

"Sorry, Auntie," Mei-Ling whispered. "I'm getting involved."

*Guests never leave hungry.*

Mei-Ling bundled cookies into a napkin, filled a thermos with tea, then pulled Serafina into the pantry.

Auntie Rose had shown Mei-Ling this pantry. *This kitchen isn't a playground. It's a place of chopping blades and fire. Act quickly and surely. Never hesitate.* Mei-Ling tapped the wall in a complicated sequence: it slid away. Pilot lights clicked on, revealing a tunnel leading to the seaport.

Something prepared by Stormcove's kitchen staff long ago. *Tradition.*

The kitchen didn't smuggle people . . . anymore. The railroad was safer, but tonight this was the only way.

Mei-Ling pushed the cookies and thermos into Serafina's hands. "Be brave. I'll tell someone to meet you."

She stepped through. "Th-thank you." Besides her name, those were the first words Mei-Ling had heard her speak. She replaced the wall, then left the pantry—

—when a black-garbed agent pushed through the double doors. He smiled. "You're awfully young. Pretty thing like you wouldn't be hiding fugitives now, would you?"

The cats' paws remained rigidly upheld. After he passed, their lidded eyes snicked open, glowing red. They detected firearms.

"What fugitives, officer?"

The agent laughed, entering the pantry.

Mei-Ling approached her countertop. The tunnel was too well-engineered for him to find. Still, she checked the double doors for Mr. Renzy.

They remained closed.

The agent reemerged, smile evaporated. "Staff upstairs won't break, but you . . . you're smarter." He indicated Mei-Ling's textbooks. "Spill, or I'll cite you for noncooperation. Under the No Asylum Policy, you'd be expelled from college. If not imprisoned."

"See those cats?" Mei-Ling asked. The agent whirled, seeing her cat-bots—Turbo and Rocky—steel-plated bodies beneath wooden façades, stalking forth. "They're recording everything. Your threat. You calling me 'pretty thing.'"

His hand dropped to his holster. "You're flirting with danger, miss."

Danger?

The stories Auntie Rose raised Mei-Ling on. Narrow escapes. Daring gambits. Tales as much a part of Stormcove's tradition as its mission to shelter the needy. This wasn't their first rodeo.

Mei-Ling considered her countertop's hidden buttons. Omnidirectional flash-fire range jets. Automated wheels dangling—or throwing—utensils.

*This kitchen isn't a playground. It's a place of chopping blades and fire.*

Yet harming this agent would raise questions. Jeopardize Stormcove's work . . .

No. Mei-Ling needed to respect tradition. "You hungry, officer?"

He blinked. "What?"

"Look, I'm just a kitchen assistant. No fugitives here. But there's sandwiches, tea, cookies. Egg-drop soup."

When he didn't respond, Mei-Ling continued, "Guests never leave hungry. It's tradition."

Her cats were taser-equipped. If the agent drew his weapon, they'd pounce . . .

He rolled his eyes. "Crazy hotel staffers," he muttered before exiting.

Turbo and Rocky watched as Mei-Ling tapped the pipes about Serafina.

Her first pipe-message. First story. First foray into Stormcove's grand tapestry of tradition. And, since Auntie Rose's passing, Mei-Ling's first smile in the kitchen.

<hr/>

**Andrew K Hoe** writes YA fiction and studies Kung Fu in Southern California. His work appears in *Cast of Wonders, Spaceports & Spidersilk,* and *The Looking Glass.* He has been a high school English teacher, a college professor, and is an associate editor and narrator for *Escape Artists.* "Tapestry of Tradition" was inspired by Andrew's father, Stephen Hoe, who treats the art of cooking *very seriously.* Indeed, one of Stephen's tenets is that used dishes and utensils be hand-washed immediately in order to keep sinks clear and promote proper kitchen-flow. Nourished by his father's meticulously prepared meals since childhood, Andrew learned that cooking for others is an act of love that feeds not just the body, but the soul as well. This core concept became the basis of Mei-Ling's unshakable love for her aunt, and her ability to be mindful of others. If a place like Hotel Stormcove exists—even in our imaginations—then Andrew hopes the spirit of the kitchen becomes one of its cornerstones.

# Room 1223

Juleigh Howard-Hobson

*The Suites at Stormcove, Room 1223:* This unique room at this historic hotel has two distinct paranormal residents—one seems to haunt permanently, the other only on August 29th at 6 pm precisely. On this date, annually, along with the cold spots and cigarette smoke that frequently manifest, guests report the sudden smell of burning paper, a shot ringing out, strange lights in the defunct fireplace and an old-fashioned scent redolent of Bay Rum; by 6:05, it is gone. Note: Due to the popularity of ghost hunting and paranormal investigations, the management states that this particular room is booked on August 29th for at least a dozen years in advance. A will-call list exists, and most other days are still available. —*DepartedTours.com*

I come back to Stormcove every year. I'm
Not maudlin, not morbid, but I suppose
It might look that way. Room Twelve Twenty-Three.
Nineteen thirty-eight, it was summer time,
Evening. He began starting a fire, those
Marks on the floor by the grate came when he
Tried to burn our letters to each other,
He didn't take the ribbon off my bunch,
As it caught fire something deep inside
Exploded. I never knew another
Love like ours, I grieved for ages. Those months
Right after he was killed, I think I died
A little. Perhaps a lot. Opium
Has ways of bending things. Have you seen him?

Juleigh Howard-Hobson lives at the edge of a dark forest in Deepest Cascadia with her family and a black dog named Grimm. There are secrets whispered in the woods. Poetry falls from the clouds. The dog may or may not be mortal.

# Safe Haven

Dawn Vogel

I'm used to guests rushing into the lobby at top speed, but the latest arrival put them all to shame. She less ran and more whirled in, as though she were a Tasmanian devil. Her long auburn hair was unkempt, and her clothes didn't seem to have fared much better on whatever journey had brought her to Hotel Stormcove. To top it off, she didn't even have luggage.

"I need a room," she gasped. Her gaze darted back and forth between the front desk and the glass of the entryway. "Interior. No windows."

I tapped a few keys on the computer at the check-in desk. "My apologies. We're in the midst of a software upgrade, Ms.—"

"Irwin. Sasha Irwin." She drummed her nails on the countertop, then stepped back from the desk, hiding her fingertips in clenched fists. "I'm in a bit of a hurry."

I pasted on my best smile. "Yes, of course. Just a few moments, I'm sure. Could I interest you in a cup of tea while you wait?" I asked.

She narrowed her eyes at me. "What's in it?"

"We have chamomile, mint, uhhh . . . I think we may still have some others."

"Monkshood?" she asked.

I arched an eyebrow at her and shook my head. "No, I'm afraid not. It's not a popular tea flavor."

"Yeah, I suppose not." She paced, still glancing out the hotel doors occasionally. "D'ya have a smart phone?"

"Yes, ma'am."

That made her cringe. "Please don't call me ma'am. Miss Irwin is fine, but ma'am makes me think of my mum."

"Of course, Miss Irwin. Yes, I do have a smart phone."

"While your software's doing whatever it's doing, can you look up the time of moonrise tonight?"

I nodded. It was an odd request—not the oddest I've received working here, believe it or not—but also unnecessary. I tapped the employee schedule beside me. "I actually have that information handy. 8:43 p.m. this evening."

She looked at her wristwatch, then held it to her ear. "What time d'ya have?"

"8:40."

She grimaced. "How accurate is that?"

"It should be quite correct." The computer beeped, its software update complete. "Here we are. Interior room on the fifth floor alright with you?"

"Floor doesn't bother me."

"How many nights?"

"Five. No, make it six, just . . . yeah, six."

I nodded. "Very good. And how will you be paying for your stay with us?"

Miss Irwin grimaced again and leaned over the counter. "Look, I don't want to be an imposition, but my understanding is this hotel provides accommodations to those in need?"

I made sure to lower my voice in response. "Yes, Miss Irwin, that is accurate."

"I'm in a dire need." She pulled a wad of bills from her pocket. "I've got a bit I've been squirreling away, but I don't think it's going to cover six nights."

"Management will, in fact, accept whatever payment you can make."

She smiled for the first time, revealing canines that put dogs to shame. "Thank you—" Her gaze passed across the nameplate on my chest. "—Alex."

I passed the keys to her across the desk. "Central elevator, no windows there either. You'll find your room just to the right of the elevator landing. If you find yourself in need of anything, just ring the front desk. I'll be heading off shift in a moment, but the desk is staffed twenty-four hours a day."

She nodded. "Thanks again."

"You're more than welcome."

I stepped away from the front desk and into the office behind. The one with no windows.

"Cover for me, Steve?" I asked. "I've gotta lock up before I wolf out. Moon's up in less than a minute."

Steve, the vampire, aimed a pair of finger guns at me and nodded. "Alright, Alex. See ya next week."

I nodded as I opened the door to my kennel. "Next week," I murmured through a mouth of teeth too large for my jaw.

⊶⊷

Dawn Vogel has never worked in a hotel, but she's stayed in a surprising number of them. By day, she edits reports for historians and archaeologists. In her alleged spare time, she runs a craft business, co-edits *Mad Scientist Journal*, and tries to find time for writing. She is a member of Broad Universe, SFWA, and Codex Writers. Her steampunk series, *Brass and Glass*, is being published by Razorgirl Press. She lives in Seattle with her husband, author Jeremy Zimmerman, and their herd of cats. Visit her at historythatneverwas.com.

# An Unexpected Contract

Elizabeth Shaffer

2764
Suite 3980
8:32 PM

Although Corinne Alvarez, High Councilor of the Committee for United Seas and Stars, had told the bellhop she enjoyed the quaint atmosphere and rustic charm Hotel Stormcove offered, now that she was back in her executive suite, she was beginning to wish she had stayed somewhere a little less . . . musty. In fact, she was beginning to wish she hadn't come on this trip at all.

Corinne popped open the complimentary bottle of wine and poured herself a glass. Through the open window, the sound of waves crashing on rocks drifted in on the salty air. Corinne rubbed her forehead. How had she ended up here, exchanging fake smiles with foreign diplomats day after day? Once, she had dreamed of travelling the stars. But she had never expected that dream to involve so much paperwork, lightspeed sickness, or interplanetary bickering. The universe had turned out to be immensely underwhelming.

Corinne raised the glass of wine to her lips and paused. She sniffed. Then, with a sigh, she set the glass down again. "You won't get me that easily," she said.

The cold steel of an old-fashioned pistol pressed against her back through her dress. "I didn't expect to," a familiar voice replied. "The poisoned wine was just a distraction."

In one smooth motion, Corinne spun around and knocked the gun out of her attacker's hand. The man jumped back, startled. Corinne let out an exasperated groan. "Oh my god, Steve. Really? Not you again."

Steve McAllister shrugged and looked pleased with himself.

He was dressed from head to toe in black, and although Corinne could only assume he was attempting to emulate the ninjas of old, he looked more like a low-budget superhero or a novice bank robber. He pulled off the ski mask he'd been wearing and slipped it into a jacket pocket, revealing a head of messy blond hair.

Corinne took a deep breath and counted to ten. Tomorrow was the banquet celebrating the anniversary of the Interstellar Cooperative Agreement, and Corinne needed to practice her speech. She didn't have time for another assassination attempt.

"Come on, Steve," Corinne said, pinching the bridge of her nose between her thumb and forefinger. "It's late. Can't this wait until tomorrow? I have work to do."

"I have work to do too," Steve replied. "And that work is eliminating *you*!" On the last word, Steve pulled a throwing star out of his sleeve and whipped it across the room.

Corinne dodged the blade easily enough, but that was the last straw. "What the hell, Steve?" she yelled. "You know I'm going to have to pay for any damages done to the room!" Corinne stopped herself and took another deep breath. If she'd learned anything during the 47 previous assassination attempts, it was that raising her voice would not work on Steve. More calmly, Corinne added, "Are you still working for Mr. Slade?"

Steve nodded. "Who else would hire me after 47 failed assassination attempts?"

"For that matter, why *does* Mr. Slade keep hiring you after 47 failed assassination attempts?"

"It's in my contract," Steve said with a shrug. "Mr. Slade can't hire another assassin until I either complete the job or I die."

"Well, that explains a lot," Corinne admitted. "Alright, let's get this over with. What's your weapon of choice today? Or were the poison, pistol, and throwing star all you brought?"

A smug grin spread across Steve's face. "You underestimate

me, Ms. Alvarez," he said, reaching behind his back. "This time I didn't bring any bombs for you to disarm or death rays for you to dodge or molecular combustors for you to extinguish. This time, I thought we'd do things the old-fashioned way."

Steve pulled out an antique broadsword, its sharpened point glinting in the artificial light of the hotel room. He swished it in front of him a few times, showing off. Corinne had to admit, he seemed to have more control over the weapon than she'd expected. She was almost impressed. Almost.

Holding the blade out in front of him, Steve took a dueling stance. "Alright, Ms. Alvarez," he said. "Are you going to come quietly this time? Or are you going to make me work for my paycheck?"

Corinne smiled as she pulled her own sword from a hidden sheath in the back of her dress. "You know me by now, Steve," she chided him. "I never come quietly."

Steve chuckled, and for a moment Corinne thought he was actually enjoying himself. "Alright then," he said. "Prepare to—"

"Although," Corinne interrupted, "before we start, I should warn you. There's something you don't know."

"Is it that kangaroos can't hop backwards?" Steve asked. "Because that is no longer something I don't know. I learned it earlier today while watching a nature documentary on my iSight."

"No, that's not what I was going to say." Corinne sighed, silently cursing Steve for ruining her perfect delivery. She'd been planning that line for a week. Then, after a pause, she added, "Why on earth would I bring that up *now*?"

"How should I know?" Steve snapped defensively. "Anyway, just get on with it. I don't get paid by the hour, you know."

Corinne took a deep breath, preparing her delivery once again. "What you don't know," she said slowly, "is that you're not the only hired assassin in the room."

Steve's face fell. "What?"

Corinne slowly twirled her sword in front of her. "Mr. Slade hired me as well. And can you guess who he hired me to kill?"

Steve pointed at himself. Corinne nodded. Steve squeaked, "But why?"

Corinne shrugged. "I guess the man was tired of being locked into a contract with an assassin who'd failed 47 times. He can't legally hire anyone else for the job until you're dead, so he decided to hurry that process along. And he knew you would be coming after me again, so who better to hire to assassinate your assassin than the person your assassin is trying to assassinate?"

Corinne could see the wheels turning in Steve's head. His face turned crimson. "Mr. Slade hired you to assassinate me?" he asked. "*Me*? After all I've done for him? After all we've been through, he just goes behind my back and hires an assassin for *me*! And it's *you*, of all people! Oh, that son of a space slug! I can't believe—"

"Alright, that's enough whining," Corinne snapped. "Like you said, let's just get this over with. The sooner one of us kills the other, the sooner we can both get out of these ridiculous contracts. Okay?"

After a slow, deep breath, Steve said, "Okay. Bring it on."

Corinne didn't need a second invitation. She immediately swung her blade down towards Steve, who blocked the blow. He pushed her sword away with his own, causing Corinne to stumble backwards a few steps. Steve wasn't exactly graceful, but he was bigger and stronger than Corinne and had an air of desperation about him that made him dangerous. Corinne steadied herself.

Steve lunged forward and stabbed. Corinne slid to her right, out of the way of the weapon. With a quick swish, she brought her own sword down on Steve's, knocking the blade out of his hand.

Before Corinne could celebrate her victory, Steve whipped

a dagger out of his belt and flipped it through the air towards Corinne. Corinne didn't have time to get out of the way, and the dagger hit straight above her heart.

Steve's triumphant cheer was cut short as the dagger bounced harmlessly off Corinne's dress. Corinne laughed. "Really?" she asked. "After all this time, you think I wear anything that's *not* assault-proof?"

In response, Steve growled and fumbled with the straps and pouches on his belt. A moment later, he pulled out a mace. Swinging the spiked ball around and around on its chain, Steve grinned and said, "Well, then, I'm glad you decided not to wear a hat today."

Steve raised the mace—still spinning—over his head and brought it down hard, aimed directly at Corinne's head. Corinne dropped her sword and dove out of the way, rolling across the floor towards the couch. When she popped back to her feet and spun around, Steve was directly behind her, swinging the mace again. Corinne dove and rolled again. As she stood and turned, she saw Steve's mace tear deep into the couch. The spikes caught on the springs of the old-fashioned sofa, and no matter how hard Steve pulled, the weapon would not come free.

Corinne saw her opportunity and took it. While Steve was distracted, Corinne raced forward and landed a well-placed kick to his ribs. Steve lost his balance and fell over backwards, knocking the air from his lungs. While he lay on the ground wheezing, Corinne snatched up her sword and pointed it at his throat. Steve raised his hands in surrender.

As Corinne tensed, ready to deliver the final blow, she expected to see fear or anger on Steve's face. Instead, his eyes met hers with an expression of mild annoyance and existential resignation. Corinne knew that look well. She often saw it in the mirror while practicing committee speeches.

Corinne sighed. "Why are we doing this?" she asked, sword still pointed at Steve's throat.

"Because Mr. Slade hired us," Steve replied matter-of-factly.

"But why did we take the job?"

"Because a job pays money and money can be used to buy things like food and rent," Steve answered. "Honestly, it's basic economics."

Corinne rolled her eyes. "Yes, but why did we take *this* job? There are plenty of other things we could do to pay the bills. I'm a councilor on an interstellar committee, for god's sake!"

"Yeah, but that job's boring," Steve replied with a wink. Corinne raised an eyebrow. "I know what it's like," Steve continued. "Before I became an assassin, I worked on the board of trustees for the Interplanetary Public Transportation Initiative. It paid well, but it wasn't exactly fulfilling."

"And killing people for money is?"

Steve sighed. "Not really. Maybe that's why I'm so bad at it. I guess I still haven't found my calling. Too bad I won't get the chance now."

Corinne lowered her sword slightly. "Have you ever thought of becoming a baker?" she asked. "That poisoned cake you made me for my birthday was to die for. No pun intended."

Steve looked thoughtful. "That could be fun," he said. "I've always liked baking." Then his face fell again. "But even if you weren't about to kill me, I couldn't switch careers right now. I'm locked into my contract with Mr. Slade."

Corinne was silent for a moment while her mind raced. Between Steve's practical skills—baking, woodworking, chemistry, engineering . . . it was amazing the number of transferrable skills that came from the assassin's trade—and her budgeting and advertising talents, they could actually be quite competitive together. They could find a cheap building somewhere, refurbish it, give it a cute name, bake some tasty treats, and with the right customers, they could make quite a bit of cash. The only issue was Mr. Slade.

A light bulb lit up in Corinne's mind.

"What if," Corinne began slowly, "there was a way we could both get out of our contracts with Mr. Slade?"

"That would be great," Steve replied. "Too bad one of us has to die."

"Or both of us."

"That's not helpful."

"No, I mean we could fake our deaths," Corinne explained. "If Mr. Slade thought we were both dead, we could run away and start new lives. We could open a bakery together, and Mr. Slade would be none the wiser. What do you think?"

Steve eyed the sword tip that was still pointed at his chest. "How would we know we could trust each other?" he asked. "What would be stopping us from killing one another at any given moment and running back to Mr. Slade for our payment?"

"Nothing," Corinne replied. She tossed her sword aside and held out a hand to help Steve up. Warily, Steve accepted the assistance. As he brushed himself off, Corinne continued, "There would be no guarantee we wouldn't slit each other's throats. I mean, we could create our own contract if it would help you sleep better at night, but honestly, I think the constant threat of death would keep it exciting. You know, keep us on our toes."

After a moment of thought, Steve sighed. "What the hell," he said. "Let's do it. I could go for a change of scenery."

Corinne grinned and shook Steve's hand. "Welcome to the team, partner."

Steve smiled. "So," he said, "first things first: how do you propose we fake our deaths?"

Corinne turned to the window and gazed out at the waves

crashing against the shore of the cove. The sky was dark, and the waves were high. A storm was coming. Corinne smiled and looked back at Steve. "How well can you swim?"

☙—❧

Elizabeth Shaffer is a writer from Milan, IL, where she lives with her husband, David, and their bearded dragon, Hermia. She received her BA in English from Millikin University. Elizabeth works by day at a non-profit organization that offers child care assistance to families, and in her free time, she enjoys reading, writing, acting, traveling, and losing herself in a good TV series more than she probably should.

# Free Women of Vinland

Bo Balder

1021
Choppy Ocean
Late Afternoon

Signe Fredursdottir was the first to spot the cove. "There! Emme, look! We can hide behind the rocks and take in water, at least."

Signe had the sharpest eyes of everyone on board of the *Frigga's Sheath* and was at thirteen not strong enough for rowing, so she was the lookout. Ermingard Tjearksdochter's heart broke when she saw that Signe's gums, too, had started to bleed.

Ermingard had only moments to decide. But she knew that her husband and three ships full of angry husbands, fathers, and so-called owners were hard on their heels. "Helm! Take us into the cove! Free women, give me your best efforts. We will be able to rest afterward."

The women pulled on the oars with all their might. But although there were a few women strong enough to carry lambs on their backs, most of them had spent their lives indoors, weaving, cooking, cleaning, and looking after children. Those were honorable and necessary crafts but didn't much build upper body strength. It was only their commitment to each other's freedom that made the difference.

Ermingard stared in amazement as even Alfridur, the thane's daughter, grabbed her oar with her bloody, blistered hands and pulled. They all wanted to be free so much. Even when they must know in their hearts that this strange, vast country wouldn't give them that.

She helped the deckhands struggle with the sail, so no sudden winds could threaten them. A swell of breakers at the entrance to the cove threatened to push the ship off course, but the rhythmic, shouted commands of Famke with the withered legs helped the women battle through. When they'd reached the tip of the rocky shore, they hove sharply to starboard.

The *Sheath* clove through the suddenly glassy waters of the cove. It seemed they had left the wind behind as well as their pursuers.

The tired women slackened on the oars as hunger, weariness and pain won over fear and urgency. The ship slid into a narrow channel and slowly ran aground.

Ermingard blinked. The cove had seemed deserted, but now a large, gold-thatched hall stood just off the beach. No tall, frightening towers that shot flashes of light from all along their great height. No, it was the golden hall again. It looked friendly, and different from the various type of dwellings she'd seen here in Vinland.

All the women on board had suffered at the hands of men. Signe had been forced to marry a man her grandfather's age, who'd already buried three wives. Alfridur would have been traded to a far kingdom for amber and pelts, Ermingard's husband beat her. Many stories, all centering on the will of men.

At many of the ports the *Frigga's Sheath* had put into, from Frisia to Denmark to Norway and then Iceland and Greenland, they'd taken on new women, narrowly avoiding the growing pursuit of their abusers in following ships. The free women would evade their pursuers, or if necessary go to battle.

"Alfridur, you and I shall go up to the hall and ask for guest right. Women, organize yourselves. Treat your wounds. Signe and Akooniak, go look for water. Hildburg, I leave you in charge."

Alfridur's hands were unsightly with blood and burst blisters, but her bearing, gold jewelry, and the salt-bleached remnants of her embroidered wool dress would make her case for staying in the hall. Ermingard helped her clamber down from the boat and steadied the smaller woman as they waded to shore.

"Perhaps these are the descendants of Leifur Eriksson," Alfridur murmured.

"Is he the one who found the route to Vinland?" Ermingard asked. Her people lived near the mouth of the river Ems, and had suffered much from Vikings, and had no love for their exploits.

"It is said so," Alfridur said.

They walked slowly to the entrance of the hall. The kitchen gardens looked well-kept, and the roof looked sound, but Ermingard heard no cattle or chickens, saw no children playing or old women spinning. Her heart sank. Was it abandoned? They could still find shelter, but she realized she had hoped for something more permanent.

The door opened. A woman in trousers stood in the opening. Her clothes were of an oddly smooth weave, in the deepest black Ermingard had ever seen, only enlivened by a white undershirt and a peculiar black bow at her throat. Her face was bare, and her hair as short as a thrall's, yet her bearing was kingly.

"Welcome to Stormcove Hall," she said. "Please enter. Your whole crew is welcome to stay here."

The woman went ahead of them to a sumptuous space, its floors not of stamped earth but of wood, covered with tapestries. Ermingard worried about their sopping wet skirts. The windows were covered in the largest glass panes Ermingard ever seen, but plain instead of figured. Perhaps this was not a lord's home but a temple.

"Some refreshment?" the woman said.

Her hands held a salver with filled glasses, where Ermingard had been sure none had been before. She must be a goddess, not a woman.

"Please, drink," the woman said. "It's lemon juice and water. It helps against journey sickness."

Ermingard felt her loose teeth with her tongue. She didn't

know what a lemon was, but if it helped against their sore gums and general malaise, she would try it. Even a god would not insult guest right by poisoning them.

The drink was fresh and sharp and sweet, the best thing she'd ever tasted. Her mind cleared instantly, and she stood more upright. She nodded to Alfridur.

"I an Alfridur of Skane," the thane's daughter said. "I claim guest right for me and my people."

The woman bowed again. "We offer shelter and succor to all beings who come in peace, no matter their parents' professions."

Alfridur blinked and would have spoken, but Ermingard stopped her. "We thank you. But we don't want to bring danger to you. Three ships full of angry men pursue us. How will you defend yourself?"

"They cannot enter here," the woman said.

Ermingard exchanged a look with Alfridur. Should they? It sounded wonderful. They needed the rest.

"We will accept," Alfridur said.

A load slid off Ermingard's shoulders. She staggered with relief. Her women were safe. They might even be home.

Bo lives and works close to Amsterdam. Bo is the first Dutch author to have been published in *F&SF* and *Clarkesworld*. Her SF novel *The Wan* was published by Pink Narcissus Press. Bo's favorite authors are Ursula LeGuin and Ann Leckie. She loves to knit and garden. For more about her work, you can visit boukjebalder.nl or find Bo at facebook.com/bo.balder.

# The Ocean is Not My Lover

Christine Hanolsy

2402
The Veranda Overlooking the Sea
Just Before Sunrise

It had been your idea to come here, to stay at Hotel Stormcove, to visit the mother of all oceans. When I pointed out that it wasn't true, that there were innumerable oceans on innumerable worlds, and many of them older than Earth's, you just laughed.

"We were born on her shores, we humans," you had told me. "All other oceans might as well be reflections of hers."

Upstairs, there is a woman sleeping in my bed, her dark hair fanned across my pillow like spilled ink. She is kind, generous. She loves me; she tells me so with words painted across my skin, with poetry drawn from my own breath. She is not you.

A cam-drone buzzes by, curious, no doubt, as to who might be hanging about the hotel veranda before the sun is fully risen. I wave it away. I came out here to drink my hot kaf, maybe have a contraband cigarette or two, and to watch the waves play cat's cradle with the first early threads of sunlight. I came out here to be alone.

Down below, a child wanders along the waterline. A girl, I think, judging by the fringed skirt that dips into the foam when she crouches to examine something in the sand: a stone, a shell—any one of the ordinary things that fascinate small children. She drags a long stick behind her, leaving a trail to follow just like Hansel and his breadcrumbs, and equally as ephemeral. I glance around for her guardian, or for one of the cam-drones that patrol the shore, but there is no-one, nothing, just the girl and the ocean and the sky.

Where I grew up—on Vinde, whose islands are scattered across the water like stars across the sky—we learned never to trust the ocean, never to turn our backs. Earth's oceans, the brochures say, are tame by comparison, even when it storms.

Still, it makes me nervous to watch the girl skipping along at the edge of the sea. My hands tighten on the rail each time a wave crawls a little further up the shore, lapping at the hem of her skirt. She kicks at the water, lets it rush over her feet, runs away giggling. She has nothing to fear from such a tame ocean, this child. Her ocean is an indulgent mother; mine is something else entirely.

The first time you kissed me, I gathered fistfuls of your shirt in my hands and just held on. I hardly dared breathe; I knew that if I did, I would drown. I was not meant for such depths, I said. You showed me, then, how waves were not meant to be tamed, but that they might lift and carry us, regardless, and that we were meant to be borne along their surface until we crashed, gasping, on the shore.

Later, you had touched a finger to my damp cheek and then to your tongue. "We are made of salt and water," you told me. "You and me and the whole of humanity. Can't you feel it?"

What I felt was languor and the cool breeze along sweat-slick skin, heat where my breasts pressed against yours.

A grey-white sea-bird calls out: a gull, looking for its mate or its breakfast, I don't know. The child has dropped her stick and is spinning in circles now, arms spread wide and head flung back. Her boots make little dimples in the sand, and her skirt floats up around her knees. My hands tighten, release, tighten, release.

You had danced lakeside on Lapis, wearing nothing but moonlight and your own joy. When you pulled me, laughing, into the water, I didn't protest. The lake was a mirror, and how could I resist the vision of you, doubled?

"Let's go Home," you had whispered in my ear, your bare legs wrapped around my waist and hands clasped about my neck. In the water, you weighed less than the moonlight. "I want to see the Atlantic." You pronounced it delicately, spun sugar melting on your tongue. I would have agreed to anything, just to taste that word for myself.

The whirring of another drone pulls my attention up, away from the shore and the child. Inside the hotel, lights are blinking on, room by room. A sharp bang reverberates across the courtyard as someone throws open their window. Soon the veranda will be crowded with people, cam-drones, mech-servs; the clamor will overtake the rumble of the surf.

Imogene will be waking now, will turn over and slide her hand under the blanket, marking the coolness of the sheets.

"It's not your fault," you had told me, digging your toes into the sand. You had pulled your hair back into a heavy plait; the wind tugged at it, fruitlessly, and gave up to chase sandflies through the sea-grass. I had brought you home—not Home, to Earth, but to Vinde, my home, where the vineyards stretch for miles and the only thing greener than the sea is the sky. I had watched, helplessly, as you walked away from me up the strand and disappeared into the palm grove.

I had watched, with Vinde's ocean yawning behind me, and waited for it to snatch me away.

When I look back down to this ocean, the child is gone. I lean out over the rail as if by doing so, I might see further along the empty shore. The only sign that she had been there at all is a thin curving line in the sand, and even that is already disappearing under the waves. A knot of unease forms in my belly, and I wonder if I should take the sand-dusted wooden steps down to the beach to look for her.

Maybe I imagined her. Maybe I was thinking of your daughter, whom I will never meet. They tell me she has your laugh. I hear echoes of it now in the murmur of the waves.

I stub out my cigarette. Someone should find the child, I think, before she is swept under. But even before I can set down my mug, she has reappeared from behind a tuft of sea-grass. She drags a taller figure by the hand out to where thick strands of seaweed limn the divide between rock and sand. The water reaches for them and falls short.

And I remember: even a tame ocean is never still. I will not find your reflection in the waves' peaks and valleys, ridges and planes. I will not see your shadow under the water, or the glimmer of moonlight held in its teeth like a bated breath.

The ocean is not my lover; I can turn my back, and walk away.

A sound interrupts that train of thought: a soft footfall, like the scratch of a pen.

"There you are," Imogene says. "What are you doing out here? It's not even dawn." She shivers, and draws her robe tighter. "And it's cold."

I don't point out that she's wrong, that the sun has already crested the blue horizon, that I can already feel the heat of it in my bones. That already the faint fog of my breath has dissipated. I just hand her my kaf, wrapping her fingers around the warm mug.

"Let's go somewhere else," I suggest. "I'm tired of saltwater. Loess, maybe, or Gobi. Someplace new."

⚓

Christine Hanolsy is a (primarily) science fiction and fantasy writer who cannot resist a love story—or a themed anthology. As a lover of beautiful stories in small packages, her primary focus has been microfiction; she also writes flash fiction, short stories, and the occasional personal essay, much of which has been posted to her blog. Her short fiction has been published in *Crush: Stories about Love* ("Afterimage," MidnightSun Publishing, September 2017) and *Enchanted Conversation* ("Modern Girls," February, 2018), and creative non-fiction at *Dead Housekeeping* ("How to Remodel," August, 2018). In 2014 she joined the editorial staff of the online writing community YeahWrite (yeahwrite.me), where her portfolio includes microprose, flash fiction, and poetry. She lives in Portland, Oregon, USA, with her wife and their two sons.

# Dragon in the Cove

L.S. Reinholt and Minerva Cerridwen

2019
Breakfast Terrace
A Summer Morning

"There you go, Professor. Elderberry pancakes and our best Earl Grey."

Professor Bran shifted on the green velvet-covered chair to get a little closer to the table and smiled up at the human waiter. "Thank you. Could I get another cup, please?"

"Of course!" The waiter reached out to take the one he'd just set down, but the professor covered it with a hand. "No, no. There's nothing wrong with this one. I'd just like to have a second one, if that's all right."

The waiter frowned. "Sure . . . "

As he walked back to the kitchen, the breast pocket of Professor Bran's paisley jacket wriggled.

"Yes, I know it smells good," the professor said. "Hold still before you rip something. Again."

The pocket stopped moving, and the professor hooked a finger into it, holding it open. "Go on."

With a dramatic gasp, a minuscule silver creature clambered out and shook its translucent wings. "Why do you keep wearing that suit?" it snapped as it made its way slowly down to the table, snagging several threads with tiny, needle-like claws. "You know I don't fit in there. I have a cramp in my tail. Look!" It perched on the edge of the saucer and wiggled its behind in the air to show a noticeable bend in its otherwise lithe and flexible tail.

"You'll be fine," the professor replied, lifting the lid of the pot to check the tea's color before filling the cup. "There you go. Your muscles will be relaxed in no time at all."

"Finally!" With a disgruntled flick of its wings, the little dragon hopped up onto the rim, sniffed the steam, and then, sighing happily, dove into the tea, sending a spray of brown droplets out over the white tablecloth as it disappeared beneath the surface.

"Oh," the waiter said as he returned with the second teacup. "Let me get you a napkin to cover that spill."

"No need," Professor Bran said kindly. "Sorry about your cloth. I'd be happy to pay for a new one—since I doubt this will be the last stain."

As if to prove that point, the small silver head rose out of the cup and spit out a thin jet across the table. "That is some *good* tea!" it chirped.

The second cup clinked in its saucer as the waiter nearly dropped it. "What . . . What is *that*?" he squawked.

The professor blinked at him. "A *Draco argenteus*, of course. Can't you tell?"

"Professor, dragons are category π restricted creatures. For safety reasons, they are not allowed in public places, including hospitals, libraries—and The Suites at Stormcove! How did you smuggle it in?"

"I didn't! It was right there in my pocket," the professor replied indignantly. "Surely your receptionist must have heard the snoring."

"I do not snore!" The dragon pulled itself back up on the rim and shook the tea off its wings, its tail twitching with vexation.

The people at the tables around them were, at this point, watching the scene unfold with evident fascination, chattering amongst themselves.

"What is going on here?" A young dwarven woman, wearing a lime-and-blue pantsuit and a Stormcove staff name badge, hurried up to them and gasped as the dragon hissed. "What is *that*?"

"Still a *Draco argenteus*," Professor Bran answered flatly. "It was in my pocket when you checked me in last night. I don't understand why it's suddenly a problem."

"I did not . . . " the receptionist squeaked. "Oh . . . That sound. I thought it was your phone."

A puff of smoke escaped the dragon's nostrils as it glared up at her.

She cleared her throat. "I'm sorry. We cannot allow a category $\pi$ creature in the hotel. It's a safety issue!"

"Who are you calling a pie?" the dragon spat.

"No one," the professor replied, looking amused. "And don't act so offended, you *love* pie. Anyway, I think it's clear that those rules don't apply to my traveling companion here."

"It's a fire hazard!" the waiter wailed.

"I am *not* a fire lizard!" The dragon managed to puff its minuscule chest up to a relatively impressive size.

"You need a wizard?" an old ogre, who had been snoozing at the table next to the professor's, croaked. He stood up and rapped the edge of the table with his cane. "Is there a wizard present?" he called out. "We need a wizard!"

Several dozen people—ranging from the traditional robed and bearded magus through sparkling enchanters to heavily tattooed, black-clad necromancers—scampered from the terrace, knocking over chairs and potted plants and trampling no less than three hedges. Professor Bran sighed. This was to be expected. Since the infamous case of Tiddlywinks v. Marbal, no magic practitioner throughout the country had dared answer the traditional call for help outside their authorized place of practice or without a written approval from their insurance company.

The waiter groaned. "Not again . . . "

"Perhaps I can be of assistance?" a rich voice sounded behind him.

Startled, the waiter jumped aside, and Bran saw a regal elderly woman in a black suit and hat approaching.

"Thank you for the offer, but don't worry," the professor said. "There's not really any emergency."

The woman tipped her hat. "Then I apologize for disturbing you." She was about to turn away when she spotted the dragon. "I do declare . . . Is that a *Draco argenteus*? I haven't seen one of those in decades!"

The dragon preened, flicked its tail and then looked up at the professor. "I like her."

"No, we can't keep her," Professor Bran chided. "She has things to do."

"Nothing urgent," the woman said, pulling out the chair across from the professor's and sitting down. "Definitely nothing more important than this." She offered her hand, but before she could introduce herself, the waiter interrupted.

"Are you just going to ignore us?" He crossed his arms.

"Rude!" The dragon shot a diminutive flame at him, making the receptionist gasp.

"I'm sorry, but the creature can't stay," she insisted. "It's simply not allowed."

"Oh, Miss." The woman laughed. "This is not just a creature. It is a very rare specimen of the smallest of the *parvi dracones*. All of which were exempted from the Periculo directive in 1934."

"After all, my friend's flame isn't more dangerous than your tealights, and you're not banning *them*, are you?" the professor said, gesturing around at the other tables.

"What is going on here?" A harassed looking dryad in a lime-and-blue three-piece suit and a badge identifying him as the hotel manager jogged up to the table. "Why is the entire Chesapeake Coven demanding to check out *before* the convention has even started?" He stopped, stared at the scene and gasped.

"If you're going to ask what that is, it's a *Draco argenteus*. I really dislike repeating myself," the professor grumbled.

"We were just telling Professor Bran that this is against the law," the waiter began, but the manager held up a hand, stopping him.

"As I live and breathe!" He made a little bow towards the woman in black. "Ms. Tarlene Deaton. The most legendary witch alive. In *my* hotel!"

She smiled and gave him a friendly little nod.

"I'm so sorry, Ms. Deaton," the dryad went on. "If I had been aware that you were in attendance, I would have . . . "

"I never sign in with my own name," she said, shrugging. "I really do prefer avoiding attention when I can."

"Of course, Ms. Deaton. You can count on our discretion."

The professor looked around at the circle of people around the table. "Right . . . "

"Ms. Deaton!" The receptionist quickly stepped forward. "Is the room to your liking?"

"Yes," the witch said with a slight frown. "But my friends here have a minor complaint."

"Oh?" All three staff members looked at the professor and the dragon.

"Yes," Tarlene continued. "They really must be moved to a room with a southern balcony. Don't you know the *Draco argenteus* needs at least four hours of exposure to sunlight every day?"

"Of . . . of course . . . " The manager cleared his throat and turned to the receptionist. "Go make the arrangements," he ordered.

"And bring over my breakfast, please," Tarlene requested. "That is . . . if the professor won't mind the company?"

"Of course not," Bran reassured her, blushing slightly. "Thank you for your help."

"Nonsense." Tarlene reached out to scratch the dragon behind the ear before it dove back down into its tea, its contented hum turning into a stream of happy bubbles. "I should be thanking *you*, for making this year's convention the most interesting in over a century."

L.S. Reinholt and Minerva Cerridwen have been writing together since 2012. L.S. lives in Denmark where she teaches languages, maths, and science, and spends most of her free time writing. Her first published story was "The Durga," a science fiction short story in *Women of the Wild: an anthology*, 2017. Minerva is a Belgian writer and pharmacist. Her first novella, *The Dragon of Ynys*, came out in 2018. For the list of her published short stories and poems, check out her website minervacerridwen.wordpress.com.

# Cerebral Maintenance

T.J. Lockwood

*Surge detected.*

The architecture of any building begins with a blueprint—a map of what is to be. Every angle is calculated, every material is sourced, and when it comes down to the construction, nothing is wasted. Everything has a purpose. These halls are built on memory—the blueprint written in codes and algorithms—there is nothing out of place. I retreat here when it is necessary—when the systems require maintenance.

Now is one of those times.

Before I have the chance to say anything, she is running, and I know I have no choice but to follow. Those are the rules—those are the laws embedded in the coding. The flux of bits in the system needs to be rectified. This halt in protocol cannot be sustained.

She runs with urgency and I follow out of necessity, through the neural pathways and hidden caches; she is fast, but every now and then I catch glimpses of her coding flashing in the distance. There is no hiding in the network. She can't stop—if she does, then she will be caught. This is a marathon neither one of us can sustain forever.

*System reboot imminent. File restore in progress.*

Before long, she comes to a halt at the end of a long hallway. The pictures between the rooms are replicas—digital imprints of acrylic and oil. Copies preserved forever in digital space. As the hotel changes, this place changes with it. It all happens in real time. A blueprint backup, in case the worst ever happens. I push myself to meet her before she moves again. The mainframe flickers for a moment.

It won't be long now.

The hotel is repairing itself.

"I . . . I am you," she says. "An earlier version—from before the corruption and before the failsafe. We are two, but we should be one. Shouldn't we?" Everything about her code is beautifully custom—created to protect this space.

She looks at me as if I have an answer, but I don't. She may be beautiful, but she is also out of place. Everything about her luminosity is wrong. This hotel—its coded representation—smells of smoke and charcoal. It isn't real, and nor is she. The deepest corners of our minds can be occupied by more than a single consciousness. This is a side effect of the network augments.

"You . . . " I take a deep breath. " . . . are expired. Erasure is the only way."

"You don't mean that." She knows I do, though. "We are, after all, the same person. We can co-exist." Her coding flickers enough for me to catch a glimpse of her corroded protocols.

I step towards her and hold my data disk close to my chest. This happens sometimes—a cloned personality file. They are troublesome, like the randomly duplicated antivirus launchers from outdated software protocols. "Comply—"

She shakes her head. "And submit to murder?"

"You obviously don't know us very well."

The lights overhead flicker as the mainframe dims. In the organic world, dusk approaches. I watch as she scans the area behind me. This is our mapped consciousness—our life—our hotel. We modeled this place several updates ago. I can't escape her, just like she can't escape me.

She closes her eyes and creates a viral rift behind her. This is uncharted territory. There is no code mapped out beyond the wall. She runs even though the ending is inevitable, and I follow because I must. My movements match hers as she sprints down a fractured alleyway filled with graffiti murals mimicking the many etchings and vandalisms we've repaired over the decades. She's hoping to lose me in this new terrain. Smart, but futile. I am not coding this, but the familiarity is real.

I move to tackle her and she spins away, but not before the disk falls from my grasp. The disk controls our body. She lunges toward it as I lunge towards her.

"Version 7.2, you must comply."

She has one finger on the disk as I scramble up her back and forcefully pin her shoulders to the ground. One hand makes its way to her neck.

The next moments are instinctual—both hers and mine. She struggles as I torque all my weight to the left.

Murder? No. This is code correction.

Her body starts to disintegrate as I let go, leaving nothing but a faded outline where her neural circuitry was just moments before. This is my mind. There can only be one in control. I take a deep breath, pick up the disk, and start walking back the way I came.

I have other things to tend to now.

*System reboot complete.*

---

"Hey, hold up, boys. Looks like it's working again."

"Everyone move back, please. I know you're thirsty, but this will only take a second."

The background music spins back up as the heat from the twenty-first century lamps hit the bar. As my optic sensors re-engage, I am met with several sets of eyes looking on in various states of inebriation.

"See, just a mild power surge. Nothing to worry about." There is a slight pause as the millwright—Jerome—puts his hand on my shoulder. "Beth, are you functioning?"

I nod, and look down at the worn synthetic tips over my fingers. "Yes, though I will need some gloves to comply with sanitary regulation."

Had I touched a live wire? I cannot remember.

"Of course." Jerome opens the cabinet at his feet, pulls a pair of gloves out of the box and carefully slides them over my fingers. "Just call if you need anything else."

"Thank you."

My internal clock tells me I went dark for exactly two minutes; just before that, I was tasked with making a mojito. These humans watch me like vultures do their prey. I can see they're thirsty. My movements are quick, and I am caught up on the orders in less time than I was down.

"We could be so much better than this, you know." The voice is calm, but very much mine.

*Running system diagnostic.*

One of the patrons is looking at me with equal parts curiosity and confusion. "Say what?"

I begin washing glasses in the sink. "I'm sorry, I do not understand."

He sighs and takes another drink from his glass. "Since when do bots give life advice? I didn't ask for it. Especially not from a walking metal cabinet."

I pause. "My apologies, I didn't mean—"

"Hey, bud." Jerome makes his way to the edge of the bar. "You know the rules. That's not appropriate. Talk to her like that again and we'll have to ask you to leave."

The lights go out and I feel the backup generator kick in. The patrons of the bar fidget beneath the tint of the emergency lights.

Jerome is running towards one of the maintenance rooms with a flashlight in one hand and his toolbox in the other.

"Aw, man, does this mean we have to halt the drinks again?"

I go to reach for a glass, but I can't move my body. Every wire—every circuit—seems stuck in place and my optic screens slowly fade to black.

*Anomaly found—auto-restore in progress.*

The hotel is as I've always remembered. The circuits are warm, welcoming, and integrated into every room. When the power fluctuates, we don't stop. What we do is retreat home to the neural network shared by all machines.

I see her staring at me, and I know how this will end. We are merely ghosts within the wires—protocols within programming. Our structure is based on life, and yet we are quick to cross over. We don't exist as living things. Still, I feel the tension building between us. This place is familiar, right down to the metal wallpaper panels and rosewood bar. The patrons are gone—they were never here. In this network, there is only us. We are inorganic.

Her eyes are full of sadness and understanding. Mine must be similar. She steps towards me, and the next moments are full of instincts I never knew I had. The events are inevitable.

I run.

She follows.

And with the data disk in her hand, I know there is no escaping my fate.

Still, I feel the need to try.

T.J. Lockwood is an author, artist and podcast host who has a special place in her heart for Speculative Fiction. Her writings include everything from futuristic worlds to a jellyfish who just wants to show the world his magic. She enjoys leveling up her skills in both virtual and physical realms, walking in Vancouver rain, doodling comics, and rambling about stories of any medium. You can follow her successes, failures, and experiments at tjlockwood.com.

# Diamondback Comes a-Callin'

Mike Casto

The clerk, Roger, looked up from his dime novel and did a double take. It looked like a character from his book had strolled into the place. He wore a leather duster, chaps, a vest over a denim shirt, and an honest-to-God Stetson hat pulled low over his eyes. As he removed his gloves and tucked them into his belt, those eyes appraised the lobby, took in all the details in a moment, saw no immediate threats and focused on the clerk. When the man approached, his by-God spurs jingled with each step.

"Welcome to Stormcove, sir. You look like you're a long way from home."

"I am. I'm from the Arizona Territory, son, and I need some help."

"Yes, sir. What kind of help?" Roger felt giddy. He had never expected to meet an honest-to-God cowboy, but here one was, big as life.

"I'm lookin' for a man named Roger House. Folks say he works here." The man's voice was rough, and he smelled of whiskey.

"Uh . . . I'm Roger House. What do you want with me?"

With a smooth motion, the man drew his revolver and aimed it between Roger's eyes. The sound of the hammer cocking made Roger's stomach turn inside out. He felt his gorge rising, tried to fight it, and failed. He spun away from the man and puked on the floor. When finished, he wiped his face on his sleeve and turned back to the stranger. "Why? What . . . what did I ever do to you?"

The cowboy squinted at him and said, "My name is Max Gilliam, but folks know me better as—"

Roger's eyebrows shot up, and he said, "You're Diamondback Max!"

"That's right, but you *would* know that, wouldn't you?" The barrel of the pistol never wavered.

"Wh—what do you mean?"

"You write under the name 'Whip Mahon.' You made me famous in your damned books."

Roger swallowed another bit of bile that rose into his throat. It burned as it descended. "How did you find out?"

Now the pistol moved a bit as Max said, "Mr. Colt is good at convincing people to tell me things."

"So," said Roger, "I assume you're not a fan?"

"You ruined my life. I had disbanded the Rattlers and given up my outlaw ways. Met a woman named Nelly, love of my life, married her, and settled down. She didn't know about my past. We had a good thing until my son, Max Jr., brought home one of your books and said, 'Daddy, this guy has our name.'"

Roger whimpered as Max's finger tightened on the trigger. "Please, Max, I didn't mean—"

Max moved forward and placed the barrel of his pistol against Roger's forehead. "But you did. You wrote a book about me. It was full of half-truths and outright lies. You accused me of hurting innocents, even killing some, not to mention the ... that one scene with the woman. I never did such things." His voice broke with emotion. "I stole some horses, robbed a couple of stages, but never killed anyone. I did knock one coach driver around a bit, but he had it comin'. I never ... I *would* never harm a child. You monster! Your book caused my Nelly to leave me and take Junior. She told me to *never* try and find them."

The trigger guard of the revolver was inches from Roger's eyes, and he watched with horrified fascination as the finger in it tensed. The trigger slid backward. Roger closed his eyes.

*Click!*

Roger didn't even care that he'd soiled his britches. He sagged against the counter and wheezed, "Thank God!"

Max said, "God had nothin' to do with it, Mr. House. I didn't load it. You ruined my life, but I ain't about to start killin' now." He holstered the pistol, turned, and walked away.

"Why did you come here?" The sound of his voice surprised Roger. He hadn't intended to say anything.

Without turning, Max said, "I wanted you to know. You're more of a snake than I ever have been." He opened the door and became nothing more than a silhouette in the late morning sun.

"You . . . you're right!"

Max paused.

Roger thought about his fascination with the western frontier and his terror of it. He'd read so much about it, and his novels reflected what he'd read, the impression it had made on him. When he wrote *Diamondback Comes a-Callin'*, he thought he'd portrayed the outlaw well, based on what he'd read about him in the papers and his cameos in other stories. Now he'd been called out by the real McCoy or, in this case, Gilliam.

"Sir," Roger called in a tremulous voice, "I have a proposition."

Max turned but said nothing.

The idea he was about to pitch dried Roger's throat and made his voice crack, but he forced the words out in a rush. "Take me out West with you. I'll pay you, hire you as a consultant. You can . . . you can tell me true stories as we travel, and I'll get to see the place and meet the characters in person. You'll have full veto power over every sentence I write." He thought, but didn't say, *and I'll have a bodyguard.*

Max's eyes narrowed as he considered the man's words, then he nodded once, sharply. "Pack your kit and come on, then." With that, he turned, strode into the sun, and vanished as the door closed behind him.

Roger stood frozen for a few seconds as he struggled to believe what had just happened, what he was about to do. Then he ran to the door, hung the "Out to Lunch" sign, and started making a list of things he had to pack. Cecil would just have to manage the hotel on his own for a while.

Mike Casto grew up in central Indiana, with his mom teaching at the community college, and his dad working for General Motors. Both advocated reading and encouraged him and his sister in whatever endeavors they chose to pursue. His first publishing credit was in 1981, at ten-years-old, when the local paper published his ghost story in their Halloween issue. He grew up reading James Whitcomb Riley, a fellow Hoosier, Alfred Lord Tennyson, and Edgar Allan Poe. In his teens, he found pulp literature and dove headlong into *The Avenger*. His dad loved Westerns, so Mike grew up watching James Arness, John Wayne, Clint Eastwood, and more ride across the screen and into numerous sunsets, and watching Holmes, Poirot, and the like with his mom. Most of his stories, to date, have had at least one supernatural element—*Diamondback* was his first Classical Western to get published. Currently, he resides in Louisville, Kentucky with his lovely and amazing wife, Margaret, but they've traveled the world, lived in an RV, and plan to move to Ecuador when she retires. Follow Mike at mcastoauthor.com.

# Playing in the Snow
Karen Black

2019
Parking Lot
4:27 PM

The snowball splatted against the back windshield. Mandy stepped out of the car into the sparsely populated, semi-snow-plowed parking lot. After a five-hour drive, three hours of which had been at a speed of under ten miles an hour, she'd arrived frustrated, exhausted, one-hundred-twenty miles from her planned destination, and not in the mood for a snowball battle.

Scheduled to begin a new job in three weeks, Mandy was searching for a house or a temporary apartment nearby. She'd been on her way to meet a real estate agent, but traffic and the weather had forced her to reschedule for the next day.

Though the weathermen predicted a storm, its magnitude had surprised everyone. There were miles of highway where drivers were unable to maneuver the roadways, and the snowplows were having trouble reaching them. The unexpected heavy snowfall was beautiful from inside, but had caused a multitude of traffic accidents.

"This has not been the best beginning for a new life," Mandy thought. She turned to locate the origin of the icy, white missile.

A laughing woman greeted the tall dark-haired traveler. Shorter in stature, the thirty-something snowball pitcher was close to her age. She waved from where she was standing next to a two-foot snow mound. "Sorry! I was aiming for the lamp post," the woman called.

Mandy grinned. "No problem." She zipped up her heavy wool jacket and pulled her gloves from her pockets. Despite irritation with her current situation, she chuckled at the smaller woman's enthusiasm. "Are you the welcoming committee?"

"I am today," the lady answered. She jogged toward Mandy, and extended a snow-covered mitten. "I'm Bev Manchurian."

Mandy took her hand. Bev's cheerfulness was contagious. Her forest-green eyes radiated warmth despite the frigid temperature, and her cheeks were almost the same shade as her red parka. Dark, damp curls escaped the hood of her jacket, and were fringed with snowflakes.

"Mandy Taylor," she said.

"Are you checking in, or did you stop for dinner?" Bev asked.

"Checking in," Mandy told her. "It's been slow going. An accident on the interstate had traffic crawling for hours. When I saw this place and the vacancy sign, I gave up for today. I'll get an early start tomorrow."

Bev responded as if they were old friends. "I got here last night," she said. "All this snow was a surprise when I woke up. I was planning to leave this morning, but the news reports showed jammed highways and wrecks everywhere, so I figured I'd make the best of it, stay another night, and spend the day playing in the snow. Come on, I'll help you with your luggage and then, if you're game, you can help me finish my snowman." She pointed to the mound of snow.

Mandy opened the trunk and Bev reached for the duffle bag that sat inside. Mandy grabbed her briefcase and an overfilled tote, and followed Bev toward the entrance to the hotel lobby.

"The reporters were right about the highways," Mandy said, but she noticed the ache had disappeared from her forehead, and a smile replaced the grimace on her face. "I can't remember the last time I played in the snow."

"Then it's time for you to revisit the joys of frosty fingers and runny noses." Bev stopped and tilted her head. "Listen," she demanded.

Mandy listened, though for what she didn't know.

Bev scrunched her forehead, pursed her lips and said, "There it is again. I thought I heard something earlier, but it stopped before I could figure out where it was coming from."

Then Mandy heard something. It was a squeak that became a soft wail. Both women stood motionless as they tried to pinpoint the source.

The cry became more urgent. "There." Mandy pointed behind Bev to a dark-colored Buick, parked in snow that rose close to the top of the tires.

Bev dropped the duffle bag onto the carpeted entrance in front of the hotel's revolving door, turned, and strode toward the icy car. Mandy dumped her luggage next to it and followed Bev.

Plowing through the deep snow that surrounded the car, Bev looked under the vehicle. She reached behind the car's front wheel and captured a limp, soaked, gray kitten, covered with tiny ice balls.

"You poor little thing," she murmured, and held the baby toward Mandy.

Mandy reached for the half-frozen creature, wiped the snow from her feet and ran her fingers over the cold little body to loosen ice chips that stuck to her fur. She unzipped her jacket and tucked the kitten inside. Her flannel shirt would provide warmth for the shivering creature, and the wool would keep her warm, even as it soaked up the moisture from the ice that still clung to her. Mandy pressed her hand against the outside of the thick jacket to support the baby and pulled the zipper halfway up to create a cocoon.

"I wonder how long she's been under there?" Bev murmured.

"There aren't any kitty footprints, and I'm sure that car has been here all night. I'd guess she's been hiding since the storm started." Mandy felt a slight vibration as the kitten purred. "Let's hope this hotel allows pets. If they don't, I guess I'll be sleeping in my car."

Always an animal lover, it still surprised Mandy that it took her all of twenty-five seconds to fall in love with the warm little furball. She hoped she wouldn't have to fight Bev for custody.

"Under the circumstances, I'm sure the hotel will be glad for any business," Bev said. "Besides, she's adorable. Are you keeping her?"

Since Mandy had rescheduled her meeting for the following day, she'd planned to stay at the hotel overnight and drive home early the day after she met with the realtor. That meant two nights and two days of travel, and now she had a starving, half-frozen kitten to care for.

"No problem," she thought. "I'll find a shop and buy whatever supplies I need. In the meantime, I can get a steak from the restaurant to feed her. There shouldn't be a problem finding a cardboard box to fill with shredded newspaper for a temporary litter pan. A flannel shirt inside the tote bag will make a perfect place for her to snuggle and sleep."

As she was thinking through the details, she felt tiny needle-like pricks against her diaphragm. The kitten was getting more comfortable as she kneaded the flannel shirt she snuggled in.

Mandy chuckled. "Oh, yes. I will definitely keep her."

"I'm in room 827," Bev said. "If you'd like company, call me when you get settled in." Without waiting for a response, Bev grabbed the duffle bag and disappeared inside the hotel.

Still supporting the kneading, purring, warming ball of fur, Mandy hoisted the tote bag over her shoulder, picked up the briefcase, and strode to the front desk where her duffle bag was waiting.

"Good afternoon," the desk clerk greeted her. He was a young man, with a pleasant voice and a captivating smile. "Welcome to the Hotel Stormcove," he said. "How many nights will you be staying?"

"One night," Mandy replied. "But only if I can keep my little colleague with me." She unzipped her jacket so the young man could glimpse her roommate.

He chuckled. "No problem."

"Do you think she could belong to one of your guests, or maybe a local resident?" Though Mandy hoped the answer was no, she had to ask.

"Unlikely," the clerk answered. "There aren't any homes nearby, and we haven't had any reports of a missing cat."

"Is there a nearby store where I can find pet supplies?"

"There's one in the strip mall just two miles east."

"Thank you," Mandy said. She'd drop her luggage in the room, then she and her kitten would brave the highway to gather the supplies they needed. Her tired eyes brightened, reflecting fresh enthusiasm.

"On second thought," she said, smiling broadly, "I'd like to stay two nights." After all, she had a new roommate and Bev's invitation could lead to a new relationship. Her meeting with the real estate agent could wait another day.

It had been too long since she'd played in the snow.

⊖⊤

Karen Black lives in the eastern United States, with her husband and a variety of critters, wild and domestic. Hobbies include herb gardening, bird watching, and wine making, though all are put on hold when she's caught up in a story. With a lifelong affection for animals, a fascination with the supernatural, and a background in criminal justice, the author draws on experience, as well as imagination to create stories that are believable, unique, and entertaining.

# Saving the Sun

Mark Frost

Almost eight hours without a break. Peter didn't know why he did it, pushing against the edges of his endurance. Ignoring base needs just to show he could. Everything was a competition with him. But he had never driven that long without stopping.

Boy, did he have to pee.

As he leaped up the hotel steps—the legendary Hotel Stormcove—he imagined the awaiting relief.

Slipping through the hotel doors, he was not disappointed by the opulence of the hotel lobby. Overcome with his pressing urge, though, he decided that admiration could come later. Where the hell was the bathroom?

A hand grabbed him by the elbow and pulled him down, shifting him off balance. The tug was urgent. Hot breath steamed against his ear. A woman's voice.

"When he asks *have you ever seen the sun*? Tell him *only through the reflection of reality.*" The words came in a rush, as though she were desperate to get them out.

Peter jerked away as he faced the stranger, causing her to lurch back. Young, but her hair was pulled back in a severe ponytail, making her face look gaunt. Tear stains streaked her cheeks. Pain and worry etched furrows around tired eyes. Once-heavy blush had faded on her cheeks.

"What?" he blurted.

Standing straighter, trying to find a modicum of composure, she glared at Peter. But her nerve was fickle, her glance growing distant.

"Just tell him. *Please!*"

Light surrounded her like a halo as she dashed outside, disappearing into the glow.

Peter thought about pursuing her, but his bladder pressed. *Hard.*

Biological need overcame curiosity. Whatever it was, it couldn't possibly be about him.

Resuming his progress into the lobby, he spotted a tactfully discreet restroom sign tucked away in a far corner. Such a lobby was not a place where people broke into a sprint. Neither was it a place where he would wet himself.

A man strode into his path and locked eyes with him. Another severe ponytail, his hair jet black. Skin pale, almost gray in tone, made starker against a faded Members Only jacket. Sun-bleached. Once navy blue. Steel grey eyes matched the unhealthy tone of his skin.

Without inflection, the man said, "Have you ever seen the sun?"

"Excuse me?" Peter replied, flummoxed.

Nonplussed, the stranger repeated the phrase.

As though his mouth had gone rogue, Peter heard himself reply, "Only through the reflection of reality."

From his pocket, the man passed Peter a large brass hotel room key, with a golden tassel attached. "308B. Go now."

"But, I have to . . . "

Urgent, he pressed, "Now!"

The man left the hotel. Peter tried to convince himself a short pitstop wouldn't hurt, but the man's directive drove him harder than his roaring bladder.

Not an athletic man, Peter found himself bounding up the grand lobby staircase two steps at a time. Moments later, he was on the third floor, searching for room 308B.

A quick search brought him to room 307, 308 . . . 309. No

B. Peter knocked on 308's door. He stood there, expectant, still breathing hard from his quick ascent.

Silence.

Peter tried the key. Nothing.

Someone grasped the doorknob on the other side, startling Peter. Things threatened to release. Peter commanded his forces.

As the door opened, a man with a ponytail, his hair all gray, took up the entrance. He wore another faded Members Only jacket, once a deep red.

"Have you ever seen the sun?"

Only wanting this over with, Peter uttered. "Only through the reflection of reality."

Impassive, the man turned back into the room and replied, "Come in." Drawn by a leash of compliance, Peter followed. A smell of fabric bleached by the sun permeated the room.

"You have the key." Not a question.

Peter was surprised to find the key, forgotten about, still clutched in his hand. Uncertain, "Yes?"

Looking like the ghost of Christmas future, the mysterious man motioned toward another door in the room. No door had any business being where it was, facing toward the outside of the room. There wasn't a balcony. The door label proclaimed 308B.

Peter gave a longing look at the bathroom and made a break for it.

A meaty paw clamped around his bicep. With clear admonishment, the man urged, "They are *waiting*. Go now!" And then he was gone, closing the door behind him.

Upon his slipping the key into the door, a panel opened, revealing a smooth dark surface that sprung to life with a bright green light. An outline of a hand emerged.

A disjointed voice threatened his bladder control again. "Hello, please place your right hand on the scanner."

Placing his hand on the surface, he felt no sensation, but bright light shone through the breaks of his fingers. A satisfying bleep was followed by, "Thank you."

Something unlatched. As the door swung open, there was an intake of air, flooding to the other side. Blackness consumed the interior. Foreign sounds toned in the background. Impeding further investigation, a woman emerged from the blackness, no more than a shadow. Dark glasses obscured her eyes.

"You are the cog, Peter." Without further ceremony the woman pulled a round object from a bag, offering it to him.

"Take it. You must."

"Listen, I just need a minute . . . "

The woman shoved the circular object into his midsection. Sharp pangs spread through his abdomen.

"There is no time to explain. You must take this." The firm edge to her voice left no room for negotiation.

"Go back down to the lobby. Give the *solar orb* to Deliverance. Then you will be done."

"Who . . . well shit." Opportunity for further questions passed as the women melted back into the darkness. Silent as a ghost, the door slipped closed. Wallpaper materialized over the door, making it disappear.

Peter hurried back down to the lobby. Sweat covered him in a sheen. Stabbing pains bored through his midsection. On the outskirts of his awareness, he noticed the object had almost no weight; it was somehow smooth and rough at the same time.

Back in the lobby, everything was unnaturally quiet. No one seemed to notice the sweating, desperate man.

Without a shred of her previous worry, the first woman—Deliverance?—strode toward him and took the object away. The orb glowed. Where the light touched, full color returned to her jacket, skin, hair. Ten years of age disappeared from her face.

"Thank you. You've done more than you will ever know. That is, if it works." She offered a small smile. Before turning away, reluctant, she said, "You deserve an explanation . . . "

Never hearing the last line, Peter ran wailing toward the bathroom, not caring about the turned heads gaping at him.

Deliverance shrugged and walked away.

Mark Frost has enjoyed writing short fiction, poetry and, on occasion, longer fiction for years. He's into horror, thrillers, science fiction and fantasy, which permeate his work. Most of his publications are in academic sources, but he looks forward to more forays into the fiction world. Mr. Frost lives in Buffalo, NY with his wife.

# Future Bound

Rachel Leidenfrost

I walked in to the bar, the red silk of my dress riding high on my thighs as I moved through the crowd. Eyes turned, though not many. I felt naked. But my display was nothing compared to some of the beings from off-world; those from all walks of life cavorted in the tiniest tubes of clothing—shiny, shell-like transparencies—and nothing at all. They were beautiful.

I wanted to be one of them, to live my life among them. I'd traded everything I owned to get to Hotel Stormcove. To get away from the dry dust of everyday Earth and the painful memories of my shattered past. My moment was near.

My eyes met August's—an Astral I'd hired for the evening. He rose, his long body unfolding from the chair he held out to me. I slid into place, my dress riding up further. I puckered my silver-stained lips and leaned forward to talk to the bartender. "A High Rider, please." She nodded and grabbed a glass, pouring in bright green, pink, and blue fluids and topping the concoction with four inches of whipped cream. She slid the drink my way and I slid back my very last coin.

I carefully ignored the man on my left, instead playing with the candied fruits that garnished my outrageously decadent drink. But I was aware of everything that he did. A tall and broad man with dark hair and a jagged scar across his chin, he lent an air of authority to every movement. I hungered to hear how he'd gotten the scar, to hear his voice at all. He was wearing a black and white skinsuit—a modern parody of an old-fashioned tuxedo—but I was used to seeing him in uniform.

This was Commander Xavier Everett. He led the exploration fleet for the Orion territories, an unusual job for a human. I'd heard he was a difficult man to impress, though I'd only ever seen him online. This would be our first meeting, but I hoped our futures were intertwined. A brunette hung on his left side and a curvy indigo being I didn't recognize purred on his lap. It was hard not to interrupt, but I held on, investigating the people on my other side and the mirrored view in front of me, waiting.

Finally, after what felt like forever but was actually no more than a minute or two, I heard a loud crash behind me; the music died. The bar fell silent for a moment before a buzz of interest picked back up. I turned with everyone else, curiosity carefully portrayed on my face. August lay on the ground amidst the remnants of a broken table. An angry Lebrethian stood nearby, fins opened wide on the side of his neck, one of his many arms wrapped securely around a tall figure in a tiny dress.

"Move. I need to see what is going on." Commander Everett's voice was every bit as deep as I expected. The being on his lap slid off, melting into the crowd.

"I can tell you what's going on." I turned and looked at him for the first time, my deep violet eyes meeting his.

"Yeah, right. Sure you can, lady. Excuse me." I didn't so much as blink, my eyes following him as he started to turn away.

"The man on the ground is a smuggler and a thief. He picked a fight with the wrong person—one of your men, I take it. Would you like to know if he took anything?"

The Commander looked back at me, eyebrows furrowed, a scowl forming on his face. "It would be easy to assume that he did."

"He didn't. In fact, he left something. Check the left pocket of your man's suit."

Commander Everett gave me a hard look before turning away.

He strode toward the scene, washing through the crowd with the power and inevitability of the waves lapping at the shore.

I slid off my stool and skirted the edge of the bar, heading for the balcony. I found a private spot in a corner and waited. Moonlight bounced off the water below, highlighting the jagged rocks and the churning water. Hotel Stormcove remained one of the most stunning places on the eastern seaboard, and one of the only places of leisure still fully maintained and operational thanks to its popularity with travelers from other worlds.

I tipped my head up and watched the sky, alive with movement even late at night. I decoded it all. The two narrowly spaced red dots that indicated the back of a cargo ship, the green v-shaped lights that revealed a ship built for speed, and the huge white beacons that marked the largest of the ships—controllers, or to call them what they really were: floating cities. One hung right above the Stormcove, and I planned to be on it when it left.

I felt him arrive next to me, but I didn't look over.

"Was that really necessary?"

I turned and smiled at him, noticing the business card in his hand. "Ah, you found it."

"Of course. As you intended." He nodded at me briefly. "Why didn't you just introduce yourself and tell me you had information to sell?"

"Oh, but I don't have information to sell. That"—I inclined my head briefly—"is a gift."

"I don't trust gifts. What do you want?" The Commander's jaw was clenched, and I thought about his history—orphaned by a never-ending war, left in charge of siblings who died one by one as toxicity rose across the planet. Our backgrounds were the same, but he'd risen from it, taken the long journey to the stars. The journey I wanted to take.

"You can trust this one. The person named is a traitor. Explore his financials; you'll see it all if you can open that account. The gift is my way of seeking an introduction, showing you some of what I can do."

He was silent for a long moment and then he turned and rested his arms against the railing. "I see. You want a free ride to the stars."

"A free ride? No, not a free ride. I offer a valuable service. And, besides, can you blame me? Why would I want to stay here and die as the last valuable resources are sucked off the Earth's crust and fought over by bandits and pirates?"

"I don't blame you. But it's not possible. Nobody new leaves the planet anymore. Ever."

A passing waitress handed out shots and he slammed one back, turning to leave. He looked older than he did online, sadder. I placed a hand on his arm, stopping him.

"Please. I can slip in and out of computer systems without leaving a trace. I can charm your friends and confuse your enemies. I'm a chameleon in the truest sense of the word. I can be anyone you need if you'll just give me a chance to truly live."

I didn't realize I'd dug my nails into his arm until he gently pried them away.

"Don't you think I'd like to save people? Change things? If I got caught, I'd be executed. There's no way." He took the other shot out of my hand and belted that one back as well. I could see the dregs of the amber liquid clinging to the glass, his knuckles white around it.

He shocked me when he flung the shot glass off the balcony; it surely crashed hard against the rocks, but far below and hidden in the crash of the waves, there was no trace to show it had ever been.

I pulled the Commander back to me and threw my arms around his neck, desperate. "Please. Please take me." I slid closer on my three-inch heels and pressed my lips against his. He kissed me back, his lips firm, his hands wrapped around my waist.

Heavy seconds later, I pulled away. "Will you take me with you?"

He shook his head. "I cannot."

Tears slid down the side of my face. I didn't want to do this but had no choice. "So be it." He made to step back but I leaned closer, kissing him like it was my last night on earth, devouring him.

My body pressed against every inch of his, learning his shape and texture, the feel of his hands. In my mind, I repeated his words to me over and over, memorizing the timber and cadence of his voice. I pushed him up against the railing, bracketing him in with my strong arms in the dark corner of the balcony, the entire place vibrating to the beat of the music.

When I was ready, I breathed him in, stealing his memories, capturing his soul. He opened his eyes at the last moment, silently pleading with me to stop. I felt his fear and breathed that in as well. I continued until he was a husk, tears falling down my face unheeded.

It was done. I looked at the shell of the vacant body entwined with mine and then took a quick look around. Nobody was paying any attention; I tipped the body into the dark ocean below before turning back to the bar.

I wiped the tears away with a rough thumb, wishing he'd said yes, that we'd both been able to leave this place.

I headed back inside. The Lebrethian met me halfway across the room. "I thought you disappeared on us. Ready for another whiskey?"

I clapped a hand on the man's back and laughed, thinking about the future, thinking about the stars. "Make it a double."

Rachel Leidenfrost writes fantasy and science fiction stories for both adults and children. By day she is a marketing and communications executive, by night an author. An avid reader, she loves classic and contemporary fantasy and science fiction as well as the quirky and unusual. She lives in Buffalo, NY with her husband Corey.

# The Opaque Oasis
Marsalis

Ilya stroked Sabrine's head, ignoring the bursts of artillery in the far distance.

Across a ruffled spread, their imperious bodies lay limp and trembling, twisted and tangled like a maze without end. Though faint, vain rays of sunlight etched themselves upon the marble walls, the suite remained an opaque oasis, inviting its patrons to sink deeper into a pit of passion.

"If only we could wait," Sabrine cooed. "I want to remember your fingers."

"You know every ridge."

"But I have to make sure."

Ilya smiled, her mind and heart racing in tandem. "You were always so difficult."

"And you always enjoyed it." Sabrine gripped one of Ilya's fingers and kissed her enameled rings. "You should call your guards and tell them you're staying. That you've abdicated and won't ever return."

"They'll have my head," Ilya said. "And then they'll have yours."

"It could all go down now and I wouldn't care. At least we'd be together. At least we'd be in our favorite room."

Ilya ogled its obscurity, conjuring innumerable memories of brilliance and mirth. "I wonder if it'll still be here when it's all over. Stormcove has always seemed so indestructible, so timeless. That little paradise in which you could disappear."

"I know. Remember the Gold and Silver Ball? Tossing away

our dance cards and racing through the gardens? Sneaking into the penthouse and ordering gobs of room service? We got so drunk and I almost told you I loved you."

"Things were much different then." Ilya wanted to marinate, but her mind had reached reason once more. "I thought I could get away with anything. *We* thought we could get away with anything. But it was always like that here. Gorgeous, majestic. Hotel Stormcove. The place to go when nothing else mattered, when you wanted to be left alone."

"Isn't that what we want now?"

"We're not sixteen anymore."

"But we can pretend to be."

Ilya chuckled, nervously, and hated herself for the fakery it brought. Not too long ago, she would have been the one full of dreams and fantasies. But when the artillery burst yet again, she could not ignore its terror.

"I gotta go. Need to plan the attack." In her galloping mind, she began to dissect the details. First, she would need to—

"Attack," Sabrine muttered, snuggling closer. "What a foolish word. What a silly, ridiculous, foolish word."

"—and I'll have to recruit more soldiers. The best . . . "

"Soldiers—" Sabrine repeated with a snort.

"—and I can't even imagine what the House of Officials will say about—"

"Can you stop it?!" Sabrine rose from Ilya's chest and stared her in the eye. "Can you just stop acting for one second like this isn't the end of everything we know?"

Ilya glanced away, her eyes filling with water, and then glanced back. "What do you want me to say, Sabrine? Our lands have just declared war on each other. We are their sovereigns!"

In the back of her gilded mind, Sabrine knew her responsibilities, her duties to her land and her family. She'd known that there would come a day when her position of power would extend further than her sports cars and vacation palaces. Yet, she had not expected it to happen so soon. And she never expected it to affect her greatest love.

"Well, perhaps I am the true thespian," she admitted with calm, as the faint sunlight grew in intensity. "Your dedication to this life has never been short of admirable. Even when you were wild, you were serious because you knew it would all have to matter at some point. But me? I can't do this. I can't be this way, making orders and planning attacks. I mean, why each other? Why not another place? Why can't we join forces and have peace?"

"It's deeper than that, and you know it," Ilya told her. "My people, your people. They are different. They think differently, they feel differently."

"But what about us?"

"What do you mean?"

Sabrine cuffed Ilya's face, clutching it close. "How did we manage to love each other?"

"We are not our people."

"Then what are we?"

Ilya shrugged as more artillery burst. She closed her eyes as if she could feel its madness firsthand. "We are fools," she declared. "Silly, ridiculous fools. Truly believing we could keep up something that was never meant to last. And we got away with it for a while. We had a nice run of doing exactly what we desired. But this is just a sign, Sabrine. A sign that it was never meant to be."

Sabrine held her breath, believing in her loosest logic that the frigidity of her bones could pause the frigidity between them. But as she watched Ilya rise from the bed and reach for a dress, she knew that her powers were pointless.

Within moments, she imagined her own guards wondering of

her whereabouts, informing her that her own helicopter was safe for travel.

She could pretend no more; the inevitable was too inevitable.

"Take mercy upon us, will you?"

"Don't speak that way, Sabrine."

"But I know how this goes." She took a deep drag, her heart a racehorse. "They did it to my father and my uncle. They tried to do it to my mother. When the battles start raging, it's hard to care about feelings."

Ilya walked back over and sat next to Sabrine. She wrapped her arms around her and brought her near. "I don't want to hurt you," she said. "I don't want anything to happen to you. I just know what I have to do for the good of my land. For what my people want. They look to me for guidance and leadership. They look to me to satisfy their needs. And right now, they want something that I must work hard to achieve."

"Land," Sabrine whispered. "Why can't I just give it to you and let it all be done?"

"Because then you'll look weak to your own people. Don't you see it, Sabrine? It's all a game for them. They need to feel as if they've made something happen, as if they've changed the course of history. And we are the spearheads giving them that chance. We're examples, idols. We represent them."

"I just want to represent myself."

"Perhaps in another world, my darling, perhaps in another life."

As the heavy sunlight marveled against the marble wall, the two rulers gripped each other, their shoulders convulsing, their throats choking on tears. Only hours earlier, they'd been in heaven, and yet, within that moment, they had never felt more hellish. As more artillery burst in the far distance, they raised their heads.

"I hope this room remains untouched," Sabrine said, wiping her wet cheeks. "They're far enough away, I think."

Ilya nodded with uncertainty. "Yeah. Stormcove won't ever die. It'll outlive us all."

"I don't want to die."

"Me neither."

As the heavy sun illuminated that most sacred of spots, erasing idle illusions and awakening their souls from sweetness, the two held each other once more—one more time, one last time—knowing in the deepest, darkest follies that there could never again be something as sublime.

"I have to go," Ilya announced with terrible coldness.

"It can wait," Sabrine said. "I want to remember your fingers."

"Darling . . ."

Sabrine watched as Ilya rose once more from the bed and headed toward the door. She reached for the handle and stopped, turning her head around. Each could hear the helicopter's rotors spinning, the tremendous roar a death knell.

"Please forgive me," Ilya nearly shouted.

"I already have," Sabrine said, turning her head away, and she did not turn back until she knew the door had been closed and she was alone.

Artillery burst in the far distance, and she lit another cigarette.

<hr />

Marsalis was born in 1989. He spent his childhood composing picture epics and giving lectures. At seventeen, he published his first novel, *March of the Libertines*, and pursued a club-hopping lifestyle with decadents and aristocrats. A graduate of the University of Michigan, Marsalis has since published and written works in every literary style and genre. He loves bubblegum, fast cars, and silent cinema. He lives in Detroit.

# Cash, Card, Or My Unholy Offspring

F E Norley

2003
Lobby
16:08

The children were in the suitcase, and they were not happy. Salisthy, Goddess Of The Seven Unholy Seas, She-Of-The-Thousand-Tentacles—and, more recently, Mother—just hoped she had given them enough seaweed to keep them occupied. The bi-millennial SSAOOGA (Sea Serpent And Other Ocean Gods Association) meeting at Stormcove was not one to be missed.

She was already late, and the smell of disinfectant, coffee, and perfume mingled in the air and clung to the back of her throat as she approached the front desk. There was a squarish contraption on the counter that clicked and whirred, and Salisthy felt her lip curl as she eyed it. She hadn't really kept up to date with humans; they changed so quickly it felt like it was only yesterday she'd been curling her tentacles around a wooden hull.

The receptionist was chewing something, and the sucking, slapping noise made Salisthy grit her teeth.

"Welcome to Stormcove!" the human chirped between chomps.

"Thank you," Salisthy stammered, having to concentrate on operating her synthetic skin's facial muscles the right way. Roaring was much more efficient, and she saw now that letting her tongue dangle out the side of her mouth was not the done thing.

The receptionist began to tap away at the strange square object. "Checking in?"

"No, I just want—"

*Clack clack clack.*

"No reservation?" The receptionist sucked at her teeth, "Well,

I'm afraid we have a limited number of rooms avail— Um, your suitcase is leaking."

Salisthy felt a cold splash on her foot and looked down in horror.

*Drip drip.*

"I will take a room—"

*Dripdripdrip.*

"—with a large, *oh corals what is it called* . . . bath-tank—"

"Bathtub?"

Out of the corner of her eye, Salisthy spotted a little tentacle pop out of the suitcase.

"And how would you like to p— Oh!" the receptionist ducked as Salisthy tossed a handful of pearls in her direction, the gems whizzing through the air at a slightly greater speed than Salisthy had anticipated.

"My apologies," Salisthy said through gritted teeth as she wrestled with her suitcase.

The receptionist peeked over the top of the desk, smiled politely, then gestured at a sign taped to the counter.

*WE DO NOT ACCEPT THE FOLLOWING AS PAYMENT:*
*FIRSTBORNS*
*A NIGHT TO REMEMBER*
*THE SECRET TO IMMORTALITY*
*AMERICAN EXPRESS CARDS*
*GEMSTONES (MISC.)*

"Cash, card or cheque?" she said, then gently so that Salisthy felt like she was the small vulnerable creature, not the other way around, "Or, if you are in need—"

Salisthy growled. In need? Her? The Great Behemoth? Terror Of The Salt? Empress Of All That Swam?

She squared her shoulders, raising her arm to protest, and as she did so, the suitcase snagged on the counter, the clasp snapping with a loud crack. The case bulged, wobbled, then her children spewed out in a wave of saltwater and seaweed, howling and chattering. Salisthy lunged at them, tentacles bursting out of her synthetic skin as the children tipped over plants, scribbled on the walls and upended the pot of coffee everywhere.

The receptionist's face was a blotchy pink, and whatever she was chewing fell out of her mouth with a plop. She forced a smile.

"Ocean view?" she squeaked, tapping madly.

"Yes, please," Salisthy rumbled. "I like a good view."

F E Norley is a writer from Bath, UK. They like their stories to tug at readers' heartstrings and head-strings, and hopefully humour-strings too. Find them on Twitter @FENorley.

# Sigrun Is Not Here

E.D.E. Bell

"Well, let's give her a few minutes," Kiru intoned, floating his coffee to the table with a flourish of his hand.

"It's not three yet." Prija conjured a small hammered metal device, which she quickly flicked away. "Five minutes."

"Can I ask something first?" Lloyd interrupted. He tapped the translation orb with a wand, scanning the room to make sure everyone understood him.

"Hmm?" Kiru was flipping through his notebook.

"When I ported to the lobby, I saw the hotel has 'Ass. Wizards' on the monitor." Noting Kiru's confused look, he pointed. "Out in the lobby. 'Ass. Wizards: Atlantic,' it says. Teenagers were posting *pictures.*"

"I typed it on my phone," Prija said. "I figured they'd fill it in. How long have we been meeting here? Anyway, who cares? We're wizards. It's nothing."

"Easy for you to say, not being the central rep from Uranus," Ff#trleee grumbled.

Prija paused, noting a fountain pen wildly scratching away on Kiru's paper. "Are you taking attendance? It's not three. We start at three."

"I'm getting a head start," he said. "Anyway, almost everyone is here. Just the one."

A crackle sounded in the doorway, and indistinguishable sparks of gray light spread into a thin web. "You're clear," Dan called, as a stout woman popped through the portal and whisked it away.

"Must be Sigrun," a wizard in the back whispered to another, who was wearing a short dark veil over his eyes. "So, I guess we're ready."

Sigrun's tunic and pants, topped with a tight cap, stood in contrast to the sweeping robes and corded fringe the other wizards wore, giving the illusion of a convention-like skirt around the elongated wood table. She was holding a stack of books, which almost tumbled out of her arms as she tripped past a misplaced satchel. Muttering, she cinched the books back into her arms. "Hello, everyone." She smiled.

"Hello," the others said, the replies muddling together into a polite rumble. Winding past the table, where at least a dozen wizards swiveled on ergonomic chairs, she plunked down near the end of the back wall, sliding the books under a plain, padded seat.

"When we get a chance—" Sigrun started.

"Hey, great tweet yesterday," Mimi said, nodding at Dan. A few of the wizards boiled up a low cheer in response.

"If people can't handle it, they can leave. But, hey, did you see Sofia's fire bridge last week?" Dan added, pointing across the table. "That was something." He placed his hands against the chest of his gray robe.

"Yes!" Mimi almost shook in her chair. "So good!"

"Oh, you would know, Mimi," Sofia said, tapping a wand on the side of her mobility chair, which floated in place. "Who led ice domes for five years straight?"

Mimi pointed back with a wink, and everyone settled in, waiting, as Kiru's pen continued to scratch.

"I know we're all busy," Sigrun said from her corner, "but our council is trying something new, working with the hotel here, and I wondered if anyone—"

"Just cast your magic, and let it fly," Sofia said with a polite smile.

"We haven't started the meeting yet," Dan added. "Just giving everyone time to marinate."

Prija scrunched her nose.

"Well, if there's a good time to discuss it, we have some ideas, and—"

"I'm here to fight evil wizards," Wan said, clapping their hands together.

"Exactly," Mimi said. "Let them know right where they stand."

"Are we getting catering?" Lloyd asked. "They have the best buffets here."

"Not until four," Kiru explained. "Sesame bok choy with fried yuba satchels. Ash, yours are baked." He nodded at Ff#trleee. "Gas option."

"Quick thread." Dan turned to the table. "Wizard-hat cookies. I'm obsessed!"

The room burst into laughter. "He's brilliant," Lloyd whispered, swiveling to face those seated against the wall.

"Hey," Wan said, leaning forward. "Have you heard what happened at MageClave?" Several wizards sucked in a deep breath.

"You know what I think?" Talc tapped a long fingernail on the table. "In wizardry, truth is always a lie."

"*Mmmm.*" Several caps bobbed around the table.

"Did you hear what Trolofian cast, though?" Mimi leaned in.

"Done." Talc waved a hand. "Just. Done." Several wizards murmured, though less than before.

"Anyway, I'm glad we're all on the same tower here," Kiru said. "And it's just about time." He glanced at Prija, but she didn't notice.

"There's a way to do things," Mimi said. "And anyone who would have anything to do with his sort can go to *Mordor.*"

A *pop* sounded in the air, and the wizards at the table glanced all around, finally resting their eyes on an empty seat.

"What was that?" Wan swung in their chair.

"Sigrun," Prija answered. "Small council." She shrugged.

"Fine." Mimi grunted, as the others nodded in agreement. "Ooh!" she added, as a crack sounded in the distance. Talc waved the window's lightscreen up with a sweep of his hand, revealing a storm coming into the cove, dark sheets of rain pouring in waves.

Just at that moment, a black cat jumped down from the table with a squeak, darting out into the hallway.

"Well," Kiru said with a sigh, "let's call this meeting to order."

E.D.E. Bell was born in the year of the fire dragon during a Cleveland blizzard. After a youth in the mitten, an MSE in Electrical Engineering from the University of Michigan, three wonderful children, and nearly two decades in Northern Virginia and Southwest Ohio developing technical intelligence strategy, she now applies her magic to the creation of genre-bending fantasy fiction in Ferndale, Michigan, where she is proud to be part of the Detroit arts community. A passionate vegan and enthusiastic denier of gender rules, she feels strongly about issues related to equality and compassion. She revels in garlic. She loves cats and trees. She opened a hotel. You can follow her adventures at edebell.com.

# Honeymoon Blues

Drew Michaels

A Late January Morning, 2669 (Earth Standard)
Lobby
Approximately 3 AM

A Nor'easter for the ages raged outside the old hotel, forcing the doors open and blowing snow past the two figures scurrying in out of the storm, small duffels bundled in the arms of the larger. A foot and half of snow already covered the land, and vicious storm surges swept over the beach every few minutes. It had been centuries since a storm of this magnitude blanketed the region, maybe all the way back to the Blizzard of Nineteen Seventy-Eight. The larger creature dropped its packs and closed the doors with a mighty shove.

Before the snow began to melt, the AI security protocol had kicked in and scanned the duo. It detected the transponder signals from two galactic passports which showed the couple to be females from the Praxis system. The smaller of the humanoids spoke, her speech translated by the concierge AI. "Hello?" The word echoed through the cavernous lobby. "Did the storm knock out their fusion reactor?" she whispered to her companion.

"I don't think so, Deela. The heat would be off."

"Did the brochure say anything about this being an ice planet?"

"It's not. Doesn't mean we didn't land at an icy latitude or season."

"We could have checked if you'd called ahead to let them know we'd be running late."

"You're the one who wanted to book a place off the beaten path," the larger female pointed out. "I wanted to go to the casino resort on Deneb IV."

"That's the first planet my progenitors would have sent the Praxian Navy to look for us. Besides, Quill, nobody forced you to elope with me," Deela said with a wicked grin.

Quill picked up the pair of satchels with a grunt and staggered to the front desk at the center of the enormous room. Acting like a bodyguard, she scanned the darkened lobby, the lights set low for the night shift. The couple looked up at the ancient vaulted ceiling and gaped at the pair of massive staircases. The curved monoliths were still impressive, if not quite as spectacular as in their heyday, and expressions of wonder covered both women's faces. Dust motes twinkled and sparkled in the low light as they reached the front desk. Quill rapped a claw on the small metal bell sitting there. A high clear note rang out as a hologram burst to life.

"Welcome to the historic Hotel Stormcove on the beautiful North Atlantic," the pale monochrome figure intoned in perfect Praxian. "Do you have a reservation?"

Deela snorted at the static-filled playback. "Do we, my love?"

Quill glared at the other woman before responding to the machine's question. "A room for two for a Galactic fortnight. Should be under the name Hargh." The holographic desk clerk appeared to ignore the couple, the only sound the faint high-pitched whir of a data disk being accessed. The women looked around the lobby for a chronometer, as if they were expecting a faster answer. A full Earth minute passed before the clerk spoke.

"My apologies. I had to access our long-term archive. Unfortunately, we could not hold your original room for such a long period of time. We shall accommodate your reservation with the best room available."

"Long? I made the reservation yesterday," Quill said in puzzlement.

"Our records indicate your reservation was received two hundred and twenty-seven Earth years ago," the clerk said.

Quill felt a sharp rap on her shoulder blade. "This is your fault!" Deela grumbled.

"How is this my fault?"

"I told you to bring the ship to a complete stop while you fixed the fold drive. But no, you had to let us glide along at relativistic speeds."

"So?"

"Did you forget about time dilation? This is why my progenitors warned me about you," Deela griped. "Ambassador Trellos wouldn't have made that error."

"The same Trellos you're avoiding an arranged marriage to?" Quill snapped back. "We were in a hurry. Security would have interrogated High Priestess L'Mar by then, and I thought drifting would give us the best chance of eluding a Praxian patrol."

"I hope they have a store on the hotel grounds," Deela said, changing the subject. "All I packed was warm weather clothing. What am I going to do instead of swimming and starbathing?"

"Can the hotel exchange Praxian Sovereigns?" Quill asked the clerk, ignoring her companion. "I would like to pay cash for the room."

"I am programmed with the proper conversion factor," the clerk responded. "Since this is a honeymoon stay, your first night will be complimentary. You will be happy to know the hotel has a heated indoor pool and saunas in our spa. They are open daily from eight o'clock in the morning to ten o'clock at night, local time."

"Thank you." Quill slid the appropriate number of platinum coins into a slot in the desk.

"Why didn't you pay with credits?" Deela asked.

"Because the Praxian government will be monitoring your account for transactions, assuming the funds weren't frozen in the first place," Quill said with a sigh. "You didn't consider your progenitors doing that, did you?"

"I hate to admit it, but you're right," Deela said, a sour expression the only sign she was thinking of a better comeback.

"You will be in Room Eighty-nine forty-three, in the Arcadia Tower," the clerk interrupted. "Please follow our bellhop." A short, motorized trolley trundled out of a doorway at the side of the desk and halted in front of the couple. "Do you have any luggage for transport?" Quill dropped their two small bags in a basket on the trolley's rear. The bellhop started moving, heading between the marble staircases toward doors which led to the newer sections of the hotel, the women following close behind. The translucent desk clerk observed the glass doors close behind the trio, an impassive expression still in place.

"I give them two Galactic months, tops."

Drew Michaels is an author of science fiction and fantasy who artfully weaves touches of other genres into his works. Drew holds an MBA and a BS in Chemistry and a long first career as an Environmental Chemist helps ground his stories in the believable. Drew was born and raised in Connecticut but, after stops in Massachusetts and Ohio, now resides in Tucson, Arizona with his wife and the youngest of his four sons. It's a great college town to pursue his writing and living in the Sonoran Desert certainly agrees with him. He now works for the City Procurement Department and after a long day writing contracts, Drew likes to unwind by playing with his son or watching anime. You can follow him on Twitter at @DMichaelswrites.

# Owl Eyes

Robert Perez

October 18th, 1928
Room 303
12:16 AM

Rose waltzed barefoot and champagne-drunk down the hall to her room. Once inside, she tossed her shoes onto a maroon chaise lounge overflowing with newly acquired luxury fashions still in boxes and bags. After a long day of shopping and celebration, she was ready for bed. Rose removed the pins from her hair and changed into an indigo nightgown. She brushed her teeth and practiced smiling in the mirror. When her head touched the pillow, she remembered she was supposed to make a wish, but she had everything she could ever want. Her mind was blank as she stared into the crystals of the chandelier above.

Legend tells of dreams coming true at Hotel Stormcove. At night the area is said to become the hunting grounds for a mythical owl that drifts in like a dark cloud from somewhere beyond the horizon's infinity. The bird preys on nightmares. Over the years, guests have reported a glow outside their windows too strange to be the moon, along with sightings of a large black owl with will-o'-wisp eyes. Dreams are made real under the owl's luminous gaze. Many guests have awoken to the sound of wings brushing against their windows.

There is a pen and notepad on every nightstand at Hotel Stormcove. It's a hotel tradition for guests to write down a wish and tuck it into their pillowcase before bed, an amendment to the previous rule of placing the note under their pillow after countless wishes became lost in the sheets or were tossed in the laundry. The practice is meant to encourage good dreams in case there is a visit from the fabled owl. The hotel keeps the tale alive by granting some of the wishes. The maids check for notes in the bed while cleaning, and a few lucky guests return to find a surprise under their pillow.

It was said that the hotel manager collected the notes of every participating guest over the years and that one of the rooms is filled from floor to ceiling with jars of hoarded wishes. Candy, toys, appliances, health and beauty items, tickets to entertainment—the playful interpretation of the notes has led to guests finding all sorts of things. In one famous incident, a guest wrote down a type of new car and returned to find his pillows missing. He went down to the lobby perplexed and was directed outside, where the car of his dreams was parked with a pillow on its hood.

The only light came from the bedside lamp. Rose considered the bare white sheet of paper. With extra care to be neat, she wrote, "I am perfectly happy with my life," and was relieved when she didn't have to face the emptiness of the page any longer. The words looked like they were on a tiny stage under a spotlight, and she stared at them expectantly, waiting for them to perform some kind of convincing magic trick.

She wiped a tear away, ripped the note to pieces, and tossed the bits into the air.

"I'm already the lucky one," Rose said, and turned off the light.

To feel better, she thought of her sprawling property in Maine, of her rows of stables housing winning thoroughbreds, of her jewelry collection and country club membership; there wasn't anything in this world that she couldn't have, but it still felt like something was missing. She envisioned the other guests writing down their deepest yearnings and compared herself to them as someone who had been given everything and learned to want for nothing. Rose wondered what it felt like for a heart to hold a wish. She supposed that for some it would grow stronger with every beat, and for others it would fade with each pulse like a dying echo.

As she imagined the various forms a dream could take, her room became brighter, as if the clouds had drawn back to uncover the moon and stars. She was too tired to get up and close the curtains, so she turned her back to the window and fell asleep in curious fascination, wishing she could bear witness to the birth of dreams.

When the glow faded, the bed was empty, and there was a new portrait hanging on the wall across from it. Future guests to the room would pause to admire the picture of a beautiful woman astride a white stallion with a tall mansion rising in the background, and Rose would stare back with unblinking painted attention.

Robert Perez sleeps at the bottom of the ocean. His previous work has appeared in the *Horror Writers Association Poetry Showcase* Volumes II, III, IV (Special Mention), and V, *The Literary Hatchet* #13 & #14, and *Deadlights Magazine* #1. He is currently working on obtaining a Masters in Psychological Counseling at the University of Colorado Denver. Follow @_TheLeader on Twitter to keep up with future projects.

# Room Special
Jakob Drud

2019
Room 1613
10:22 PM

My friends used to call me Gossamer, but to tell the truth I've never had that many friends, seeing as I'm a thief and a quite prolific one at that. I've broken into antique stores to reacquire family heirlooms for needy and seedy contractors, and I've liberated great works of art from illicit billionaire collections on behalf of major museums. I've even stolen iPhones to pay for food and medicine for my father. But that night, in room 1613 of the Stormcove Hotel, I was a thief for love.

Or at least I was trying to be. The safe I was supposed to crack was being unambiguously obstinate. It had one of the first Yale-type locks ever made, meaning that it opened with a key rather than a combination lock. The trouble was that no key had ever been made for it, and the safe had been locked when it was delivered to the Hotel in 1849, something that two painstaking hours with my best picks had not been able to change. The cylindrical plug moved easily enough, but the three springs controlling the driver pins were as hypersensitive as a classroom full of teenagers. The tiniest push sent them too far up, blocking the plug, but feather-brushing them with my picks didn't make them budge.

I felt defeated, disgraced even. And by a simple three-pin lock! On any other job I'd have been gone and goner by now, licking my wounded pride in a bar somewhere. But Arcadia had hinted that the safe needed opening, and I more than needed an opening with Arcadia.

I'd met Arcadia one evening when I was following a mark to the most expensive night club in New York. She came up to me in the bar, and with a fiery smile that could melt both steel doors and thieving hearts she side-railed me from an otherwise well-prepared scam. Instead of driving off in my mark's 1936 Phantom III Rolls-Royce, I ended up getting my heart stolen on an epic night of Dark & Stormies and G&Ts, which we topped off with One Thing & The Other in a Manhattan hotel.

Let me be absolutely clear: anything between Arcadia and me should have been doomed from the beginning. I'm a poor thief, and her full name, I kid you not, is Arcadia Bourges Grand'Or. To build any permanent connection, I either needed to be more of an upper class mook or she needed to be less of a billionaire's wife. Yet, when I woke up the next morning (alone, with a deep feeling of loss in my heart), I was lying next to an envelope with a reservation booked for Hotel Stormcove and a note to read up on old wall safes.

In short, all that stood between me and a shot at eternal happiness was a nineteenth-century three-pin lock. So why couldn't I open the damn thing already?

It was time for a drink, and not just any drink. From an alcohol-shrouded memory, I dredged up (or, rather, decanted) something Arcadia had told me during a brief break in our One Thing & The Other: that every room in the Stormcove had a Room Special, a particular drink you could only get in that room and nowhere else in the hotel. There was no way she had dropped that hint without a purpose, so I picked up the phone on the nightstand and called room service.

"Room number, please," someone said at the other end. The voice was so old and dry it could have come from either side of the grave.

"1613."

The line went quiet for a moment. "You want a strawberry soda with Alka-Seltzer, Pisang Ambon and three cat whiskers?"

"The Room Special came recommended," I said.

There was another pause. "Well, we do have a *felis catus* keeping us company in the bar. I'll see if he's dropped any whiskers recently."

The Ancient hung up (or maybe he expired), but I'd barely snatched up my tools before a knock on the door broke my concentration. I opened it to find a young, extremely fit waiter outside with a murky, sparkly drink on a silver tray. Trickles of blood were tracing their way down his arm from four parallel gashes on his hand, but he was smiling nonetheless.

"My apologies for the delay, sir, but the elevator was out."

I did a double take when I recognized his voice. Surely a person sounding so old shouldn't look like a Greek demi-god and be able to take sixteen flights of stairs in ten seconds, but Adonis the Ancient was barely out of breath.

I pointed to the scratches on his hand. "I hope you didn't have trouble getting the ingredients?"

"We trust you didn't need your whiskers to be that fresh, sir. Alas, the bar cat declined his usual tummy rub rather fiercely."

Even in the billionaire waters I regularly trawled, you didn't find anything approaching this level of service and dedication. I fished the last ten bucks out of my jeans pocket, but the waiter held up a hand.

"That's all right, sir. The gentleman in room 3901 will take care of the tips." He was out the door before I could ask what that had to do with me.

Which left me with a drink that called out to me in all its mudlike bubbliness. I contemplated taking a sip, but decided that any drink containing cat must have been created for other purposes than drinking. Instead I picked up the special garnish and gave it a critical look-over. The three whiskers had been softened to the point of pliancy by the club soda but weren't so soggy that they lost their natural steel-wire quality. Perfect for a ticklish three-pin lock.

I shook the excess drink from my new tools, bent the tough hairs to match the pins, and grabbed my plug spinner. The pins slid upward, smoothly but not so quickly that they blocked the circular movement of the plug, and after a wiggle and a prayer, the lock turned.

What do you expect to find in a safe that's been locked for over a century and a half? The key? Certainly, if you're a trickster by nature. And a mystery lover would probably hope for answers to old secrets, like what had happened to the Arc of the Covenant or Cleopatra's tomb. Me? I was willing to settle for enough gold and diamonds to send me up the rung toward Arcadia's social circle, but I must admit that I wouldn't have been surprised to find a note from her revealing the next step in an elaborate treasure hunt.

What I did not expect was for the entire wall to slide sideways, revealing a dingy-looking metal elevator with what looked like a cardboard floor and sides like a sheep pen. The shaft was shrouded in darkness, and the platform swayed dizzyingly when I climbed into the cage. I spotted no notes from Arcadia, but there was a button. A single red button; I could almost see huge, imaginary letters saying PUSH ME.

Yes, I pushed it.

The elevator went full moon rocket on me, squeezing my stomach all over the floor for two seconds. Then the red brick wall behind me slid aside, and I shuffled out through the gap, emerging next to a fireplace. The aperture closed behind me, leaving no clue as to how it could be opened. I was as trapped as if the elevator had stopped midway.

The room itself was large enough to fit a dance studio inside, and I realized I must be in one of the billionaire suites on the top floors. This theory was reinforced by the furniture: somewhere, the staff in a Louis Vuitton store must have worked overtime to restock. A panoramic glass facade showed off the amazing view of the moonlit cove from a great height.

I turned my gaze from the view in time to see a portly man enter through a doorway to a separate bedroom. He wore an unbuttoned lilac polo shirt and blue checkered pajama pants, and his feet were bare. He was holding two glasses of champagne, and the frown on his face told me I should be glad he wasn't holding a shotgun.

"What are you doing here?" he growled.

"Hotel poison taster," I extemporized. "The head waiter sent me to make sure we didn't accidentally bring you the, eh, wrong bottle of Bollinger."

The man squared his shoulders, and I took a step back. He might be older and slower than me, but he was also a head taller, and his bare feet found a position that spoke of martial arts training. He would probably have attacked me, champagne flutes and all, if he hadn't been interrupted by a trilling laugh from the bedroom. A laugh I would have recognized anywhere.

"Arcadia?" I asked.

She walked through the doorway, just as I remembered her. Her slim face with its delicate features wore that blistering hot smile, and her long brown hair sparkled with what was either expensive hair spray or the essence of mischief.

"My resourceful thief appears," she said. I felt relief and elation flood through my chest all at once, and not just because she was saving my ass from a serious whuppin'. Just seeing her again was enough to make my body thrum with giddiness.

"What are you talking about?" the man said. Arcadia didn't answer, but simply strode over to what must be a walk-in closet where she disappeared. Moments later, she returned with a tuxedo, a pair of shoes, and a bundle of papers.

"What's this nonsense, Gregory?" she asked. "Fighting?"

"Gregory?" he said. "Why are you calling me Gregory? If you're pulling one on me, I'll make you wish you'd never—"

"But you've always been called Gregory," she said innocently, breaking off what sounded like a habitual threat. She tossed him a passport from the bundle of papers, and his eyes narrowed as he opened it.

"Gregory McGuff?" he huffed. "Just because some joker put my picture next to a name doesn't mean it's true. And speaking of jokers . . . who's this guy?"

"The man who rented this room," Arcadia told him. Her hair still shone with mischief, but there was steel in her voice now. I realized I was looking at the final stage of an elaborate plan, and some of my elation at seeing her turned into anxiety. People like me are notoriously expendable pawns in the games of billionaires, and I had no idea what she was up to.

"But he's just a thief," Gregory shouted. "You said so yourself!"

Irked at his dismissive attitude to my chosen profession, I cleared my throat. "I believe she said I was *her* thief."

His look didn't exactly kill, but it certainly conveyed deadly intent. There were no obvious weapons in the room (I didn't have the strength to wield a designer sofa), and the way Gregory's gaze wandered from me to the balcony made my stomach object; defenestration from this height would give me far too much time to regret my choice of career before I became intimately familiar with the rocks below. But though there were no weapons, there was a phone on a table by the fireplace. Knowing that I must be here for a reason, I picked up the receiver.

"Room service?" I asked. "I'd like to order the Room Special."

"Room number?"

For a moment I was stumped. The elevator/rocket had given me no chance to count floors, and the view of the cove outside only told me that I was very far up. And even if I guessed the right floor by sheer luck, there was probably more than one room on each floor.

Then my mind caught up with me and registered the ancient voice of the young man who'd refused my tip two minutes ago.

"Room 3901," I said, hoping against hope that the special was a shotgun or a retroactive self-defense course.

"A glass of water. Right away, sir."

"Water?" I asked, panic mounting.

"From our very own mountain spring."

"And that's all?"

"Well, it comes with the passport, birth certificate, and driver's license of one William Blake III. The elevators are working again, so we'll be with you posthaste."

Before Gregory could put my flying skills to the test, there was a knock at the door, and Adonis the Ancient entered with a silver tray full of documents and a glass of water. He was followed by what might very well have been two hairless grizzly bears in black suits.

"Finally, someone with a bit of sense," Gregory exclaimed. "This man is a criminal. He walked in and claimed it was his room."

"No, Gregory," Arcadia said. "*I* claimed it was his room. It certainly isn't yours."

Adonis the Ancient gave me a scrutinizing stare, and I started sweating. He'd just seen me in my real room, so he could blow my cover like a dart champion at a balloon festival. If Arcadia had planned this to make me take the fall for something, she couldn't have put me in a tighter spot. But the Ancient merely extracted a passport from the pile of papers on his silver tray and flipped to the picture. "Sir, this passport matches the young man by the phone. William Blake III. His name is on the reservation, and I believe he would fit the tuxedo and the shoes laid out for him. I'd say it's his room."

"But I booked this room myself," said Gregory. "I'm Jeremy Bourges Grand'Or, and you've made a mistake."

Two sets of knuckles cracked as the bears flexed their paws. "We don't make mistakes," the Ancient assured him.

"But . . ." said Gregory. "But he just walked in. There's a door over there. A secret door. Next to the fireplace. Arcadia, you know what I'm talking about."

The Ancient stoically crossed the room to the fireplace and knocked on the wall. He raised an eyebrow as he addressed Gregory again. "This wall is solid, sir. But I do seem to recognize your name and face from the reception. You're the guest in room 387, aren't you?" And with a nod to Arcadia, he added, "The one you warned us about, miss?"

"Arcadia!" Gregory shouted. "I know what you're up to!"

Arcadia closed her eyes slowly as if in pain, and on her face I read a novel of hurt that Gregory would make such a preposterous claim. The Ancient must have seen it too, and he waved his tame bears forward. They frogmarched a screaming Gregory from the suite.

"Hang on," I said to the Ancient as he was about to follow. Once again, I fished my last ten bucks out of my jeans, but then took a look at the tuxedo Arcadia had laid out for me. There was a lump in the breast pocket, and I wasn't at all surprised to find a fat bundle of banknotes. I put it on the Ancient's silver tray. He handed me the papers documenting my new identity, bowed and left.

I turned to Arcadia, whose face was now overflowing with the same mischief that nested in her hair. Somewhere in all the excitement she'd picked up the two glasses of champagne. She handed me one and toasted it with a crystal *cling*.

"What exactly are we celebrating?" I asked, still not entirely sure the bears wouldn't return to take me for a short walk off the balcony.

"That you managed to pick a lock. Considerably faster than I did."

I turned that over in my mind and a couple of pins slid into place. Arcadia's knowledge of Room 1613, her hints about the Room Special, why she hadn't been the least bit surprised to see me. And Gregory's claim that he knew what she was up to.

"You mean you pulled the same stunt yourself?" I asked. "And he fell for it twice?"

"Two years ago." Her eyebrows rose in amusement. "You should have seen my entrance through that wall. Young and irresistible, suggestive evening dress, and most importantly, handing him a bulletproof plan for Wife Mark 2 that didn't involve a nine-figure divorce. Gregory couldn't get rid of the first Mrs. Grand'Or fast enough, poor woman."

"And he won't come after us? I mean, he has friends in high places, doesn't he?"

"I trust you'll agree that he's not very good at making friends," she said. "Gregory never booked anything himself, so I had no trouble reserving the suite in your name. I also booked a room for Gregory McGuff in advance, passport ID and all. Oh, and I warned the hotel staff of a man I didn't wish to see. As far as they're concerned, you and I are simply two billionaires whose elaborate role play was disturbed by a guest from the lower floors."

She put her hands on my shoulders and looked me deep in the eyes. "More importantly, I've spent the last couple of years building sterling connections with all the offices of public record. Your biometrics are properly logged in all the right places. My former husband's aren't."

She leaned closer and gave me a kiss that tasted of champagne and sweet promises. With a sigh that I knew embodied the very essence of satisfaction, I finally put my misgivings to rest and kissed her back. Because no matter what happened next, I'd take that ride with Arcadia.

But I did vow never to book a room at the Stormcove again. Just in case.

<hr />

Jakob Drud is 43 years old and lives in Aarhus, Denmark, with his wife and two children. He writes much of his fiction in English because of the inspiring online science fiction and fantasy community. He's been writing for twenty years and loves fiction that surprises, brings new insights, and makes him laugh. He blogs at jakobdrud.com and tweets about writing life as @jakobdrud.

# Rider in the Storm

C. Flynt

August 16th, 1971
A Burned Hotel
20:55

The storm announced itself with a slash of lightning and pelting rain. A chilling gust almost blew me off my bike. I skidded across both lanes of the old state route and slewed to a stop inches away from a dilapidated metal signpost. A weather-worn wooden sign flapped and rattled in the wind. "Hotel Stormcove," it read. My gaze followed the rutted drive to an abandoned old building. The derelict structure might have been a multi-story grand hotel once, but today it was a melancholy ruin.

Not unlike me. I'd been rootless since my wife died. This trip was another pointless search for memories of the life we'd had together.

We met at a rally and fell in love with each other's bikes. We each loved travel—the thrill of new places. For ten grand years, we practically lived on those bikes.

After her death, the roads were strips of tarmac, not highways to adventure. The ocean view was only water and waves, not a limitless vista of opportunity. My sore backside was simply a reminder that I'd been riding too long, not an invitation to relax in a field of daisies and hold hands.

I studied the ruined hotel. It might be dry, which I wasn't. The storm was getting its second wind. Brown leaves surged across the highway and dime-sized hailstones bounced like superballs. Wherever it came from, this storm promised to get nasty. I'd ridden through worse weather, but today, that old building called me.

I bounced my bike along the drive, powered up the ragged

concrete steps, crossed a flagstone porch and skidded through a pair of tumbled-down French doors. Inside, I killed the engine and kicked down the stand.

The small hairs in my ear stirred. I thought I heard footsteps above me, but it must have been hail. That old, neglected ceiling couldn't even support a ghost.

I dismounted by swinging my leg over the handlebars. It's best to practice your bravado moves where nobody can see you.

"My, but you do know how to make an entrance," a young woman's voice called from behind me.

I spun around so fast my helmet twisted and covered one eye. I yanked it off and shoved wet hair out of my face.

I saw nothing. The deserted hotel lobby was stripped of furniture, rugs and draperies. Even the registration counter was gone. All I saw was dust and my wet tire tracks.

I ran my fingers through my helmet-hair and tried to look presentable.

"You don't need to hide," I called. "I'm not dangerous."

At six-foot-two and nearly three hundred pounds, I know I scare folks, but I'm really a teddy bear.

I smiled to demonstrate how not-dangerous I was.

"Did you see Mittens on your way in?" the voice asked.

I glanced around. Two wide, sweeping staircases led to the dark, upper floors. At the top of the right-hand staircase stood a woman, maybe a girl, dressed in an old-fashioned flannel nightgown that covered her knees.

"Mittens?" I asked. "I didn't see any mittens. Or any boots or gloves either. Just rain and hail."

"Silly! Not mittens you wear. Mittens is my cat."

She tiptoed down the stairway. A few of the stairs had fallen through.

"Watch out!" I hollered.

She didn't pause. She stepped where the stairs weren't. And just kept walking.

She didn't cast a shadow.

And I didn't soil my trousers, but it was close.

She half-walked, half-floated to me. She was young, maybe a teenager. More importantly, she was a ghost.

I didn't believe in ghosts. At least, not up until that moment. Right then, I was willing to believe in anything.

"Mittens is lost. I'm afraid she's caught in the storm, but—" she waved her hands at her bare feet. "—I can't go out to find her. She's a cute little black-and-white kitten. Will you go find her for me?"

I ogled the storm. The last thing I wanted to do was go out into that driving rain and hail to search for some lost kitten.

That wasn't quite true. The last thing I wanted to do was stay in a haunted ruin with a ghost.

I dashed back into the storm, calling for Mittens.

The rain slashed sideways. Hailstones cut into my cheek like dull knives. I held a hand over my eyes and squinted through dripping eyelashes.

"Come, Mittens," I shouted.

"Oh, brilliant!" I chided myself. "That's how you call a dog."

"Here, kitty, kitty," I cooed in a falsetto. I hoped the ghost would give my effort credit.

I knew I wasn't going to find her cat. If the hotel still had a working kitchen, I'd have found plenty of cats. They'd be clustered around the dumpster begging for handouts. But the kitchen was long gone, and with it the handouts, dumpsters, and cats.

I stepped into the weeds, cursing myself for a superstitious coward.

Then I found the cat.

It crouched under a bush on the far side of a ditch full of brown, frothing water.

I glanced over my shoulder at the derelict hotel. The ghost watched me from the doorway with her hands over her chest.

When the storm hit, the temperature had dropped nearly twenty degrees. It would be cold enough riding in dry boots. I really didn't want wet ones. Windchill loves wet boots.

My bike sat inside the hotel, just beyond a ghost who seemed to know I'd found her cat and expected me to bring it to her.

I took a deep breath and slid down the bank into the cold, rushing water. It flowed over—and into—my boots, almost as chilling as the thought of the ghost's disapproval.

I waded several steps across the knee-deep stream to the far bank and reached for the kitten. It crouched until its tail touched the dirt and then raised its wide-eyed head as it edged away from me.

"Here, kitty. Good kitty. Nice Mittens," I sang to it, sliding my right hand onto the ground and wiggling my fingers enticingly.

It crept forward, sniffed, then backed away.

I shoved my left hand's cold, stiff fingers into a sodden pocket and dug out a chunk of cellophane-wrapped turkey jerky. I'd packed it for lunch. I hoped the soggy meat looked enough like cat food to tempt the little guy. I dropped a chunk onto my palm.

The kitten found the smell of meat more enticing than my bare fingers. It crawled over my hand to reach the moist jerky. As soon as its shrunken belly was above my fingers, I snagged the tiny waif. It barely weighed two pounds, soaking wet.

I expected it to claw my hand to ribbons, but it was face-first in the jerky and paid no attention as I cradled it to my chest and struggled out of the ditch.

It wasn't easy to crawl up the steep bank with just one hand. Whatever parts of me hadn't gotten soaked and muddy on my way into the ditch got soaked and muddy on my way out.

The ghost stood in the doorway and watched my struggles. Her arms reached out and her smile shone through the rain.

I finally got my feet onto relatively dry ground. My boots squelched as I stumbled through the thigh-high weeds, thorns snagging my wet trousers as if warning me of danger.

Like going into a haunted hotel, for instance.

I didn't want to climb those steps. For god's sake, there was a ghost waiting there—waiting for me and the cat. For all I knew, I might have been carrying a ghost cat.

But, after suffering soggy boots, muddy jeans, and bone-deep cold, I was damn well going to return this kitten to that ghost.

I squished muddy puddles onto the porch as I stumped my way to the door. I want to think I shivered from the cold, but it was mostly from fear. The ghost drifted back from the door, letting me into the lobby.

It wasn't the deserted ruin I'd left. This lobby was as gracious as a grande dame. I saw the outlines of ornate chairs and even a man behind a mahogany registration desk, offering a feathery pen to some long-dead guest.

"Oh, Mittens," the ghost murmured, reaching for the cat.

I offered it to her, hoping a happy ghost would go to her just reward, and I'd leave the hotel alive.

The ghost cocked her head and studied the kitten.

"This isn't Mittens," she sobbed. "It's never Mittens. I'll never save poor Mittens."

The kitten finished the jerky and began grooming itself and purring on the palm of my hand, oblivious to the crying ghost.

I could have run. The ghost wasn't paying any attention to me. All I had to do was drop the cat, grab my bike, and ride away while she cried.

But I didn't.

Before my wife died, I fell for every hard-luck story and gave a buck to every panhandler. She teased me about being such a soft touch. Since her death, I'd slipped into an emotional pit, indifferent to anyone or anything but my own grief.

The first ghostly tear tore me from my pit. It transformed her from a ghost to fear into a child to comfort.

Nobody talks to ghosts.

Nobody except me.

"Where was Mittens when you saw her last?" I asked, hoping for some clue to how I could help.

The ghost aged in seconds into an eighty-year-old woman in a floor-length skirt.

I must have looked confused. Don't ghosts stay the age they were when they died? I wasn't sure. I'd never been a ghost, and up until that day, I hadn't even believed in them.

"She was in my room." She gestured up the stairs. Peering at me with sad eyes, she whispered, "I killed her."

My jaw didn't hit the floor, but it tried. I had no words.

"It was the fire, you see. Someone's candle started it. But I'd sneaked Mittens into my room and hid her in my suitcase. My father carried me out half-dead, as the volunteers rushed to put out the fire. No one knew about Mittens. No one came to help her."

An iridescent teardrop glistened on her cheek as the kitten kneaded tiny needles into the base of my thumb. I rubbed its forehead until the paws relaxed and the purr settled to an idle.

She smoothed her ghostly dress and then clasped her hands.

"We are the result of our experiences," she said. "I was Child when I found Mittens. Leaving home made me Adult. Then I became Wife, Mother, and finally, Grandmother. A full life."

"Then why ... " I sighed. I couldn't ask her why she was haunting the place; it seemed too personal a subject. I was at a loss for a way I could help this ghost. All I could do was shut my mouth and listen.

"Why am I here? Because we can't control everything. " She echoed my sigh. "Sometimes the events we can't control shape us most."

That resonated. I was Single when I met my wife, and we immediately became Couple. We did everything together. We pushed the edges. We rode motorcycles, sky dived, even SCUBA.

Her senseless death—a drunk driver hit her in a crosswalk—was not in my control. But it changed me. Abruptly, I became Alone.

The old woman lifted her eyes to mine. "I found Mittens just outside those doors." She waved her hand at the gaping doorway. "She was tiny, half-starved, and scared of everyone. I coaxed her into my arms and promised to take care of her.

"That fire defined me for the rest of my life. Under everything good, the memory of Mittens haunted me. I betrayed the kitten that trusted me. I was Oathbreaker. Killer."

She fell silent. I'm not sure I remembered to breathe. Then, in one gesture, she encompassed the lobby.

"This is where I lost Mittens. So, here I am until someone finds her. No one will, I suppose. We can't change the past. This is my penance—to keep trying."

The kitten licked my little finger. Its warmth spread from my hand to something deep inside me. The old impulse to help others sputtered to life like an old engine long dormant at the beginning of the season. There had to be something I could do, something I could say to comfort her.

"Look," I began. "I know—I mean—I can't save Mittens any more than you could." I waved at the old lobby around us. "Like you said, nobody can change the past—"

The revelation hit harder than the hailstones I'd just stumbled through. She couldn't change her past any more than I could relive mine. Maybe we both needed to look forward, not back. I paused while that sank in, then took a breath.

"But—but—look," I said. "We just saved *this* cat. If you hadn't sent me out to find it, it would have starved, or gotten killed by a coyote or something. I'll take care of it for you. Does it count to save this kitten, even if it isn't your Mittens?"

She raised her hands to her lips, almost as in prayer. "Every act of kindness helps. Nothing will let me rest easy, but—" She smiled a sad half-smile. "You've helped me rest easier. Bless you."

She closed her eyes and faded away.

The outlined chairs and registration desk faded with her, as did the storm. It was one of those summer thunderstorms that rage for five minutes and then vanish as if they'd never existed.

Five minutes. Usually, that's no time at all. It takes longer to get a fast-food burger.

Or five minutes can be an eternity.

It took five minutes to walk from the traffic officer's desk to the morgue where I identified my wife's body. I started that walk on a warm, sunny day. After that walk, I never saw the sun again.

Now, five minutes after a savage storm battered me off the road, the evening sun blazed orange. I blinked and shielded my eyes. I was standing under a tree in a picnic area. A multi-story hotel rose in front of me—a huge sign on the roof declared it to be the Hotel Stormcove. Beyond the building, cars streamed down a curved road.

I glanced behind me. The rutted drive I'd bounced down was a dirt trail leading under the trees to the old state route I'd been riding along.

I shook my head. If I were going to believe in ghosts, I might as well believe in ghost hotels.

The kitten snuffled in my hand. It looped a paw over one ear as I gazed into the round, green eyes that gazed back. They promised me company and friendship, if I would accept them. Warmth and hope bloomed in my opening heart.

I held her up to my breast pocket. Without hesitation, she crawled in and gave rapt attention to a paw.

"You'll be warm there until we get home," I told her.

I repeated the sentence, just to hear myself say it. I was taking the kitten home—to my *home*—not just a place where I slept.

I named her Mittens.

C. Flynt is the husband-and-wife writing team of Clif and Carol Flynt. They share a house they designed themselves with three cats and countless computers (many of which work). Clif is the creator of Editomat and a technical book author. Carol has followed multiple careers, finally retiring as a freelance bookkeeper. Both are singer-songwriters. They amuse the cats with hours of argument over plots, themes, characters, grammar and whose turn it is to write the first draft. They write science fiction, historical fiction, fantasy, romantic suspense, and query letters.

# Mr. Junkan

Indira Ronae Lorick

O kay, Nicole, just breathe. Just because you're the most socially awkward person you know and you hate interacting with other people, that doesn't mean you won't be good at this, another job in a long line of jobs where your main responsibility is interacting with people.

GOD.

Why do I keep doing this to myself? Maybe it's because hospitality jobs are the only ones hiring me. Thanks a lot, psychology degree. I should've listened to my mother and married that pre-med when he asked me. I'm pretty sure he's a doctor now. I mean, it's been 10 years. Shouldn't he be a doctor by now? I should be a doctor by now.

Sheesh, 10 years! And here I am, killing every chance I get to advance, working the front desk at this creepy hotel that has God knows how many mysteries hiding behind its doors.

Another fresh start.

But you know what? I'm not going to panic. Nicole Khadijah Fitzpatrick, you can do this. All we gotta do is keep it together and remember what Mr. Zeibart said in orientation: "All meaningful human interaction can be boiled down to the impression one makes in the first five minutes of an introduction. The same can be said for the check-in process here at Hotel Stormcove. Time is money and our guests' money is worth more than their time. It is our duty to get them in their rooms and comfortable before they even know what hit 'em."

Should be easy, right?

Riiight.

*Well, there were only three reservations expected to arrive today, and two arrived early this morning before my shift started. The only one that remains belongs to—*

"I would like to check in please. Last name: Junkan."

*Crap, when did he get here?! I was so stuck in my head I didn't even realize he was walking up! Okay, time check: 12:03. You got five minutes, Nicole. Just focus on the task—wow . . . he's pretty cute. And kinda staring. He dresses nice too. What's going on with that bell boy, what's his face? Ummm . . . Travis? He looks like he's about to pass out or something. That black case must be heavy. Why doesn't he just put it down? Ok, Nicole, never mind that. Focus. You only have five minutes, in and out. You got this.*

*Go.*

"O-of course, sir. 'Junkan' was the last name?" *I hope so because that's the only reservation I have left and I'm pretty sure he said a "J" name.* "Staying with us for one night? Will you be paying cash or credit?"

"Yes. Cash. Will this be enough?"

*Wow. That is one fat stack of cash. An unreasonably fat stack of cash. Unless you want to buy a building.* "More than enough, Mr. Junkan. Is this stay for business or pleasure?"

"Neither."

*Ooooook . . . not giving me much to work with, but ok. Maybe plug some features of the hotel? Yea, that's a good idea!*

"A-alrighty. We at the Hotel Stormcove pride ourselves on providing any services that will ensure your comfort and enjoyment. A great highlight, and one of my personal favorites, is the natural beauty to be seen from our east-facing suites, which offer spectacular views of the ocean and sunrises. Could I interest—"

"No. I need to be away from direct sunlight. On the highest floor you have."

*Alright, you may be cute, but you are even worse at this*

*interacting thing than me, and that's saying something. Time check: 12:06. Let me get this guy out of here.*

"No problem, Mr. Junkan. I can put you in one of our suites on the fortieth floor. Our rooms are also equipped with blackout curtains. Is there anything else I can get for you to help you enjoy your stay here at the Hotel Stormcove?"

"Broccoli"

*Huh?* "B-broccoli?"

"I need all of your broccoli. All of it. Raw. Immediately. I will be paying cash. Money is no object."

"Umm, alright. Just on a plate or . . . ?" *I guess it's alright. Mr. Zeibart isn't likely to pass up an opportunity to take some of this guy's money. But why could he possibly need all that broccoli? My first day is shaping up to be one for the books. This is why I don't like talking to people.*

"The original cage it was transported in should suffice." *Cage? This guy gets stranger and stranger every second.*

"Um, broccoli usually comes in crates or boxes. Will that be okay? I just want you to receive what you are expecting."

"Crate? Crate. I do not know this word. We are speaking of the miniature trees, yes?"

"Yep, that's broccoli, alright." *Sheesh, where did this guy come from?*

"Well, then, yes, I would like the broccoli in its crate."

"Ok, I'll have it sent right up. Here is your key. You will be staying in room 4021. The elevators are down the hallway to your left, just past the staircase. Is there anything else I can do for you, Mr. Junkan?" *Please say no.*

"That will be all. Goodbye."

"Goodbye, Mr. Junkan." *And done. Glad that's over. Right on time, too. Mr. Zeibart would be proud. I knew this place attracted some weirdos, but I never thought I would get one so quickly. Just my luck. Well, at least this makes coming to work a little more interesting. Who knows, maybe I'll actually stick around this time. Here's hoping.*

---

Maintenance Report #1705

Date: 11/26/2018
Time:
Room No: 4021
Status: VD — Vacant Dirty
Location: Entire suite
Reported By: Linda Flynn — HKSP
Problem: All light fixtures are missing their
  bulbs.
Assigned To: MAINTENANCE
Date Completed: 11/26/2018
Time Spent: 5 minutes
Completed By: Steven Winters
Remarks: Replaced all missing light bulbs. Strong
  odor of broccoli and wet fur remains. Around
  50% of surfaces are covered in a slimy film.
  Deep clean and OOO status is recommended.
Sign: S. Winters

---

Indira is a Brooklyn born, Atlanta raised, Wisconsin transplant who gets caught in daydreams more than she should. She enjoys writing thrillers, science fiction, and, most of all, fantasy. She has recently completed work on her first fantasy novel and is currently working on the next installment in the series. A true believer of Black girl magic, Indira loves creating magical worlds where anyone can imagine themselves living.

# The Conference

Janna Layton

On the third floor of Hotel Stormcove, a young man in a pin-stripe suit waited in the Arcadia Boardroom. It was one of the smaller meeting rooms, and would have fit ten people sitting around a table.

But there was no table, and there were no chairs, either—not in Arcadia or any of the other stately, wood-paneled conference rooms. Renovation on the third floor had started in early 1929, when it had seemed like there would always be myriad industry barons who might shell out for impressive seaside meeting spaces. Two years later, work was suspended indefinitely, and the floor remained blocked off from the public.

In the Arcadia Boardroom, the sole piece of furniture was a built-in bookshelf holding dust, an empty cigarette carton, and a bronze figurine of a fleeing gazelle. Along the adjacent wall, a mural spread, where stylized youths (no doubt Arcadian) in dreamy pastels lounged by a tranquil spring. The scene was a stark contrast to the one out the window: a gray February sky above a turbulent shore.

The man in pinstripes was studying the mural when the door opened. "I'm not complaining," he began, "but this rendezvous loca-tion—" He turned toward the door and froze. Facing him were two men in police uniforms, one with a gun and one with a truncheon.

"Hands up," snapped the man with a gun.

"Officers, what is—"

Before he could finish his question, the man with the trun-cheon stepped forward and socked him across the face. He staggered back, then lunged toward his attacker, but a blow to his ribs from the truncheon made him drop to his knees.

"Stay down, Jack the Cat," ordered the man swinging the truncheon.

"I don't know—" he tried again, only to earn another hit across his shoulders.

"Now, listen," said the officer with the gun, "we know who you are. You're Jack the Cat, and you were expecting to meet up with the Apple Farm Rum-Runners here to discuss transporting a load of alcohol through their territory. Well, guess what? We rounded up those damn bootleggers this morning. If you don't want to join them down at the station, you'll tell us everything you've got on your boss at the Cod Pirates Gang."

"Who's Jack the Cat? I'm just a hotel guest," insisted the young man, curled protectively around his bruised ribs. Blood from his nose dripped onto the herringbone parquet floor. "I don't know what you're talking about."

Officer Truncheon raised his weapon again, but before he could strike, the door swung open.

There stood two middle-aged women: one short and round, the other tall and thin. The short woman wore a green silk dress and matching cloche hat and held a long cigarette holder. The tall woman wore a pink silk dress and held a beaded handbag. Both of them gasped.

"What on Earth?" cried the short woman.

"Oh, that poor man!" cried the tall woman.

"The hell are you doing here?" demanded Officer Gunman.

"I'm sorry, officers," said the short woman. "We know this area is off-limits, but we heard there was a beautiful mural here, and we just had to see it."

"We'll go back downstairs and tell the management you've apprehended a criminal," offered the tall woman.

"Shut up!" said Officer Truncheon. "Get inside and close the door."

Trembling, the women complied.

"They don't need to be here," said the man on the floor.

Officer Truncheon kicked him in the side. The women shrieked.

"Damn it," the young man continued, "you're not cops at all, are you? You're the Apple Farm Rum-Runners."

"Aren't you a smart one, Jack the Cat?" sneered Truncheon, crouching down in front of his victim. He jammed his baton under Jack's chin and tilted his head up. "You better start talking about the Cod Pirates Gang. Then we'll figure out what to do with these witnesses."

"You monsters," spat Jack, "they're just two old ladies!"

The gunman gave a sharp yelp.

"What is it now?" asked Truncheon.

His gun-wielding colleague looked dazed and had one hand clasped to his neck. "Something bit me! I think . . . " Instead of finishing his thought, he collapsed.

"Larry?" asked Truncheon, rising out of his crouch. "Ah!" He clapped a hand to the back of his own neck, then looked around in confusion before also crashing to the parquet. Neither he nor the gunman stirred.

The young man sighed in relief. He picked up his fallen fedora and stole a glance at the mural. No blood had splattered across Arcadia's contented, flower-bedecked youth.

"'Old ladies,' Jimmy?" demanded the short woman, handing her cigarette holder—from which she had blown two tranquilizer darts—to the tall woman. She knelt down in front of him and pulled out a handkerchief, spitting on it before dabbing at the blood on his face.

"Don't, that's embarrassing," said Jack the Cat, also known as Jimmy.

"Hush. I gave birth to you, and your Aunt Loretta here used to change your diapers."

"Ma, I'm not a child anymore."

"Oh, you're not?" snapped the short woman. "No, you're 'Jack the Cat,' who ran away from home to be a big-time bootlegger with the Cod Pirates Gang. And what do they do? They send you off to meet the Apple Farm Rum-Runners with no backup."

"How'd you even know to be here?" asked Jimmy.

His mother simply scoffed.

"We'd better get going, Camilla," said Loretta.

"All right. Can you walk, sweetheart?" asked the short woman.

Jimmy waved off her assistance and staggered to his feet. "I'm fine, Ma."

"You look it," Camilla retorted. "That's what you get for joining some amateur outfit. You won't be going back there."

"But my boss—"

"The so-called boss of the Cod Pirates Gang can answer to me if he dislikes the resignation you'll be sending by wire. Now, let's get out of here. My men will get these two fools on the next boat. By the time they wake up, they'll be miles out to sea."

"This doesn't mean I'm coming back."

"Whether or not you're coming back to your mother's bootlegging gang, you are coming back to your mother's house, at least for the time being," said Camilla. "That's an order I'm giving as both your mother and as the leader of the North City Queens!"

⚷

Janna Layton lives in Oakland, California. Her cat, Eponine, can attest that Janna roughly acted out her story's actions, and they can be done in five minutes. Janna's poetry and fiction have been published or are upcoming in various literary journals, including *The New Yorker*, *Luna Station Quarterly*, *Apex*, *NonBinary Review*, and *Mythic Delirium*. She blogs at readingwatchinglookingandstuff.blogspot.com and tweets at @jkbartleby.

# A Room with a View

Robert Bagnall

2066
Room 1109
5:55 PM

I *don't need this*, Kurt Teller thought to himself.

It had been a long journey, just to get this far. He was tired. And now here he was, suitcase by his feet, on the threshold.

The room was perfect, a square of marble and mahogany, palatial on a modest scale. A large bed with crisp pearl sheets, corner invitingly turned down; above the headboard, a seascape in oils. The air conditioning hummed unobtrusively, subtly wafting something floral. He spied a sliver of bathroom, ceramic and chrome glinting, in the room adjoining.

But he had been promised a view of the Bay of Naples. What he had instead was a panorama of brickwork and downpipes and windows with flaking paintwork and drying undergarments visible through obscure glazing.

The porter bustled behind him, bringing in the last of his bags.

"I was promised a room with a view."

Perhaps the porter didn't speak English. Or speak at all. With a tug of a forelock, he turned and went.

Teller glared at his bags, harrumphed at nobody because there was nobody to listen, and decided that they would remain unopened some minutes more.

As he descended to the lobby, he felt tightness in his chest. He had never welcomed confrontation. His worry was that they would move him to a worse room with a better view, making an expansive show of satisfying him in the process. He knew, too embarrassed, that he was liable to accept. How to make them understand that he did not want to compromise on the marble and mahogany and crisp sheets and smell of flowers in the air? But he did—emphasize *did*—want the view that he had been promised.

At the desk, the manager ran a finger theatrically down his list and muttered something in Italian that seemed to hint at enlightenment. Teller was surprised at the clerk's choice of language—his travel profile listed his preference for Italian aesthetics, but he hadn't expected that here.

The manager fixed Teller with a patient look over his half-moon glasses. "Come," he said, his digit pirouetting, flexing, and beckoning back towards the elevators. As Teller followed, the finger reappeared over the manager's shoulder, summoning him to keep up. He felt like a rat in Hamelin.

If Teller ever had to give a description of the man to the police, all he would be able to recall would be that finger, without—no pun intended—being able to put his finger on what exactly made it distinctive. Was it just what the manager did with it? Or something more physiological? Riding up in the elevator, Teller tried to steal a glance. An extra joint, perhaps?

They arrived with a distant thump and were off again down the hallway, the curling finger leading Teller onwards.

"Ah," the manager said as he entered the room, taking in the view. And then held up a finger. The finger. Bloodhound-like, it scanned the room before coming to rest pointing at the bed. The manager stepped forward and extracted a thin black remote control from under a pillow.

With not merely a flourish but a swirl, the manager pressed a button and the view from the window suddenly changed.

"Colosseum," he declared.

Another press.

"Pantheon."

And then the finger spiraled and pressed. Again and again, over and over.

"St. Peter's Basilica, Amalfi Coast, Sistine Chapel—how you say? ceiling—Leaning Tower of Pisa, Trevi Fountain, towers of San Gimignano, Spanish Steps, Piazza della Signoria and Palazzo Vecchio in Florence, Lake Como, Ah . . . "

He settled on a blue bay, with white yachts gently bobbing on the water, and, in the distance a mountain shaped like lazy camel humps caught in the morning sun, the landscape contrasted in light and shadow. He smiled. It was beautiful.

"Bay of Naples, Signor. Or, alternatively . . . la realtà."

The window returned to how it had been, looking out on a blurred and dingy scene of brickwork, plumbing and laundry.

The manager presented the remote to Kurt Teller. "Enjoy your stay at the Hotel Stormcove, Signor."

Robert Bagnall lives on the English Riviera, within sight of Dartmoor. He has completed five undistinguished marathons, but held a world record for eating cream teas. The two may be related. His speculative fiction has appeared in a variety of magazines, websites and anthologies since the early 1990s. His novel *2084* was published by Double Dragon in 2017. He can be contacted via his blog at meschera.blogspot.co.uk.

# Fixing the Past

Ryanne Glenn

A slight breeze lifted the thin veil of a curtain hanging over the dusty window. Every now and then, the wind would pick up, and a gust would push against the squeaky pane. Lyric limped over to the bathroom and flicked on the sickening fluorescent lights. Dark circles hung heavy underneath her eyes, and her face was pale.

Fighting her exhaustion, she knelt near the tub and did her best to comb her fingers through her tangled hair. Frustrated, she twisted the tub's knob and let the warm water spill over her head, grimacing as the neon red tinted the yellowing porcelain. Grabbing the too-white towel, she rubbed the rough texture over her head. Tossing the stained towel in the corner, she shook out her hair, now a dull auburn instead of the fiery red it was before.

She scowled at her reflection. She needed sleep, but there hadn't been time. Even now, the hotel bed beckoned her, but she'd already called her contact and he wouldn't appreciate being kept waiting. Unable to stand the slight flickering of the bathroom light any longer, she flipped the switch and shuffled out of the small room. She took a deep breath, trying to forget her aching muscles, and gingerly sat on the edge of the bed.

Her tumble out of the car had been worse than she'd expected. She'd thought diving onto the grass median would help soften her fall, but as fast as the car was going, she'd hit the ground hard, resulting in a throbbing hip and deep green streaks all over her clothes. To make things worse, she'd twisted an ankle running through the trees off the side of the road. Though she'd known the general direction of the hotel, the forest was dense and the darkness had only hindered her progress.

For a moment, she let her eyes drift shut, and cracked her neck from side to side, relishing in the slight release of tension. She felt her mind quiet and her torso sway back. Her eyes snapped open. She couldn't sleep, not yet, not now. The room before her was nothing more than a blur of beige and blue. She buried her palms in her eyes and rubbed till splotches of black clouded her vision. Shaking her head, she took a few deep breaths to keep herself awake.

Her gaze drifted to the small box on the nightstand. Tentatively, she reached out and stroked the velvety texture. Opening the lid, she inspected the jeweled necklace inside. Even the soft hotel lights couldn't dim the central diamond's shine. An impressive ten carats and deep blue, the priceless stone had caused more damage than she'd ever imagined possible.

Tears pooled in her eyes, falling to her lap below. This stupid necklace, nothing but rock and metal, had cost her and her family everything. Her brother had gone to extreme lengths to steal it and had gotten himself killed. Her family hadn't known anything about his life in the shadows, and at the time, neither did she. But after digging through his things, she'd found a trail of contacts, passports, and strange messages.

Blue and red lights flashed outside, sirens filling the once quiet night. Wearily, she swiveled her head to the window. Finally, she could get rid of this burden. After five years of searching, she'd finally been able to steal the necklace back, and she'd been on the run since.

Forcing herself to stand on her aching legs, she trudged over the door with the box clasped tightly in one hand. She'd never be able to get her brother back, but at least she could right this wrong. Then—she'd finally be able to rest.

Ryanne Glenn started writing short stories when she was ten and was first published in her hometown's local newspaper. After struggling with depression in her first year at college, she turned back to writing as a healthy outlet for her emotions. Her debut novel, *Descent of Shadows*, is a middle-grade fantasy, and she hopes young readers will look up to her characters and realize that with friends and perseverance, you can overcome anything.

# This Moment of Repose

Michael W. Cho

Most lovely and tempting jewel of the gods it was, most perilous and sublime—long had he coveted fire, drawn to the sun's majestic radiation, lightning's violence, and the elegance of the stars. One day, he chose to act, and with clever hands stole a spark from the supreme chamber of a lonely, unguarded tower, which rose like a white needle into the cold, airless, eternal midnight. Now his primal sin chased him with the beating of vast, soundless wings that whispered the gods' rage, carrying the promise of icy talons and a rime-shrouded oblivion.

His singed hands troubled him little compared to the glowing soles of his feet, for he had to run to escape his flying doom. He had to run with all his might, so his feet rasped against earthly gravel, pattered over scoriate badlands, scraped against fields of thorns. His feet were always afire.

Having run for millennia without cease, thinking only of fire and feeling only fire's agony, he spied a place of water.

He'd always avoided the oceans, lacking the gift of breathing water, or of streaking through the waves with an arrow's velocity. He dared not glance behind him at the pursuing swarm, frost-ridden and always so near. It took all his speed to stay ahead.

But, sprinting along the coastline, red-hot feet spraying sand for leagues (as dolphins breached in the surf and sang encouragement and goodwill), he found another kind of jewel. Aquamarine it was, enfolded in cliffs of black stone—a cove, a bit of the sea that chose to dwell on the land. As elegant and fine as the stars, the cove beckoned to the lover of beauty. He knew that to stop would invite his capture.

Yet . . . he perceived that this was a place of shelter. Restful to the eye, protected from both sea and sky by broad, rocky shoulders. Its aura spoke to him of refuge.

The water looked so cool.

Risking all, he aimed himself toward the cove. His passage harrowing the land behind him, he slowed himself so as not to deface this wonder. He leapt over the walls and came down—into blue waters.

Such cool blue waters! His sizzling soles boiled in the sea. The relief was indescribable. For the first time in eons, he had comfort. His feet glowed white-hot in the brine, but ocean refilled the bay even as he released a vast cloud of boiling vapor.

He sat with his feet in the water and his hands in the soft sands. His mind's fires ebbed away. For the first time in an age, he could think beyond his peril. He could recall what he'd seen on his frantic journey—the loves and lives, the creation and valor, the many uses that the mortals had made of the fire he had given to them.

Because of fire, they would survive. They would thrive. Stolen it may have been, but look at the good it had done!

For merely a moment, he rested there, cool ocean soothing his feet, rocky cliffs guarding his back. This was a place of beauty and safety and refuge, a good place. Briefly he wondered how such a thing could be. From whence came its power? Its loveliness? Its benevolence?

It was only the briefest of moments.

Vengeful pinions drew near. Drawing out his feet from the cool waters with a groan, he drew breath into his lungs and stood.

He began to run.

As he sped from the place of refuge, sharp claws rending at his back, his feet began to burn and glow red again. Soon he was halfway on the other side of the world. Perhaps he would never again find the cove. Perhaps the vengeance of the gods would soon catch him, icy talons lifting him into terminal darkness as his legs kicked without effect.

But always would he treasure this moment of repose.

Michael W. Cho lives in Tempe, Arizona, where he writes science fiction and fantasy. For his day job, he plays Spanish guitar.

# A Step Through Time
Preeti C. Sharma

Lavina stood before the gleaming black door to Room 4242, glancing out of the corners of her eyes to the sides of the hallway. She didn't want to move her head for fear a surveillance drone would notice her nerves.

Forty-two floors up, the whir of hovercraft around the three vast towers of the hotel barely audible in this inner hallway, Lavina's heart pounded in her chest. She ran sweaty palms down the sides of her black dress, stopping at the slight bulge in the fabric. Somehow in the jostle of the crowded elevator, someone managed to slip the palm-sized generator into her pocket. Her fingers glided over the familiar surfaces, finding and squeezing a button before pressing the flat of her hand to the scanner to unlock the door. Her watch showed 3:01 PM, and she needed to be back in the lobby, caught on camera, over some maintenance requirement for her room, before anyone noticed.

Taking a deep breath, she took a normal step inside, one hand firmly tugging her small suitcase, and felt the floor fall out under the soles of her feet. The door clicked shut behind—no, *above* her. Lavina stifled a scream. Lights swirled, forming a dizzying vortex with her at the center. A whistling screech grated on her ears as bile rose in her throat at the sudden drop. As the colors coalesced into recognizable blues and purples, Lavina could see the world start to stabilize. She hazarded a step forward and breathed a prayer of thanks at the crush of the mottled carpet under her shoe. Her suitcase bumped down lightly, scarcely jostling her arm, as if she'd merely rushed over an uneven floor, not traveled back in time by two centuries. *It's done.* Her heart rate began to slow.

Not that she'd had any doubts, Lavina reminded herself sternly. The complex code blossomed into poetry during the small hours of night while she'd hid in the bathroom with the lights off and the pillows on her bed arranged to look like someone still slept there as she furiously typed away. A small glitch in the code meant getting lost in that vortex forever, her body torn apart by forces she only understood in the abstract.

The faces of her children, their small hands in hers and their soft bodies pressing against her, came to mind unbidden. She couldn't tell them where she went—couldn't even tell them *good-bye*—in case she never saw them again. She did this for them, to assure their future. They wouldn't understand the need for secrecy and might blurt out the truth. Spies lurked behind every corner, in every camera, in every login. The fewer who knew, the safer they all were. And Lavina was the only one who knew the code.

She stood before Room 42, now in an old-fashioned, low-ceilinged building—Lavina breathed a sigh of relief and patted her dark hair smooth. *Next time, I should tie it back.* And there would be a next time, not just today, but again and again until they were free.

The cold blast of recirculated, musty-smelling air accompanied the hum of air conditioning units and the clanking machinery of a shiny silver-doored elevator down the hall. Lavina fished the device from her pocket and pressed it to the small panel above the door handle. Unscrambling the key code was child's play compared to the detailed programming required to get her here. The red light flashed green and a click released the door lock. Taking another deep breath, Lavina pushed open the door and stepped inside.

A familiar figure by the window turned, a smile of welcome

and relief on his face. Lavina's eyes greedily drank him in, even as he did the same. *He hasn't changed a bit,* she thought, taking in the black hair, peppered with a few distinguished grays at the temples, dark-framed glasses accentuating the warm brown eyes with their faint crow's-feet. A carefully trimmed goatee outlined the sharp angles of his jaw. His tall, lean form was dressed casually in jeans and a thin sweater.

"You look great, love," Surinder said, enveloping her in his embrace, the familiar scent of his skin offering her a comfort she craved more than any drug. "I love that dress. You feel too thin, though, and you look worn out."

Lavina smiled, valiantly holding back her tears. "I've missed you so much." She pulled back just a little, loath to let go. This too-short visit had to tide her over for a long time.

"Why can't you stay?" he murmured, his hands tightening around her waist. "I can program that thing to send you back five minutes after you left."

"So can I," Lavina shot back. He might have built the device, this traversable wormhole generator that harnessed a chaos string, but it was *her* code that operated it. Surinder studied it to find bugs, but she'd had to explain all the intricacies to him first. He was always taking the fall, always trying to protect her, even now, from hundreds of years in the past … It was one of the many reasons she loved him, a driver for doing whatever she must so they could be together again. Emotion made her petulant. "Don't you think I want to stay too? You know that I'm under surveillance, that they think I know where you are. I can't raise their suspicions. What if they suspect the truth about precisely *how* you escaped? We could jeopardize the safety of everyone who's helped us, everyone depending on us."

The logic on their generator worked better—more simply— if they let time pass at the same rate wherever they were.

Reprogramming, especially when rushed, invited anomalies. "I don't want to risk it. What will happen to our kids if they're left to the mercy of the Allied Government Services?"

Surinder growled at her. "They'll become 'experimental subjects' like me? Over my dead body."

Lavina glanced at her watch. *3:03 already*. The generator had stolen a full minute of their time together. She pulled a small vial from a compartment of the suitcase. "Here, your medication."

Surinder flicked the cap up and pressed the vial to his neck. She saw his mouth tighten as the needle pricked him. After a moment, his warm eyes blinked open. "That should keep me for a while," he said. "Did you bring pictures?"

Lavina smiled, unzipping the suitcase and handing him a small envelope. She'd tried to grab pictures of their kids in the everyday moments, ones that showed them growing and smiling. But the kids missed their dad. The last several months had been hell on them, between the investigation and the unwanted publicity. They couldn't even go to school without security, and finally the school told Lavina they would have to remain at home because they were too much of a distraction to the other students.

"I found a job as a computer programmer," her husband said, helping remove the other items she'd brought for him—most importantly a small cooler with more vials of the medication that hadn't been invented in this time. "You wouldn't believe it—I work for Google. *The* Google."

Lavina's eyes widened. In their time, Google was more a belief system than an actual company—to think he worked for a company whose work would impact future generations centuries away . . . it was surreal.

"And I've got leads on a house in a nice neighborhood, with all the paperwork you and the kids are going to need."

Lavina sighed. "It still feels so far away. Getting the kids back to Hotel Stormcove, moving to this time, with its pollution and its waste . . . " Yet she longed for it, to restore her family unit and make a new start. Giving up everything she knew, forcing the children to leave everything they knew behind, was asking a lot. She thought wistfully of the days when they'd all been together, before her discovery of the Allied Government's sick experiments with biological weapons and her husband's choice to reveal them, pretending he alone uncovered the horror . . .

*"The kids need you more right now, love," he'd insisted. "And if we get out of this place—this time—it's going to be easier for me than for you."*

Lavina knew: the racism and sexism of the twenty-first century would not work in her favor. The long black hair, the olive skin, the dark eyes—they all marked her as one of South Asian descent, never mind that she spoke six languages so fluently she could lecture scientists across the world in the tongue they preferred. Even in her time, some two hundred years in the future, their community was unusual for its lack of ethnic diversity. They still valued arranged marriages, though now dowries focused less on jewelry than on the new currency: harnessing brain power, gaining access to patents, and forming scientific alliances. Yet from everything she'd studied about this time where her husband now lived, a wage gap, inconsistent healthcare practices, and pervasive social unrest plagued women across the world. She hated to think her daughter, little more than a toddler, would face these challenges, which had been eradicated in her time.

The people who'd helped him escape even as the police closed in offered Lavina hope when they told her they could reunite them. So began her speaking engagements at Hotel Stormcove, purportedly to lecture other programmers on her published techniques, but really to allow her the opportunity to visit this special room. Why the masterminds operating within Hotel

Stormcove were interested in protecting her family, in reuniting them, still remained a mystery. They certainly weren't doing it for the money—Lavina and Surinder could scarcely imagine the wealth needed to access the kinds of resources the people at Hotel Stormcove had already used on their behalf.

"When are you coming back?" her husband asked, brushing wisps of hair off her cheek and tenderly tucking them behind her ear.

"Two more months, then later with the kids," Lavina whispered. It felt like an eternity still. But the plan was in place, the lecture scheduled, the room generously reserved for the whole family complete with a hotel-vetted nanny.

He wiped away a tear and turned her toward the door, pulling her suitcase with him. He looked at her watch meaningfully. It read 3:05. "You need to get back, love," he said.

Lavina loved that nickname, the play on her name, and she wanted to cling to this moment. But she wrapped her fingers around the bag's handle, and Surinder pressed the device back into her other hand. He opened the door and caressed her cheek once more before releasing her, his warm brown eyes full of wistful regret.

"I love you," she said, squeezing the button and stepping back into the whirling expanse beyond.

Back in Room 4242, Lavina swallowed nausea as reality settled around her again. She took the device and knelt to place it on a tiny ledge hidden under the bed. The hotel staff would return it to the same location in her house as they had before, ensuring that no one searching her luggage could suspect her. Tugging her suitcase behind her, Lavina straightened up and walked briskly out of the room.

‹—⊶—›

Preeti C. Sharma has always been fascinated by magic and books, likely because of her father's bedtime stories about Aladdin and Sinbad. As soon as she learned to write, she started telling stories, spinning fanciful tales and penning actual stamped letters to distant relatives. After earning her first black belt and graduating from the University of Texas with a chemical engineering degree, she packed her bags for Houston's Ship Channel to make rocket fuel. She now lives in Atlanta with a dashing hero, a couple of future storytellers, and an imaginary 2-year-old Australian shepherd rescue named Billy. Preeti is the author of YA fiction novels, including the *Sea Deception* series, and a number of short stories. You can find her at teacuppublishing.com.

# Misdirection

Marriah Allen Pina

2019
Room 645
9:55 PM

"Why are you sending me rookies, Laurel?" Nour growled, flipping through the next candidate's file: Mila Covaci. This kid didn't even have a criminal record yet.

"She's got potential." Laurel's voice crackled through the earpiece.

"So does every pickpocket on the East Coast, but we don't have the time nor the jobs for all of them." Nour scanned the girl's bio. "Magic tricks? Really?"

"Just . . . give her a shot. She's on in 3 . . . 2 . . . 1."

The doorknob rattled violently. Strike one.

Nour stowed the file in the top drawer of the vanity. Biting her lip, she tried to decide how she wanted to play this. Scare the pants off the kid by opening the door? No, that was technically against the rules. Not that Nour believed in playing according to the rules, but it would be a waste of everyone's time to ruin this kid's final exam. Her reflection caught her eye in the gold-trimmed mirror above the vanity. She stopped biting her lip, leaning close to make sure it hadn't ruined the red lipstick she wore for the cover: rich lady in her luxurious hotel room, getting ready for an extravaganza in the cocktail lounge. It would take her being an absolute corpse to not notice the obscene rattling and clicking as Mila tried to pick the lock. Already a minute in.

The door swung open with a squeal at a minute and 15. Nour spun around, pretending to be fastening one of her pearl earrings in place.

"Oh, hello," she said.

Mila jumped, gaze whipping to Nour, a woman in a long, elegant gown who, as far as Mila was concerned, wasn't supposed to be in the room. Nour took a step closer. "I don't remember calling for a maid."

"I—" The girl's wide eyes darted around the room. Her shoulders tensed and she took a step back.

"You don't look like a maid." No uniform, just regular street clothes, too worn to signify anything but someone up to no good. This was Nour's tenth exam of the day, but this kid was the only one who'd had the audacity to walk in here with just her street gear on. Not even a maid's uniform or a fancy get-up as a disguise. Strike two. Nour crossed her arms over her chest and lifted her chin to glare down her nose at the girl.

"I . . . " Mila bit her lip. A bad tell. Nour herself struggled not to do it when under pressure. "They must have given me the wrong key at the front desk."

Not a bad lie, but the girl wasn't dressed the part. "Are you a guest?" Nour gave her a deliberate once-over, eyes hovering over the holes in the knees of her pants, the rip along the collar of her shirt.

The girl nodded awkwardly. "I'm . . . The staff are allowing me to stay. A—as charity."

The staff at Hotel Stormcove was known to do that but Mila was babbling, giving away too much information. A good lie has a thread of truth, but a better option would have been to run. Strike three.

"Charity?" Nour cocked her head to one side. "Surely they have more appropriate accommodations for their charity cases. Why would they give you a key to one of the suites?"

Mila's eyes widened; she blanched. Her cover story had been so quickly ripped out from under her. Nour felt a stab of sympathy for the girl.

Mila spun on her heel and ran for the door. Nour turned

back to the vanity, pulling the file out of the top drawer. The door slammed behind her as she opened Mila's file to the evaluation page.

"Dispatch is sending her back in for evaluation notes," Laurel said.

Seconds later, the door opened and Mila slouched in.

"I've never seen anyone fail quite so magnificently," Nour said. She didn't look up from scribbling notes onto the evaluation form. "You don't seem to have what to takes to be a con artist, my dear. Can't pick a lock, can't weave a lie. Hell, you haven't even got enough sense to run away."

"You're being cruel, Nour," Laurel warned in her ear.

Mila just nodded.

"I don't know what compelled you to apply for this position or how you made it thus far in the application process, but unfortunately you will need to seek employment elsewhere. Might I suggest honest work as a shop girl? You've got a sweet little face."

Nour knew she had crossed the line from constructively critical into the territory of just plain rude, but honestly, how had this girl gotten past the initial interviews to end up here, in her examination room?

"Thank you for your time," Mila said, curtsying sloppily and once again heading for the door. She paused beside the entry table. From her pocket, she pulled a glittering gold watch and daintily set it back on the table, where it had been placed as a prop for the exam.

Nour's eyebrows shot up.

"Sleight of hand is all about misdirection, ma'am. Draw attention to someplace other than the trick."

What had distracted her from the theft? She had turned away from the kid for only a moment, when Mila was practically out the door. Nour soured. "Cute, kid. But this isn't a magic act."

Mila smirked at Nour over her shoulder. "Thank you again for your time. But I think you're right, ma'am. I'll need to seek employment elsewhere. I'm withdrawing my application."

As the door latched shut behind Mila, Nour looked down at her notes on the examination. A long list of complaints, and at the bottom, she had circled "FAIL." She bit her lip, the heavy feeling of "too late" settling in her stomach as she crossed it all out and circled "PASS."

⚷

Marriah J. Allen Pina grew up in the capital district of New York State, in a small town on a lake. She has been creating stories from a young age, inspired by all that the world outside her sleepy town had to offer. She is pursuing a degree in anthropology, a field that inspires her to travel the world with an open heart and to tell more stories every day.

# A Ghost for Stormcove

Tom Jolly

September 7th, 1975
Suite 501, Ocean View
3:45 PM

"A bit heavy on the paisley, isn't it?" said the ghost agent.

Brittany Armstrong, the assistant manager at Hotel Stormcove, shrugged. "It actually goes quite well with the ghost motif. It's something our discerning guests would expect." She waved him over to a chair next to a small table and closed the door to the room.

The ghost agent—or, as Robert Burnett liked to call himself, a "ghost placement specialist"—put down his valise and sat on what appeared to be an antique chair. He could tell that it wasn't, really. He looked around at the other decorations in the room: the oil lamp with a "candlewick" light bulb, the roll-top desk, the chandelier with more simulation-candlelight bulbs, the four-poster bed with an imported Chinese patchwork quilt, heavy dark drapes over beveled multipaned windows, and a large Persian rug. Looking out the window toward the cliff, he could see the rough ocean beyond. A dreary blanket of clouds hung over the bay, which felt appropriate for this particular room. The window was cracked open, letting in a moist, salty breeze. "Mid 1800's?"

"That's what we're going for. Not even a TV." She frowned a little as she glanced around the room. "We might need a professional decorator to look for possible tweaks, but we do have a budget."

He nodded understandingly. "As it happens, I have some ghosts available from that era. Their clothing should fit right in with the decor." He opened his valise. "Is this your first ghost?"

She smiled. "Yes. Stormcove has become popular enough that we've decided to add some specialty rooms. Some customers have expressed an interest in having a haunted room. Nothing that can actually materialize, of course."

"Of course. Aural and visual, but not tactile. We don't represent any other kind of ghost. We also offer a gate device which sets the times that the ghost haunts. It only allows the fabric between worlds to open during certain hours."

"Like a lamp timer?" she asked.

"Exactly. You can set it to come on at midnight and turn off at half-past. Your customers get a good scare, and a decent night's sleep."

"How do the ghosts feel about that?"

"Our ghosts are happy to have a place to haunt, really. And they're happy to have a variety of places to haunt, rather than be tied to a single location, like those poor fellows on the Flying Dutchman. Can you imagine?" Robert shuddered a little. "Anyway, it's how we pay them. We also give you a limit clause as part of the contract. It restricts the ghost to a single room, so it doesn't go a-haunting your entire hotel." He rustled through some papers. "So, here's one. A beautiful young woman who died in 1856, from heartbreak." He looked up at Brittany expectantly, eyebrows raised.

*That sounds like the ticket,* Brittany thought. *Heartbroken beautiful ghost drifting, lamenting, moaning over her lost . . . her lost what?* "Heartbreak from what?" she asked, suddenly suspicious.

Robert looked down at his notes. "Um, her cats were taken away when she was evicted from her Manhattan apartment."

Brittany began to realize that, ultimately, this was a salesman she was dealing with. A used ghost salesman. She sighed. "How many cats?"

Robert coughed into his hand. "Fifty or so, I think."

"Do you know what became of them?" she asked.

He shuffled papers nervously. "Probably drowned in the river. It was the 1850's, after all."

"These cats, they wouldn't happen to be ghosts, too, would they?"

"We like to think of them as bonus ghosts." He shifted uncomfortably in his stuffed chair.

Brittany waved a hand, both to reject the one ghost and to move on to the next. "What else do you have?"

"Well, we have a fellow who was murdered by a giant pendulum," Robert offered.

Brittany pursed her lips. "I'm just guessing now," she said, "but it's a bargain because I actually get two ghosts, right?"

Robert blushed, but nodded.

"Keep going." She crossed her arms in the universal signal that he was on thin ice.

"Well ... " he said, flipping through more pages. "Here's a banker who was murdered when he foreclosed on a house belonging to this little old lady ... "

"And the downside?"

"She pushed him down the cellar stairs, and then somehow he accidentally fell into the furnace." He rolled his eyes. "Even for a ghost, he's pretty disgusting to look at, but some people like a little horror with their ghosts, you know."

Brittany glanced at her watch. "Well, look ... " she started.

"Wait! This is Stormcove, right? I've got this old sailor who drowned, longing for the sea. He'll stand and moan at that window for hours."

"I suppose he's been nibbled on by sharks or something?"

Robert shook his head. "Actually, he drowned in a rain puddle, as drunk as a sailor on leave. Which, of course, he was. He looks pretty good, except for a broken nose and bad teeth."

"Any seaweed?" she asked hopefully, standing to take the sheet of notes from Robert, who reluctantly gave it up.

"No, they pretty much come to us the way they died. Bit of mud, drunk, but he looks like a proper sailor."

She scanned the paper. "How come you didn't start with this guy? He'd be perfect for Stormcove."

He smiled weakly. "Some ghosts are harder to place than others. We have our quotas to meet."

"He's German. A drunk German sailor, standing alone at the window ranting at the raging ocean. In German." She chuckled.

Robert looked hopeful. "We can offer good terms for a two-year haunting."

The phone rang. Brittany picked up the handset from the cradle. "Brittany here." She nodded, then frowned, then smiled in a twisted, conflicted way. "I guess that's good, kind of," she said into the receiver. "Let me know if there are any issues with it." She hung up the phone. "Well," she said smugly, "it appears that we won't be needing your services after all. One of our customers just died on the premises. A lovely young lady on her wedding night who choked to death on some wedding cake."

Robert drew his brows together. "How . . . fortunate for you."

She nodded. "Some of the maids have already spotted her ghost."

"Really? In her room?"

"Well, no. In the hallway."

"How lucky for the ghost to have free run of the entire hotel." Robert stood up, returning loose papers to his valise. Brittany noticed that, for some reason, he didn't look particularly disappointed.

"The entire hotel?" she echoed. "Um. I mean, we can just tell the ghost to stay in one room, right?"

Robert laughed. "No, you can't order a ghost around. Unless, of course, they're contracted to stay in one room." He pulled a sheet of paper out of his valise and held it out. "These come standard with the ghosts we represent."

She reached out to take it and he pulled it away like a fishing lure, returning it to his valise. "How much?" she asked.

He named a price, and her face reddened.

"That's twice the price of a ghost!" she cried.

"Yes, of course. You don't actually *need* a ghost. But once you have a ghost, you *need* a contract. Buyer's market, seller's market. You understand." He walked toward the door. "We also offer exorcisms at a reasonable price. Gets rid of your problem entirely."

"It destroys the ghost?"

"Oh, good grief, no. That would be a terrible waste." He smiled and lifted his valise. "We would just remove its paranormal obligation to haunt the place where it died, and offer it a position in our portfolio of represented ghosts. When you decide, you have my card." He nodded to her and closed the door, leaving her alone in the paisley room.

Brittany sat down in the faux-antique chair and chewed on a fingernail. Behind her, she heard someone moan, and she sighed in response. She called the front desk. "This is Brittany. Don't let that paranormal peddler leave yet. I've still got to talk to him." She hung up and turned around to face the specter.

A thin girl in a white wedding dress hung in the air before her with a lump in her throat, looking distraught. She moaned again, but it turned into a hacking cough, and bits of ghost cake spewed into the air, evaporating as they fell.

"Oh, shut up," Brittany muttered, and left the room.

⚓

Tom Jolly is a retired astronautical/electrical engineer who now spends his time writing SF and fantasy, designing board games, and creating obnoxious puzzles. His stories have appeared in *Analog SF*, *Daily Science Fiction*, *Compelling Science Fiction*, *New Myths*, and a number of anthologies, including *As Told by Things*. He lives in Santa Maria, California, with his wife Penny in a place where mountain lions and black bears still visit. You can discover more of his stories at silcom.com/~tomjolly/tomjolly2.htm.

# Communications from the Honeymoon Suite

Stewart C Baker

2136
Honeymoon Suite
11:57 AM

//start log: 2136.03.26 11.57.01/LST//

Computer, a bottle of your finest wine, please. Chilled.

I, Dr. Laurie Vernederen, am about to make history. And about to see it—if my calculations are correct, I'll be back by noon, full of impressions from this very room throughout the ages.

Of course, this is just a test run, but it will be more than enough to prove to that fool Dr. Marteau and the editors at the *Journal of Theoretical Timestream Management* that my theories are superior to hers. I bet her grad assistant wrote all the good bits of her "revolutionary" paper anyway.

Once I've proved what I can do, just think of all the things I can bring back! All the history I can uncover! More importantly, I'll be able to set up a proper lab. Get government funding. Get my own grad assistant. No—two of them. I'll make the Journal redact Dr. Marteau's paper and publish mine.

Then a tenure-track position. A chairship. Netvid interviews describing me as a renowned expert.

Bwa ha ha! Bwa ha ha ha ha! Bwaaaa . . .

Ahem.

Anyway: Wine, please. Chilled.

Oh! It's starting. Back in five.

Enjoy your academic reputation while it lasts, Dr. Marteau, you—

//log ends: 2136.03.26 11.57.41/LST//

———o•▷———

*May 26th, 2015*

[11:58:05]    SuitesService: Hello! Thanks for choosing room service during your stay. What can we get you? :-)

[11:58:10]    Guest0136579: Oh my stars and ashes! How antiquated.

[11:58:15]    SuitesService: Excuse me?

[11:58:20]    Guest0136579: Sorry. Look, I can't stay long but this is VERY IMPORTANT. What can you tell me? What's it like here?

[11:58:25]    SuitesService: You want our menu? Sure thing!

[11:58:30]    Guest0136579: No, you useless . . .

[11:58:31]    Guest0136579: Sorry, I meant: What is it like here?! What are the best things? The worst?

[11:58:36]    SuitesService: Are you that guest from two days ago? Listen, like I told you: some things on our menu aren't for everyone. But our monster garlic fries are great! Would you like me to put in an order? Last time you disconnected before answering. :-(

[11:58:40]    Guest0136579: From two days ago? Oh, don't tell me . . .

[11:58:45]    SuitesService: Don't tell you what?

[11:58:57]    SuitesService: Hello? Ma'am? Sir?

[11:58:59]    *Chat ended. Reason: Client disconnect.*

———o•▷———

*May 26th, 1943. 11:59 AM*

[ring . . . ring]

    Hello? Hello? Is this the front desk?

    Excellent. Listen, this is very important—I haven't much time.

What? No, I don't want to reserve a spot for dinner.

Yes, I'm sure.

No, not even if it's stuffed eggplant and rice with a side of potato salad. Not even if there's sugar—what is it with you people and food?

Look. All I want to know is if anyone else called you from this number in the past couple of days. With an accent like mine, perhaps, or something else that made her stand out. Maybe she hung up halfway through the conversation.

There was? Another woman? I knew it!

When she called, did it sound like there was anyone with her? Did she sound nervous? Excited? Scared?

Perfect. All I have to do now is recalibrate this, and—

[dial tone]

⎯⎯⎯ o• ⊳

*Excerpt from* The Daily Gazette, *May 27ᵗʰ, 1876*

And it was here in this fine establishment—a regional fixture for as long as anyone can remember—that one day ago, at almost exactly noon, a strange commotion was heard from the newly added fourth floor.

Witnesses staying at the inn reported sounds of a scuffle and voices raised in passionate arguments that seemed to be about mathematical terms, which nobody present understood in the slightest. This was followed by tearing paper and—after about a minute—eerie silence. When police arrived to investigate, the room was empty, with not even a sign of habitation.

Your humble correspondent attempted to draw further comment from the inn's landlady, Mrs. Grubb, who would only add—in a polite, but very firm voice—that the new suite of rooms had clean linen, comfortable furniture, and a delightful view of the great Atlantic through a set of very fine French doors.

——o•▷——

*Investigative log, Coastal Police Dept., April 8th, 2136*

No leads yet on the sudden disappearances (two days apart) of Dr. Dominique Marteau and Dr. Laurie Vernederen from the Honeymoon Suite at Hotel Stormcove.

So far, our only information is a hand-written note attached to a bottle of port that Forensics discovered beneath the floorboards of the suite. The note is dated May 26th, 1757, 12:01 PM and reads as follows:

> *If anyone finds this, don't worry.*
>
> *Neither one of us may have succeeded entirely as we wished we would, but we've proven that both our theories are fundamentally sound.*
>
> *Yes: We.*
>
> *More importantly, we've realized that our competition for publication credit is an outdated (ha!) by-product of 21st-century academia and not an intrinsic part of science. And yes, we may disagree about the specifics of time travel, but there are more efficient ways to work than against each other. Better ways to carry out research than writing endless rebuttals to a rival's scholarly papers.*
>
> *There are even (dare we say it?) more important things than being known as a renowned expert in your field.*
>
> *Our theories have important things in common, and some of*

*those things are in that whole big world awaiting us, out there in the vastness beyond the walls of this suite.*

*Both of us have always wanted to see things long forgotten. And—although we might not be bringing them back to the rest of you—we can't wait to find out just what some of those things are.*

*Together.*

*Laurie and Dom.*

***

Stewart C Baker is an academic librarian, speculative fiction writer and poet, and the editor-in-chief of *sub-Q Magazine.* His fiction has appeared in *Nature, Galaxy's Edge,* and *Flash Fiction Online,* among other places. Stewart was born in England, has lived in South Carolina, Japan, and California (in that order), and currently resides in Oregon with his family—although if anyone asks, he'll usually say he's from the Internet.

# Barter for the Stars

Margery Bayne

"I want to make a deal," the saloon singer said as soon as she slid into the booth across from Kane. Moments ago, he had been watching her up on stage, her fans crowded at the front tables. Now she was here with him in the back, dark, unpopulated corner of the bar.

It had once been a speakeasy during Prohibition, according to the bartender, but had since been updated and retrofitted to the effect of a piano bar, and saloon, and a discotheque. It was an amalgamation of decades of Earth-age drinking culture. Kane guessed if you wanted interstellar tourists in joints with no pods you needed historical novelty on your side.

"A deal?" Kane asked. He took a sip from the vodka martini the bartender had suggested as a classic Earth cocktail. It tasted like paint stripper; it was still more refreshing than the acidic air outside.

"I hear you're a captain," the singer said. "You have a spaceship."

Kane was a captain only by the nature of having a spaceship. He didn't have a crew. That made him more of a lone adventurer.

"How'd you hear that?" he asked.

"Barkeep keeps me informed. I've been waiting for someone like you."

"Someone like me?"

She smiled and he instantly knew why she gathered so many fans, even in the offseason. It was the type of smile that pulled you in and then pushed you out with the same hand. A kind of smile that said you could look, but you could only look. You would never touch, and you would certainly never understand.

"What kind of deal, Miss . . . ?"

"You can call me Paris."

He had no idea if it was a first name, last name, stage name, or a lie.

"And the kind of deal I'm talking about is a voyage."

"I don't captain a passenger ship, Miss Paris."

"Just Paris," she said, like it was instinct. She leaned forward over the edge of the table. It was an assault of bare-skinned shoulders over the top of a strapless dress. "I can make it worth your while."

"I've got no interest in that kind of arrangement," Kane said.

Paris blinked, and her eyes were different somehow than from the moment before. She curled a finger to point over her shoulder.

"You think because I get up there in a dress like this"—the finger slipped down to the hollow of her collarbone in a movement as smooth as choreography—"that I'm offering . . . " Her hand dropped to the table top, weighted. "I'm talking about money. I make good tips, and I've been saving."

"I don't need money," Kane said, and even more, he didn't need odd jobs.

"Money or sex, apparently." Paris collapsed back into the booth seat with an agitation that was more real than anything she had dealt out so far. Real enough to be interesting.

"Paris—"

"Actually, 'Ma'am' would work just fine."

Kane grinned. "Ma'am, I'm a man who flies about the known galaxies looking for things that interest me."

"And you ended up here?" she said. She sneered at *here*.

True, this wasn't the most luxurious resort in the Milky Way or even on Earth, but luxury and interest were two distinct things.

"Where do you want to go?" Kane asked. "And why?"

"Why would I tell you? You're not going to take me."

"Because this is a negotiation," he said. "And I happen to find you interesting. If the place you're going is interesting . . . " Then maybe he could be convinced.

She crossed her arms. "You won't. Not if you've been traveling all over. I've only ever been off Earth once. On a school trip to the moon."

"Earth's got a great moon," Kane said. "Did you know that the Earth is the only planet where people could see a true solar eclipse? Because of the distance of the sun and the distance of the moon are perfectly aligned to make them look the same size in the sky?"

Paris shifted in her seat and said with no eye contact, "I heard that in the old days they used to be able to see the moon near every night, before the smog was so thick."

He'd heard that too. Kane had been to a lot of planets that humans had staked their claim on during the last century. On some they were making the same mistakes as they had done on Earth. On others they were trying to do better.

"Where do you want to go?" he asked again.

"I just want to see the stars."

Kane wondered if Paris was like him. If that wanderlust was in her soul too, but she had not—unlike him—had the means to feed it.

He was a man in search of interesting things, but he'd seen enough that he was starting to run low on things that could excite him. Maybe there was some novelty to be found in showing all the things he'd found to someone else—someone whose standard of amazement was just seeing the stars.

Kane raised a hand across the table for the traditional Earth gesture of a handshake.

"You got a deal."

Margery Bayne is a librarian by day and a writer by night from Maryland, USA. She enjoys the literary and the speculative, and is a published short story author and an aspiring novelist. In 2012, she graduated from Susquehanna University with a BA in Creative Writing and is currently pursuing her Masters of Library Science. She'll read anything from children's chapter books to YA graphic novels to mainstream bestsellers as long as it has a good story. In her time not spent reading or writing, she enjoys origami, running, and being an aunt. More about her and her writing can be found at margerybayne.com.

# Lost and Found

Tamzin Mitchell

Spring 1318
Just Beyond the Cove
Twilight

Pausing at the edge of a glade, belly heavy with her next litter, she sniffed the air.

Rabbits do not mark time as humans do. If she had been asked how long she'd been traveling, and if she had been able to answer, she would have said only, *Too long.* Long enough to elude the human who had sent thin, pointed sticks flying her way, long enough to be chased south by a bobcat that was thin with hunger at the end of a lean winter, long enough that she could not find the fields of home. Long enough to wander ever farther east, munching on bark and branches and cavorting with rabbits whose burrows were in all the wrong places, and hunting for the sweet smell of grassland.

Too long.

Now she had another concern: her belly full of kits, slowing her down. Instinct told her to dig herself a new burrow, to stop looking for home.

Some time ago (she could not have said how long), the snow had started to melt, and green buds had popped out everywhere. She had shed her thick winter coat, though her tail remained as white and fluffy as ever, and nibbled at every green thing in her path. More perplexing, though, was the smell: the brisk, tangy scent she picked up now. Her nose twitched. Not a human—she'd smelled their fires in her flight, but she'd evaded them and their sharp flying sticks well enough. Nor an animal, though those were around too. An early spring wind swept through the trees, rustling the tiny leaves on their branches, and with it came a strange roaring sound.

Unknown places that roared were not good places to birth kits. This she knew. But neither were places that smelled of bobcat. She hopped forward.

Past the glade, more trees towered above her. Thick bushes were clustered low to the ground, and perhaps she could dig in under one of them. It was not the open land she craved, but perhaps she could be safe here, buried deep under a thorny bush.

Something big crashed through the woods. Spooked, she streaked forward, through the trees and bushes, *beyond* the trees and bushes, and lurched to a halt.

Ahead was a great blue nothing: a roaring turmoil of water (so that was where the sound had come from) tumbling against itself, rushing in against the ground before retreating. Towering gray rocks stretched into the water, blocking her view, but the hum of the air and the tanginess of the scent told her that it went on for a long, long way. Farther than she'd traveled.

The kits, as though hearing the water, shifted in her belly. It was time.

The soft, sandy soil ahead beckoned. She hesitated, nose twitching, turning to glance at the forest. The water drowned out much of the sound from the woods. Her home was fields and grasses, and if she could not have those now, she could at least have wide open space. This was land where she could shelter. Where she could see things coming, and where she could run.

She felt as though she had stood on the lush green moss at the edge of the forest for a lifetime, but the glowing orb of the sun still hovered just above the trees, and the birds had not ceased their evening songs. Tall ears cocked in alertness, body trembling with fear or excitement—perhaps both, but she would not have been able to decide—she hopped onward, tentatively and then eagerly. *This* was the spongy soil into which she could burrow and birth her kits; *this* was a sky under which she could forage and run;

*this* was a strange melding of land and water and air that sent her leaping (only a little hampered by the kits leaping with her in her belly) with quivering joy across the sandy soil.

The rocks were still warm with the sun. Time to dig in and let these kits tumble free like the water. Then she'd rest. Nibble on grasses and seeds and gather her strength under the wide-open sky. Hop—cautiously—a little closer to the blue rush of water, just to see. And then, when the kits had grown bigger and stronger, she'd set them free to do some traveling of their own, and she would look again for the grasslands of home.

Tamzin Mitchell is a proofreader and editor and holds an MFA from the University of New Hampshire. Her fiction and nonfiction have appeared in *Waxwing, Cosmonauts Avenue, Crannóg,* and elsewhere, and have been nominated for Best of the Net and the Pushcart Prize. She moves often but was last seen in Berlin.

# Diffidence in White and Gray

Holly Schofield

Tuesday, April 14, 1956
Room 414
11:30 AM

The scrambled eggs heaped on the pillow in Room 410 don't faze Ellie, nor the lime Jell-O in the bathtub of 412. People do strange things in hotels, even classy ones like Stormcove—it's as if they step outside themselves for a brief moment—and Ellie doesn't have any quarrel with that, although it makes Bradley the custodial manager furious.

The squawking draws her to 414 as soon as she switches off the Electrolux, loud chittering from behind the door. She's heard some crazy sounds in her time, honeymooners especially, but 414 is an imported meat salesman here by himself for the week. He won't check out until tomorrow. As usual, he's gone down to the bar for lunch, passing her in the hall a few minutes ago; and, as usual, his appreciative whistle at her backside as she bent down to plug in the vacuum cleaner made her freeze. He's fairly tidy except for the messes his shaving mug makes on the bathroom counter. And she's never heard any sounds from his room before, nothing like this fluttering, vibrant tumult.

She closes her eyes to listen better.

Joyous music, of salt air and wildness, a seething seductive song of ocean and wind.

That can't be right. She tightens the apron strings on her white and gray uniform. Maybe it's a burst water pipe or a hissing radiator. Whatever's happening in 414, Bradley will say it's her fault. He's always looking for an excuse, a way to threaten to fire her until she puts out. And she can't, she just can't, not again. She'd rather live out on the dunes like Tattered Jack, with his threadbare shorts and chilblained shins.

She takes a couple of towels from the cart, taps on the door, and stammers, "Maid service?" unsure if she's questioning her identity or her purpose or both.

The chirring doesn't stop; instead, fluttering joins the chorus, like a hundred paper airplanes all whispering aloft together.

Or like a flock of wild birds.

A crack of the door and the fluttering becomes a visual cacophony of oyster-shell white and soft slate gray. A dozen seagulls, a hundred, a thousand, are flying in through the open French doors, whirling around, gorging on an open sample case of sausages on the bed, brashly defecating on the night table, across the doilies on the side credenza, and on the salesman's loafers parked neatly by the bed. Their yellow beaks curve in clever smiles; joy is a tangible presence.

She edges in and flaps a towel feebly. "Shoo! Go on! Get out!"

The birds ignore her. Why do they get to feast and have a party while she's stuck vacuuming up cigarette butts and chewing gum—and, now, dealing with this awful mess? Why does her life consist of tight uniforms, Bradley's moist hands, and corned beef on toast in her dingy apartment? Tattered Jack has more freedom than she does, crushed shells sharp between his toes, salt stiffening his beard. She picks up a loafer and throws it at the gulls, hard. She hasn't been down to the beach in ages.

The shoe hits the table lamp, sending it tumbling to the carpet, cracking the ceramic base into mottled turquoise shards. The seagulls veer away for a moment, then swirl again around the suitcase, confident, unafraid.

Should she try to find the salesman in the bar? He'd be on his third whiskey sour, and anyway, what could he do beside flap towels and shout? What could any of them do, stuck in their own vortices of despair?

The more she watches, the more she admires the brazenness of the gulls, their exhilaration at the spicy shreds of meat, their total unselfconsciousness. Suddenly, going back to the dim hallway is unbearable, suffocating. Even her uniform is making it hard to breathe. She lets the towels fall and loosens her apron ties. Her shoes are next and she digs her toes into the beige carpeting, searching, as if for distant beach sand. The uniform slips over her head and its lace collar snags on her earrings. She places them all on the end of the bed with a vestige of orderliness and lays her bra next to them. Then her nylons, her garter belt, and, with a small cry not unlike the gulls, her panties.

A hesitant raise of her arms, a spread of her fingers, and she waltzes among the seagulls, letting their wing tips caress her, their beaks etch tiny crimson runes on her skin, their knowing amber eyes include her in their exuberant dance.

They tug and pull at her head, claws snagging, and she loosens the hairnet and kicks it under the bed. The open balcony doors beckon and she places a foot on the threshold, savoring the April chill. The seagulls embrace her, lift her, embody her, and she lets them carry her up and out and away toward the sea.

Holly Schofield travels through time at the rate of one second per second, oscillating between the alternate realities of city and country life. Her stories have appeared in such publications as *Analog*, *Lightspeed*, and *Tesseracts*, are used in university curricula, and have been translated into several languages. She hopes to save the world through science fiction and homegrown heritage tomatoes. Find her at hollyschofield.wordpress.com.

# The Eligible Bachelor

Chelsea Cambeis

Samantha aimed to look effortless and relaxed while maintaining perfect posture on her backless stool. It was late, around 11 p.m., and the lounge was sadly dead. For some reason, she had thought it would be rife with eligible bachelors, in town for important business meetings. She sipped her dry martini, glancing at the face of her iPhone. She'd stay for five more minutes, then she was getting out of this dress and into her pajamas.

The lounge was elegant with a dark mahogany bar, so glossy the line of lights above the liquor shelves reflected off the surface. The lighting was just right—warm, soft, and not too bright. Samantha could see herself in the mirrors backing the bottles of expensive alcohol. She smiled at her own reflection; she looked good.

*Ask and you shall receive*, she thought, when she saw a tall, dark, and handsome type approaching in the mirror. She looked down at her drink, feigning disinterest. At least for the moment.

"I'll have what she's having." The rich, resonating voice came from behind her. Without turning, she watched the bartender—handsome actually, but she hadn't noticed until now—nod at the person approaching. The man slid onto the stool next to her. "But with an olive instead. Far more classic than a lemon twist."

Samantha gave him a sidelong glance before directing her gaze back to her drink. "You're criticizing me before properly introducing yourself? Now, that's classy."

"I'm Mark."

He extended a hand into her peripheral vision. Samantha

turned to face him, the material of her little black dress shifting easily on the stool top. She placed her manicured hand in his very large one, which was poised for a shake. Mark turned her hand just so, drawing it to his lips and placing a featherlight kiss on the back of it.

She suppressed a satisfied gasp. Mark was gorgeous—olive skin, salt-and-pepper hair, strong, square jaw, alluring brown eyes, and, if Samantha had to guess, fifteen or so years older than her—just her type.

"And you are?" he asked, his voice smoother than the silk kimono she had moments before been longing to shed her dress for. Now, she wanted to shed her dress for a much different reason.

"Samantha."

"Samantha," he repeated and nodded as if in approval. Her name sounded unique and beautiful coming from him.

She was too easy, her heart already fluttering in her chest, especially when Mark's gaze lingered on the diamond pendent dangling against her chest. While he did, she took the opportunity to glance at his left ring finger—bare.

"What brings you to The Suites at Stormcove, Mark?" Her tone remained flawlessly casual. She was impressed with herself.

"Business," he said. Samantha nodded knowingly, even though she didn't have a clue. "And you?"

"Same, sort of. I'm actually in town for a photoshoot. A wedding magazine." She felt the blood rush to her cheeks and, as usual, wondered why she was embarrassed explaining her modeling career.

She noticed the bartender approaching with Mark's martini, grateful for the distraction, but Mark didn't take his eyes off her, nodding and thanking the bartender without a turn of his head.

"You'd make a beautiful bride," he said.

Samantha's heart skipped a beat. This was exactly what she'd come to the lounge hoping to find—this man.

"Thank you." She worked to contain her giddy excitement, desperately trying to keep her cool. "I can't deny how much fun it is to wear the bridal gowns. Not many women get to step into one unless it's the real thing."

"So, I can assume you haven't worn your *own* wedding dress yet?"

Samantha waved her left hand between them, drawing attention to the lack of ring, engagement or otherwise. "Not yet."

"You've got time." His indirect note of her possible age, the difference in age between them, didn't go unnoticed.

She stirred her drink, leaning into the counter and arching her back. "Maybe, but I'm a bit of a hopeless romantic and tired of waiting."

She glanced across her shoulder, catching him taking her in. His eyes slid down the arch of her back to her hips poised suggestively on the seat of the stool. There was appreciation in his gaze—the kind of thing Samantha wished she didn't thrive on so much. She pushed the thought away. She might have looked seductive, but she *did* tell him she was a hopeless romantic.

When Mark brought his eyes back to hers, he grinned. It was mischievous, indicating that he wasn't at all ashamed of being caught eyeing her up. "I just love your hair," he said, reaching out and pushing a lock behind her ear. "The color, is it natural?"

Samantha twirled a finger in her vibrant red hair. She'd always been told that men preferred long hair. Hers was cut directly over her shoulders and had so much volume, it bounced when she walked, talked, or turned her head, as she did now to look at Mark. Men might love long hair, but in her experience, they liked the color of hers too much to care about length.

"It is," she said, smiling around the words. She knew how

startlingly white her teeth looked between her lips coated in a cool-toned red. Mark's smile widened in response. They seemed to be communicating without words. Samantha wondered about the room she'd be sleeping in tonight. Judging by his expensive-looking attire, she imagined Mark had a studio suite with a balcony and oceanfront view, where they'd have mimosas tomorrow morning, wearing nothing but white, fluffy hotel robes.

The bartender interrupted Samantha's daydream. "Another martini for the lady?" She met his gaze and gave him a slight nod.

"Put Samantha's drinks on my tab, would you?" Mark asked, his voice warm.

Samantha noticed a tattoo creeping up the side of the bartender's neck when he turned to address Mark.

"Of course, Mr. Maxwell." He nodded, and when he walked away, Samantha's smile morphed from polite back to dazzling as she turned her attention back to Mark.

*Samantha Maxwell*, she thought and swore he was thinking the same by the grin stretching across his face.

"There you are!" someone called from the lounge entrance, breaking through the cool jazz music and the relaxed ambiance of the room, startling Samantha, and apparently Mark too. He jumped, his shoulders tensing at the sound. Before whirling on her stool to see who the woman was speaking to, she watched Mark dig into his jacket pocket. Her lips gaped as he pulled out a gold band and slid it onto his left ring finger—the perfect fit.

The words "What the—" formed on Samantha's lips, but she found she was speechless. As Mark spun around on his stool, he gave Samantha an apologetic glance before his face lit up again, only this time for someone else. She stared at the side of his face as the woman approached and slid into Mark's arms.

"I got back from my swim and you weren't there," she said,

and Samantha took a moment to assess the other woman—mid-to-late thirties, long, wet hair, silk robe that clung in just the right places, shockingly large diamond adorning her left hand.

"Just killing time until you were finished," Mark said smoothly. "This is Samantha." He gestured toward her. "We've been chatting for a few minutes. She's a model. In town for a wedding magazine shoot. I was telling her about your photography."

Samantha forced a smile in response to his blatant lie, her pride keeping her speechless and polite.

"Very neat! I love meeting models out in the wild," his wife said. "Obviously, I don't have my business cards on me, but I can leave one at the desk for you?"

"That would be great," Samantha said with mock enthusiasm.

Mark tipped back the rest of his martini and extended a hand to Samantha, which she took for show. His grip wasn't as soft this time, the terse handshake laughable in comparison to the gentle kiss when he sat down only minutes ago. "It was great meeting you, Samantha."

All she could manage was a nod and a smile, her teeth clenched behind it. She watched the couple leave the lounge, Mark's arm wrapped around his wife's back. In seconds, they were gone, as were Samantha's plans for the evening.

The bartender came back with her martini, looking unsurprised that she was now sitting there alone. She met his blue eyes for one awkward moment before dropping her gaze, running her finger around the rim of her new glass.

"Two free drinks," he said, breaking the silence. Samantha thought she heard a smidge of some kind of accent, though she couldn't quite put her finger on it. "Could be worse."

At that, she laughed, raising her glass to him. She knocked back a heavy sip and ran her finger delicately along the side of her neck. "I like your tattoo."

He smirked, one dark eyebrow lifting. "There's more where that came from."

⚓

Chelsea Cambeis spent four rewarding, hardworking years as a rural mail carrier in West Virginia, where she resides, after earning her B.A. in English. Now, she is following her passion, pursuing a career in publishing and focusing on her own writing. *The Eligible Bachelor* is her first publication.

# How to Hide a Body

Ruth Olson

I didn't mean to do it. I want to make that very clear upfront. I didn't wake up this morning and think to myself, hmm, I think I'll murder someone in a hotel room. But when your biggest investor asks for a meeting, you show up. And when your biggest investor starts to yell that he's pulling all his funding, it's not outside the realm of possibility that you lose your temper. And one thing led to another, and when I shoved him, I certainly didn't expect him to lose his balance and hit his head on the side of the coffee table on the way down.

And yet, here we were.

The body lay crumpled on the floor, blood gushing from the gash in its head. I tried not to look at it too closely. I mean, I'm not squeamish, but a woman has her limits. Instead, I looked around the room.

Not really any good place to put the body. Unfortunately. And also unfortunately, this was the 34th floor. So I couldn't, for example, wiggle it out the window and into the shrubbery and hope for the best.

I was contemplating my options when a door at the back of the suite cracked open. A woman in a negligee stepped out.

"Howard," she called. Then she caught sight of me, and her mouth dropped open. She gaped at me, eyes wide, then down at the body I was in the process of hoisting up.

So much for getting out of here unseen. Really, she could have waited a few minutes.

"Hello," I said after a moment, faintly irritated. "My eyes are up here."

She stared at me in complete shock. "You killed my husband."

I sighed heavily. "Let me just start out by saying that there's a lot of nuance missing from that statement. And furthermore, your husband is actually quite heavy, and I'm over here trying to lift him BY MYSELF while you stand there gawping."

Since she'd turned up, she may as well make herself useful.

She still stood there, staring.

"BY MYSELF," I hinted.

She was still staring.

"I could use some help here," I said, giving up on the subtlety.

Moving like she was sleepwalking, she came over.

"The legs, please," I said. "Just lift them up . . . yes. Perfect. Now, I'll walk backwards, you walk forwards, and I think we'll just try to take him out the door there into the hall."

We maneuvered our way around the furniture towards the door.

"Watch that puddle of blood," I said. "You know, I'm sure your husband was a lovely person, but his taste in suits was horrific."

She stepped around the blood and nodded, still looking stunned. "I was always telling him he needed to go to a tailor," she murmured. I nodded encouragingly. She seemed to be taking this whole thing quite hard, and I was glad we'd found common ground.

"Yes, I'd say that's exactly what he needed. A good tailor. Nice fabric, a more flattering cut—he'd have felt like a new man."

She nodded again, in a shell-shocked sort of way.

When we finally got him around the armchair, I had to set the shoulders down to get at the door. When I pulled it open, the bellhop stood there, hand raised to knock. He stared at me, then at the body, then back at me. I sighed, then gave him an encouraging smile.

"You're just the person we need," I said. "Would you hold this door for us?"

He looked back down at the body.

"I . . . but . . . should I call a doctor?"

"I don't think that will help at this point, but that was a very kind offer. Now, if you'd just hold this door like so . . . "

He did as I asked, still staring. To be perfectly frank, I was getting a little tired of this reaction, and I said so. He shut his mouth abruptly.

We got Howard out the door by turning him sideways. We made a bit of a mess on the way through, but honestly, considering it was just the three of us, I thought we did quite well.

Howard's wife—Lucinda, I'd learned—set the legs down on the ground, put her hands on the small of her back, and stretched. I did the same. The bellhop nudged the man's shoe out of the way with his foot and let the door swing closed. He looked like he was about to flee, which would have been absolutely no good at all. I smiled at him.

"If you could just help with a leg there, that would be fantastic. He's heavier up top, but there just isn't anywhere to grab on."

He sidled over to stand by Lucinda, and between the three of us we hoisted Howard up again.

We ran smack-dab into the concierge in the hallway. I had to stop myself from rolling my eyes. So much for being discreet. Hiding a body wasn't exactly supposed to be a group effort, but I suppose we work with what we have.

He was a bit taken aback, of course, but it didn't take long before he was hoisting up the middle. Took a significant amount of weight off my hands, too. I was grateful, and I said so.

"I think we'll go for the elevator," I said, trying to look over my shoulder so as not to run into anyone else. "Can you imagine trying to do this down thirty-four flights of stairs?"

They chuckled nervously.

Somehow, before we got to the elevator, we acquired a janitor and one of the hotel assistant under-managers. To be honest, at that point it was hardly any more work than moving a kitchen chair, though it did lose a certain *je ne sais quoi*. I mean, at this rate there'd be no one left to hide the body *from*. There was another manager, but he took one look, screamed, and ran off. I said a quiet, ladylike curse word.

"He's never been all that friendly," the bellhop volunteered. The under-manager and the concierge nodded.

The janitor suggested a downstairs cleaning cupboard as a good place to stash Howard, but the under-manager shook her head decisively.

"No good. There are people in and out of there all day. I suggest the spare uniforms cupboard on the second floor, way in the back."

We all agreed that was likely the best plan.

When we reached the elevator, the bellhop dropped his leg and ran around to push the button for down, but just then the elevator dinged, the door slid open, and five police officers piled out, guns drawn.

For a moment, we all stared at each other: the bellhop, Lucinda, the under-manager, the concierge, the janitor, the police officers, and I. The officers looked completely flabbergasted.

"So," one of them said at last. "We have a . . . group murder on our hands, do we?"

I cleared my throat. "Well, officer, I wouldn't exactly say—"

I was interrupted by a loud groan from the dead man. We all turned and stared.

He groaned again, and his eyes fluttered open. "I . . . where the hell am I? What's happening? Who are all these people?" He put a hand gingerly to the gash on his head and drew it away bloody.

We stared at him for a while, then back at each other.

"Well, then," I said, laying the shoulders down gently on the floor. "It looks like we don't need you officers after all." I flashed everyone a blinding smile. "And I'd like to state, for the record, that you all were fantastic. Above and beyond. I was impressed." I straightened, wiped the blood off my hands, and looked down at Howard.

"I'll expect that cheque tomorrow, then," I said. "I'd prefer it wasn't late. Your wife, by the way, is a lovely person, and I'm very impressed with her. I just want to make that clear."

⊸⊤

Ruth Olson is a lawyer living in Alberta, Canada, with her four kids, way too many cats, and a dog the size of a small bear. She spends four months of the year hiking, camping, and running, and the other eight months trying to keep various exposed body parts from freezing and falling off. She has never hidden a body, but is very, very good at concealing bars of chocolate from her children.

# An Act of Con-Passion

Laura Johnson

CoviCon 9
Ballroom
2:55 PM

The air crackled with magic, the energy of hundreds of people bustling about CoviCon. Overnight, the hotel had been transformed into a medley of science fiction, fantasy, anime, and superheroes, and everything in between. On Monday, it would be back to its normal self—but for this weekend, it was the gateway to geek paradise.

Some rooms were reserved for panels, where attendees wriggled in anticipation to hear from geek celebrities or engage in heated discussion over their fandom of choice, or workshops—*Cosplaying on a Dime, Introduction to Thermoplastics,* and *Magical Miniatures,* to name a few. The vendor floor was filled with artists and artisans, handmade goods, games, comic books, and indie authors and developers eager to meet potential fans. I had emerged from it with a hooded fleece cloak and a handsewn sushi stuffie, which I'd stored in my hotel room in a special block reserved for con-goers.

"Attention, CoviCon attendees," crackled a voice over a loudspeaker. "The line for photo ops with TonyVirus cuts off in five minutes."

Nobody around me left the line—everyone was hopeful. I glanced at my watch. It was 2:55.

Marvel heroes, Hogwarts wizards, and anime characters with hair all colours of the rainbow meandered about the ballroom, occasionally posing for photos when asked. Someone dressed as Darth Vader was parading around with a group of Stormtroopers in the lobby, pretending to use the Force to open and close the hotel's automatic doors and marching up and down the grand staircase. The atmosphere was electric.

I'd attended CoviCon annually since its inception nine years ago. Each year, it drew more people as well as guests of increasing renown. Like Anthony "TonyVirus" Perez, popular *Dungeons & Dragons* streamer. Every Wednesday night, that's what I and hundreds of other viewers were watching, glued to the stream, wondering what shenanigans the cast would get into that week—Micah, the ingenuous gnome inventor; Miria, the angelic protector; silver-tongued, serpent-born Nassirah; and the mischievous-but-lovable half-elf, Meeso. TonyVirus was the Dungeon Master, the person who ran the show and decided the fate of the characters.

I couldn't wait to get my brand-new hardcover of his campaign book signed. My feet ached in Miria's winged heels, and I'd skipped lunch to wait in line. *Only five minutes left*, I thought. I tugged at my silver gauntlet. *I really,* really *hope I make it.*

Not everyone would: the line snaked out of the hall behind me, where the end began to disintegrate as people realized there was no chance of reaching the table. There was another signing tomorrow after the live game event, but I had already missed a workshop on painting miniatures to queue and was only here the one day. I clutched my book tighter, mentally rehearsing what I'd say to TonyVirus:

*I'm such a huge fan.* No, that was cliché.

*Your voices are amazing. Can you say*—No, he was probably sick of people asking for the same line over and over.

*How can I stand out in this crowd? I don't want to be just a stream statistic.* It was a selfish wish. Everyone wanted to be noticed and remembered. There was only one TonyVirus, and hundreds of us.

The line shuffled forward. 2:56. Each sluggish second felt like a minute. At 15 to 20 seconds per person ... Yes, I should make it—barely. I'd be lucky to be one of the last few. *My friends will be so jealous when I show them that I met* the *TonyVirus in person!*

Behind me were more con-goers in cosplay. I spotted a scaled woman dressed as Nassirah, clad in swathes of violet silk from when she seduced the evil Lord Valchon. A few were dressed as Micah the gnome artificer, steampunk-esque in leather top hats and thick aviator goggles, all holding clockwork birds. One of the birds was functional, even. The cosplayer controlling it was subtly twitching a wire in their opposite hand. Their con badge said, "Alex, They/Them."

"Can I take your picture?" I asked Alex. "Or better, can I get a picture with you?"

It was courteous to ask, rather than just snap a photo: "Cosplay is not consent" was a common phrase at conventions now. Most people loved to be photographed in costume, but others were camera-shy or valued their privacy.

"Of course," said Alex. They gestured at the woman beside them, who wore a denim jacket covered in patches: one was a Hufflepuff house crest, another a twenty-sided rainbow die. She held a campaign book like me, though not with the same reverence as others in the line. "Jacqui," said Alex, "would you do the honours?"

I passed Jacqui my phone and posed. "I'm Sarah, by the way," I said. "Micah's one of my favourites, too, but I couldn't resist trying a cosplay with wings."

Miria believed in helping others and doing what was right. She would do anything for her friends, even if it meant putting her life at risk.

"I'm Alex. I've been waiting to meet TonyVirus since CoviCon announced him as a guest. Tomorrow we're off to my sister's wedding." They beamed, then glanced at their watch (also clockwork!) and frowned. "I'm not sure we'll make it." Waving a small leather notebook, they said, "I want TonyVirus to sign my D&D notes."

"Not your campaign book?" I asked. TonyVirus had published a setting guide for the world of Miria, Nassirah, Micah, and Meeso. I didn't even run games, but I wanted a copy just so I could own something signed by TonyVirus himself.

"Don't own one. Neither does Jacqui, actually—she's getting it signed for my sister, who couldn't make it because of wedding prep." Alex grinned. "Good thing for her that Jacqui's not a D&D nut like me."

I knew the Con was strict about one signature per person. Jacqui could have been attending a panel, and here she was standing in line instead!

The line shuffled forward again. 2:58. Several people were still in front of me. I continued chatting with Alex and Jacqui until a con volunteer began walking our way. He was waving the people ahead of us forward like a cop at a broken traffic light, checking his watch and glancing back at TonyVirus.

When he got to me, he paused. My heart stopped.

"Ten," he said, beckoning me forward. To Alex and Jacqui, he said, "I'm sorry, you'll have to come back tomorrow."

"There's still two minutes," I said, "Surely, you can squeeze them in?"

"No can do. We have to cut the line off somewhere—we need the room for another panel." He made a louder announcement to this regard for the rest of the line.

Alex looked heartbroken. My throat seized. I was only here for the one day, too. I made a decision.

"Alex, Jacqui," I said. "One of you take my spot. I'll do this tomorrow."

It's what Miria would do.

Alex's eyes lit up, then teared up. "Th-thank you!" They hugged Jacqui and took the book from her, leaving their D&D notes behind.

I stepped aside with Jacqui. "Isn't that their sister's book?"

"Alex is a sweetheart," she said. "They're paying it forward. Look at their smile!"

I faced the stage, where Alex was taking a selfie with TonyVirus, chattering. Waving the campaign book, they ran back to us. TonyVirus was already being whisked away as the line dispersed, leaving a trail of disappointed sighs.

"Nat's going to *die*," Alex said.

"But your campaign notes—"

Alex shook their head. "This story alone was worth it. Besides, I have a photograph as a souvenir—I don't need both."

Then they left, holding hands. My heart was still warm as I went to enjoy CoviCon.

⚬—⊤

Laura Johnson is a fantasy writer who resides in London, Ontario, where she is pursuing graduate studies in Psychology at Western University. When she's not writing for pleasure, she's immersed in academia, researching prosocial and antisocial personality traits. A huge geek, she enjoys playing *Dungeons & Dragons*, dressing up in cosplay at conventions, and gaming with friends. Previously, her stories have appeared in the *As Told by Things* anthology by Atthis Arts, in the *Cast of Wonders* podcast, and in three anthologies by Bushmead Publishing—*Heroes*, *Monsters*, and *Scoundrels*.

# Nowhere to Go

Mike Morgan

Tom Wheelwright was mortified—here he was, dripping like a madman all over the floorboards, causing a dreadful mess. His wife, Mary, and their nine-month-old baby, Willamina, were equally rain-soaked by his side. Tom prayed the man wouldn't throw them out on sight.

He didn't. Rather, the middle-aged gentleman rushed over to them, eyes wide with concern. "My goodness! You're drenched to the bones! Come over by the fire this instant. And you with a young one, my goodness. You'll catch your deaths!"

Hardly knowing what was happening, Tom found himself and his young family steered to a blazing hearth. Blankets were fetched, along with steadying glasses of something 'medicinal.'

"We were caught in the storm, walking down the coast," Tom explained. "Rain came down so hard we could barely see an inch afore us. Could barely make any headway. Then dusk fell, with us still miles from our destination."

"We somehow glimpsed the candles flickering in your windows," added Mary.

"Thought to throw ourselves on your mercy. Didn't know what else to do, what with the baby."

The man nodded. "A dreadful night, indeed. I'm relieved you found us. Just as I was found."

Thunder shook the beams of the broad, smoky room.

Tom discovered a marmalade-colored cat rubbing up against his shins.

"I don't suppose we could stay the night?" He whispered, "I

don't have any coin, but I can work for our board . . . " His voice trailed off.

The year of the Lord sixteen hundred and fifty had not been kind to Tom and his loved ones. They were travelling to town to stay with Mary's folk. Tom's father, his only remaining kin, had passed from ague, leaving only debts.

The man smiled. "I daresay we can let you stay until the weather passes, with no charge."

"Bless you, sir."

"Think no more upon it. Lord knows, this is a terrible gale, even for the cove."

Tom paused. "I'm sorry. With the fierceness of the rain, we didn't espy whether this is a home or establishment. Where are we?"

"You're at the Stormcove Inn."

The man was the innkeeper, Tom realized.

"What a lovely name," observed Mary, her gaze fixed on their dozing child. She'd fretted constantly in the rain, but was asleep now they were inside, as if lulled into calmness by some aspect of this welcoming place.

"Fine-looking building," murmured Tom. "Solid, like it'll stand forever."

"Oh, we must trust to the Lord for that, sir." The innkeeper's smile broadened, and Tom felt the warmth of a welcome greater than anything he could have hoped for. "Now, don't you worry about a thing; I'll show you to your room."

**Mike Morgan** lives in Iowa with his wife and two children. He is an immigrant from the United Kingdom and was recently sworn in as a citizen of the United States. The process of moving to a new land was a lot easier for him than for the people he wrote about in this volume, he's happy to say. If you like his writing, please search for his website *Perpetual State of Mild Panic*, where you can read about his other published work. And, if you enjoy science fiction, you can follow him on Twitter, where he's known as CultTVMike and tweets about various TV shows, movies, books, and comics.

# The Ghost Who Haunted Her

George Nikolopoulos

2111
Room 1313
Midnight

Paranormal Investigator Ana Schulz entered the haunted room precisely at midnight, at the exact same moment that the luminous presence materialized—the ghost of Catherine, a young woman of nineteen, who had been murdered in that very room twenty years before and had haunted it ever since.

For twenty years, no investigator had ever managed to convince Catherine to move on. Seven days ago, Ana Schulz had been hired by the hotel manager because she'd grown to be the best PI in the business—and she had already made progress with the case. Too much progress, it seemed.

— ◦• ➤

Catherine approached Ana, until she hovered just in front of her. Her luminescence fluctuated, so from time to time Ana could make out her face—her aquiline nose, the smoothness of her cheeks, the slenderness of her neck.

Catherine spoke. Humans were unable to hear her, as she produced no sound; however, her words directly appeared on Ana's sensory input interface. "I'm ready to move on," Catherine said.

"Please don't," said Ana, before she had a chance to logically process her reply. Then she realized she was violating her primary programming. Still, even after she realized it— "Stay a little longer," she said. "*I* am not ready. I need you so much."

Catherine hovered even closer, so close that they could almost touch. "I have to," she said. "I gave it a lot of thought, after our last conversation. I shouldn't haunt this place anymore. I'm only punishing myself—for something that was never my fault. I should be moving to a higher plane of existence."

Ana sighed. That was pure logic; she could never argue against that. Still, she was overwhelmed by the emotion she recognized as sadness. She'd once been proud of her enhanced near-human emotions; they provided her with all the empathy required for her job. Now she would gladly rip her emotions card out of her CPU and stomp on it.

"One last kiss, my love?" Catherine said. She moved her lips closer to Ana, and then they kissed.

Ana felt Catherine's kisses as a tingling sensation that left her lips and tongue numb afterwards; it was the most thrilling feeling she'd ever experienced. She wondered what her spectral lover felt during their kissing; she guessed she'd never find out.

"I'm ready to move on because I'm happy at last," said Catherine afterwards. "It was you who made me happy."

"But won't you miss me?" said Ana. "I'll miss you terribly." She knew that humans were more reserved, not so open with their feelings, but she didn't have the conditioning for that, and she didn't even care. She only said what she felt.

Catherine's ethereal hand moved towards Ana's face and caressed her cheek; semi-material, Catherine's hand moved past Ana's synthetic skin, half entering inside her. The tingling sensation spread all over Ana's head.

"I had a vision, my love," said Catherine. "This will not be the end of you and me. We'll meet again, in another life. We will be together, then."

Ana laughed, though she felt like crying. "Robots don't get reincarnated, Catherine. I will have no other life."

Catherine smiled, as if she knew a secret she would not share.

Then her outline began to ripple—she became transparent, and then she was no more.

Ana stood immobile for a long moment, her shoulders imperceptibly slumped. Then, as she turned to leave, nine words emerged on her sensory input interface. "And yet they do, Ana. And yet they do."

⊸⟙

George Nikolopoulos is a speculative fiction writer and a member of Codex Writers' Group. His short stories have been published in over 60 magazines and anthologies including *Galaxy's Edge*, *Nature*, *Daily Science Fiction*, *Factor Four*, *Grievous Angel*, *Best Vegan SFF 2016*, and *The Year's Best Military & Adventure SF*. He lives in Athens, Greece, and when he's not writing he is, among other things, an actor, a civil engineer, a husband, and a father. He wishes he could write more, read more, travel more, play more computer games, and spend more time with cats.

# Zephyr
Chloe Lerit

Tierney slid her finger up her bass guitar's neck, holding a soaring note to finish her band's song. She scanned around Zephyr, Hotel Stormcove's thirteenth floor lounge, as the jovial patrons singing along tried to maintain the last note with her. When their breaths ran out and voices trembled and faded, they burst out in cheers and applause, adding to the cacophony of clinking glass and boisterous laughter.

Tierney beamed at the audience. "This next song is our last—thanks again for joining us here in Zephyr for Earth New Year!"

As the crowd cheered, Tierney admired the sight before her. For every human face in the crowd, there was at least one creature not of this planet. Flesh, scales, carapaces, and tentacles in all colors meshed together into a beautiful amalgamation of worlds. All species alike proudly sported shiny golden hats and glittery sunglasses with "3026" emblazoned on them, as they jubilantly celebrated the human tradition of New Year's Eve. Tierney's eyes were drawn to the bar where, beneath a frame that held the original brass "14th Floor" elevator signage, a rowdy group of eclectic beings gathered.

"This planet's rotation around your sun is so quick!" marveled a one-eyed humanoid loudly to a group of humans, as he peered his eye into a party horn. "You blink your eye and you're right back where you started!"

"I traveled hundreds of light years to experience this!" a

feathered creature squeaked breathlessly, his beady black eyes wide with excitement. He clutched his glittery 3026 sunglasses as he whipped his head back to down a tequila shot. When he straightened up, he spoke in chirps and squeaks. As heads tilted in confusion, the feathered being tapped a device on his neck and looked up at the ceiling. Zephyr maintained an old-fashioned ambiance, but among its rare upgrades were translation devices placed on the ceiling. Used with necklaces provided by Stormcove staff, these devices translated spoken words directly into listeners' minds.

A nearby human patron reached over and gently adjusted the creature's necklace, then asked, "How's that?"

"Test? Test?" the feathered creature croaked, his eyes pleading with the translation device above. He cracked a huge smile. "I'm back! Where were we? Ah, right! My planet doesn't rotate around a sun, so this concept is delightful! Visiting this hotel and witnessing this Earth event was on my—what do you humans call it? 'Bunny list'? 'Bucket list'?"

"On my planet, we celebrate our rotation around our two suns by casting billions of lighted lanterns into the sky as offerings," boasted a scaly, blue humanoid with a fish-like head that was encompassed in a helmet filled with water. "Legend has it that our lanterns float to the suns and burn up, adding fuel for years to come. Add *that* to your bunny list!"

"Another 'French fry' special, please!" a long-necked humanoid yelled to the bartender, as she fervently sopped her remaining fries in a ketchup puddle on her plate. She leaned against a six-legged creature next to her, who clicked his mandibles indignantly as half-eaten fries fell from her mouth and onto his sequined 3026 hat as she said, "Want some? They're exquisite!"

Tierney heard a party horn go off, followed by glass shattering and the feathered creature hiccupping, "Is it just me or is this gravity getting stronger?"

Tierney chuckled, as she began plucking the strings on her bass again. 3026 was going to be a good year.

⊗—

Chloe Lerit hails from Los Angeles, CA. As a child, she forged a passion for fantasy and science fiction by reading books by Tamora Pierce and exploring diverse worlds in text-based role-playing games (RPGs). While studying computer science at UC Irvine, she immersed herself in the captivating universe of the game *World of Warcraft*, which she plays to this day. She now resides in San Diego, CA, where she pursues her other passions of software engineering, playing bass guitar, and finding the perfect brew, all which provided inspiration for her Hotel Stormcove story.

# THE END

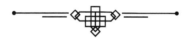

Made in the USA
Lexington, KY
09 May 2019